JOSEPH KERTES

WINTER TULIPS

A NOVEL

Doubleday Canada Limited, Toronto

Canadian Cataloguing in Publication Data

Kertes, Joseph, 1951–
  Winter tulips

ISBN 0-385-25185-8

I. Title.

PS8571.E778W56 1988   C813'.54   C88-094117-0
PR9199.3.K4737W56 1988

Lyrics from "THE LION SLEEPS TONIGHT" (Mbube) (Wimoweh). New lyric and revised music by Hugo Peretti, Luigi Creatore, George Weiss and Albert Stanton. Based on a song by Solomon Linda and Paul Campbell. Copyright © 1951 (renewed 1979), 1952 (renewed 1980) and 1961 by Folkways Music Publishers, Inc., New York, N.Y. Used by permission.

"BLOWIN' IN THE WIND"
(Bob Dylan)
© 1962 Warner Bros. Inc.
All Rights Reserved
Used By Permission

"A HARD RAIN'S A-GONNA FALL"
(Bob Dylan)
© 1963 Warner Bros. Inc.
All Rights Reserved
Used By Permission

The publishers gratefully acknowledge the assistance of the Ontario Arts Council.

Cover design by The Dragon's Eye Press
Printed and bound in Canada

Published in hardcover by Doubleday Canada Limited,
105 Bond Street, Toronto, M5B 1Y3.

This book is dedicated
to the family
and friends
who encouraged me to write it.

ONE

The morning I was to leave Montreal for Toronto, we were all awakened two hours early by the ringing of the telephone. It was Crazy Sarah, my father's first cousin. She said she'd heard on the morning news that "they" were going to gouge her eyes out in three and a half years. My father told her to call us back a bit closer to the time of the gouging, and hung up.

Then through the wall came my mother's voice—twice as shrill as the telephone: how could he be so cruel? How could he joke about a thing like that? And not about *her* cousin—but *his*?

"She bothers me," said my father. "She's been bothering me for forty years."

"She's *sick*. Can't you understand that? Last week she wrote a letter to the Queen for help."

"So why does she call *me*? Why doesn't she call the Queen directly? Her Royal Majesty is in a different time zone and already has on her hat and medals waiting for any possible calls from subjects."

At breakfast, while my mother made the beds and my father made water buffalo noises in the bathroom, my younger brother, Sammy, sat at my side glowing like an heir apparent. "Are you taking your stereo with you to Toronto?" he asked as he crunched through his toast.

"I'm not going to carry it with me on the train, no, but

1

Dad's going to drive it down in a couple of months. I'm leaving most of my records, though."

"Great — what? — Beethoven's Triple Concerto in R Major? . . . Are you taking your stereo headphones?"

"Yes, I'm leaving my stereo, but I'm taking the headphones. I'll be plugging them into my ass every night to listen to it rumble."

"Are you taking your desk chair?"

"On the *train*? I'm not taking *anything*! I'm moving into a furnished apartment."

"You should take your red rug anyway. I hate it."

"Put it in the spare bedroom."

"You don't mind if I stay in your room while you're gone, then?"

"Sammy, I'm going to be gone a long time. You can *have* my room."

The crunching stopped. "Are you coming home over the Christmas break?"

"Probably." The crunching resumed.

"Oh . . . I was just wondering."

The kitchen seemed more friendly that last morning in Montreal than I had ever seen it in all the eighteen years I had lived in my parents' house. The once hideous serviette holder before me, with "Shalom" printed on it in a brass design like that on a castle gate, now shone like Byzantine goldwork. Beside the fridge hung the perennial calendar from Rotstein's Bakery, with the Jewish holidays, Rotstein's business hours and his three locations marked on it. On the window sill was a china flamingo with "MIAMI BEACH" emblazoned in gold on its wings, and toothpicks—like spears—sticking out of its back. A green Buddha with a clock in its belly—cracked since the time Sammy's volleyball struck its smiling face—looked down from above the sink, ticking eternally in its bed of patterned wallpaper. Kosher paper. Rumor had it that, when my parents bought the house, the unmentionables who had sold it to them had hung wallpaper printed with baskets of food on it: peaches and bananas and jugs of milk *and* lobster *and*

2

shellfish and, as the story aged, whole pigs with apples jammed in their mouths. *In the kitchen. Where everyone ate.* Now, instead, over the *traife* wallpaper was hung a pattern of sing-song paper in *my* honor, with treble clefs and half-notes and children huddled together, their enormous mouths round and open, with strings of still more notes trailing out of them.

"If you're putting up a Buddha clock," said my father the day he had to hang the wallpaper, "what the hell difference does it make if you've got kosher paper or not."

"What are you talking about?" my mother said.

"The Buddha clock. That's a religious symbol too. You might as well put up a crucifix clock with one of Jesus's arms as the hour hand and his leg as the minute hand."

"What kind of nonsense are you talking," she said. My mother had a simple view of the world. Kind though she was to almost everyone she met, for her, people fell into two categories: Jews and Christians. There were no Buddhists or Hindus or Moslems. The Christians made it as a category only because they had broken off from the Jews and because they looked like Jews, some of them. They were created either to persecute or to shelter Jews—they had their pick. And just as the religions were created in descending order of acknowledgment by my mother, so were prospective spouses for Sammy and me. In fact, in the matter of spouses, there was to be no descent whatever from the first category.

My father had now joined my mother in the bedroom and she initiated one of those audible whispering sessions directed at everyone but the listener. "He couldn't find enough music in Quebec. Montreal is not musical enough for him."

"He wanted to go to the U of T. He says it's a good school."

"And McGill is a *bad* school?"

"Forget about it already." My father was no sentimentalist. "And, besides, maybe we'll have some quiet around here."

3

"That kind of quiet I don't want!" she whispered at the top of her lungs. "Ben is not a loud boy! You don't even know what *loud is!*" And here, for the second time that morning, the conversation broke off.

It was still more than two hours before my train was due to depart but, since emotions seemed to be running high and since my father was going to be driving, I insisted that we leave. My father was easily the worst driver in Montreal—no, second worst, after the guy who gave him his license in the first place. His basic problem was that he considered driving the approximate equivalent of a nap. The minute he climbed behind the wheel, he'd start whispering to himself, as if he were having a bad dream. He'd carry on full conversations with business associates, with people who bothered him, with bridge players; he'd also shrug his shoulders (his hands leaving the wheel) and thump the dashboard if he was making a particularly pertinent point.

Once, when I was driving with him, he seemed, from the expression on his face and the rapid movement of his mouth, to have gotten so angry at the person he was talking to I thought he was going to get up and leave the car. We were rolling toward an intersection and his feet altogether left the accelerator and brake. He put his palms on his knees, his elbows out and, just as he was about to hunch forward—he was a man of pride and wouldn't sit there to be insulted through an entire conversation—terror froze my voicebox and we crashed into the car stopped at the red light ahead of us.

"Now *that* is a true idiot!" my father shouted at the man he'd just hit and he jumped out of the car to yell at the driver. Except for my knees, which were still shaking, I sat paralyzed. Even my eardrums were paralyzed. I did not hear a word until my father once again opened the door: "I'll see you in *court!*" he yelled over his shoulder.

In court I testified against my father.

But the story only ended there. Between the accident

and the court appearance, my father and I went to pick up the car at Berkowitz Auto Body:

HAVE A SMASHING HOLIDAY
ALSO EXPERT MECHANICAL REPAIRS BY
OUR TRAINED SPECIALISTS

We walked into the shop; my father spoke to Berkowitz; we got into the car; my father's eyes glazed over; he consulted his mirror momentarily; started the engine; backed up; smashed into the pillar of the body shop; drove back in; got out of the car; spoke to Berkowitz; turned to me and said, "Let's go." We took the bus home; walked into the house; he kissed my mother; said (without the trace of an expression on his face) that the car wasn't finished; sat down and asked if dinner was ready.

This was the man who was driving us to Central Station. My mother sat in the front, and Sammy and I climbed into the back as we'd always done. I was thinking—just as the doors whumped shut—that this was the last time we'd drive like this—that, even if the four of us assumed these positions yet another hundred times, it would not be as it had been: driving north to the lake, or south to the mountains of Vermont, or downtown to Sainte Catherine Street to shop, or to Schwartz's Deli for a smoked meat sandwich. And we must all have begun to think the same thing because nothing was said after the usual opening remarks: "Would you mind keeping your eye on the road just once?" said my mother.

"Please, Rita, I can drive in my sleep," said my father.

"Spare us the demonstration," she said.

I noticed my mother was wearing the blue dress with white polka dots that Sammy and I had bought her for her fortieth birthday. It must have meant a great deal to her because, as often as we'd all criticized her for not doing it, she rarely spent money on herself. Generally, she wore about $5,001.79 worth of attire: $5,000 worth of jewelry (bought for her by her two American brothers) and a $1.79 dress she'd selected from a bargain counter at Kresge's.

5

She never scrimped on *our* food, *our* clothing, *our* entertainment, but, when it came to herself, she would buy lime green blouses with collars that were seventeen inches out of style and, in the fall, those horrendous knit sweaters with Niagara Falls cascading down the back—made, as the manufacturer pronounced proudly on the label, of polyester, acetate, nylon and unknown fiber. What *was* unknown fiber! Crystallized sewage? Sammy once said that, if a terrorist squad ever wanted to hold Montreal hostage, all it would have to do is to hold a match near my mother's wardrobe.

What a rat I felt in the back seat of the car with my brother pondering his new role as an only child, my father talking to the hood ornament and my mother sitting silent and statuesque, her hands folded neatly over the imitation patent leather purse in her lap. What a revolution this must have seemed to her—my *choosing* to go to Toronto when I could have studied at McGill, the very institution her Czechoslovakian ancestors held up as the pinnacle of success, the landmark of liberty! *Me.* Her first born. For whom she had washed the pesticides off grapes with Ajax, on whose watermelon she spat halfway down the slice (so I wouldn't get near the green and develop diarrhea). I couldn't stand myself at that moment in the car, and I wished my father had learned to drive so that we could be at Central Station already. I was sensitive to every motion. I was afraid someone would turn on the radio and strains of "Anatevka" would fill the car.

This was not to be the end of my agony. We got to the station so early there would be an interminable wait for the train to leave. We headed for one of the marble benches, and my mother instantly produced a neatly folded dishcloth, laid it out beside her and signaled to my father to sit down. (The cloth was so he wouldn't develop hemorrhoids.) "In a minute," he said. He was reading the train schedules.

My mother nudged Sammy. "Give it. Give it," she

whispered—the whisper resounding to every corner of the station.

"Not *yet*," said Sammy. "When he leaves." Sammy got up and headed for another section of the station.

My mother looked me up and down as I stood before her. She sized me up as only she was capable of doing. "He has a gift for you—and it's wrapped. He wrapped it himself; I wasn't even allowed to look at it and I wouldn't have dreamed of asking him." She'd probably asked fifty times. "Shall we call him back?"

"Leave him. Let him surprise me." She went back to sizing me up. Her boy. The musician. The person she had probably told all of Notre Dame de Grace would take over as conductor of the Montreal Symphony the minute Franz-Paul Decker retired or died — whichever came first. The person for whom she had sat for countless hours, listening to his "sweet viola," when my father had slammed doors between us to shut out the racket. She was an extraordinary woman who had made it her life's work—her *job*—to see to it that I replaced Franz-Paul Decker, and I stood before her, viola case in hand, heading for Toronto, about to lay her off. This she would certainly not tell N.D.G. She would say McGill had a bad department; it rested too much on its laurels. She would say the *family* had decided Toronto would be a *much* better idea—especially since Fred Haydn (apparently a direct descendant of Franz Josef himself) had taken over the string class in Toronto — and besides . . . besides, it's not a good idea for a boy to be stuck at home all the way into his twenties. *I'm surprised your Saul is staying home and going to McGill.*

As the hour of departure approached, my family alighted on the original bench. My father and Sammy flanked my mother and both were hidden by the *Gazette*, Sammy with the sports section. All you could see were three pairs of legs, two enormous newspapers, the ends of sixteen fingers and a dishcloth. My mother sat smiling at me mostly, but always read a headline when my father turned the page.

My train was finally called and, before the announcement ended, I began my good-byes. A great gust of wind swept at our backs as I shook my father's hand. "I guess it's my job now to say something significant," he said, "so I'll tell you what my father once told me: when you're fighting racism, disease and hunger, when you're trying to figure out what it means to be a Jew in the twentieth century, you're facing the hard truths of life, Benjy. But when you're only deciding which girl to date next or what color pants to wear, those are just the soft truths. You got that?"

"I think so, yes." He gave my hand an extra couple of shakes.

Then I turned to my mother, who said, "It may be a soft truth to decide which pants to wear, but it will quickly become a hard truth if you boil your flannel pants with the rest of your laundry so they won't be big enough for a canary to wear." With this, she hugged me and whispered, "Never mind. I'll come down to help out once in awhile." She was crying when we separated.

Sammy took my hand.

"I'll be seeing you, Sammy."

"My boy," he said, "when our forefathers capsized on the shores of this great land—"

"Good-bye, Sammy."

"As a token of appreciation for vacating the house," he said, "I cultivated this gift for you." He handed me a package. "It's a giant hair ball from beneath my bed."

"Thanks, Sammy."

"Don't mention it, my boy."

I hugged him.

I boarded the train and found myself a nearly empty car. I began to arrange all my gifts and luggage—taking only sidelong glances at my family still standing on the platform. Sammy had withdrawn a large white handkerchief from his jacket and was already waving it at me melodramatically and feigning tears, even though the train had not yet begun to roll. Sammy took after my mother's side of the family, the blond, blue-eyed side, while I had my father's black curls and brown eyes. "Thank you on behalf of future generations of our family," Sammy often said to me, "for carrying on the dark and primitive colors of our people."

Beside him, my father signaled surreptitiously at my mother to leave. He'd certainly waited long enough. But my mother stood firm, staring through the window at me, her patent plastic purse suspended from one hand, and the newspaper (which Sammy and my father had obviously been willing to leave at the station) neatly refolded in the other.

Odd as it may seem, the newspaper she held was actually a source of comfort for me. It meant that life would go on after my departure, that she would go home, start supper, and later sit in the den beside my father to read some article about an ambassador's wife who had learned to live with cancer.

When the train finally grunted to a roll, I was relieved, too, to find I was practically alone in the car, except for two other passengers: a middle-aged man with regulation-sized breasts behind a T-shirt marked "Yes, we have no bananas," and a slightly older woman with caked makeup, teased, dyed blonde hair and false eyelashes—what some people refer to as a fluff ball. Only, this woman's fluff did not seem as resilient as it once must have been. There comes a point in life, I guess, when fluff turns into lint. The man settled at the front of the car near the toilet, squared his elbows and was instantly jiggled to sleep. The woman sat across the aisle from me one seat back, safely out of regular eye contact.

I knew the picture of my parents and Sammy on the platform would stay with me a long time, so I tried to block it out of my mind by thinking about Crazy Sarah. The poor woman had made it her principal daily activity to call my father and several other relatives to be reassured that her landlady was not going to evict her from her home in four and a half years or remove her liver while she slept; or that

Julia Child was not going to put her in a blender on her next show and make a sauce out of her; or that the man who read the weather on the eleven o'clock news was not going to put bamboo shoots under her fingernails and drip water onto her forehead *until she went out of her mind*. This was the funny part of it: she thought the world was a cruel place and that everyone in it was crazy except for her. To some extent, her view was self-fulfilling, partly because there was no point in talking to her or dissauding her from hearing and seeing things. She'd simply think it over and call you back with a new story.

She called Cousin Harry at his shoe factory every day to tell him what she'd heard. He'd say, "No, Sarah, it's all right. I'll call Prime Minister Trudeau myself to make sure he stops Chief Dan George from scalping you next Thursday. . . . Yes, he returns my calls." Or, "It'll be fine, Sarah. Max is not going to put you up before the firing squad July eighteenth; now, if you'll excuse me, I have a shipment to get out."

One day, though, in the middle of a shouting match Harry was having with a supplier, the phone rang and Harry was in no mood for Sarah. "What? What? What?" said Harry, when he picked up the phone.

"Harry, I heard on the news the salesclerk at Eaton's at the hat counter is going to have me hanged in the Old City where everyone will see," said Sarah.

"I heard that too," answered Harry, and he hung up. She never called him again.

Some of the family members — my father included — began to think she was having us on. "Think of the advantages!" Cousin Harry once said. "You pretend you're crazy. Everyone feels sorry for you. You don't have to work; the government will pay all your bills — including mandatory rest in Florida two weeks every winter — and you've got it made! Sarah's not as mad as we think she is." To substantiate their case, these relatives, who had nothing better to talk about at Bernie Spivack's Bar Mitzvah or Marty Langer's graduation party, always recalled Sarah in her early years when she was "nowhere near as mad as that Kaufman kid—what's his name?—Murray, who makes noises like an ambulance siren every night before he goes to bed."

"Poor boy," said Aunt Ida, the resident genius at changing the subject. "What's going to happen when that Murray's parents go?—heaven forbid. He'll be lined up for soup at the Sal-i-vation Army."

"Never mind Murray," continued my Aunt Ruth from Czechoslovakia. "I hear Bernie Spivack has some tendencies himself."

"What do you mean *tendencies?*" said Ida. "He's subnormal?" she asked, thinking she was using the medical term and pointing to her temple.

"No—worse," said Ruth, leaning into Ida. "I hear he's a *hoimosectional*. And I wouldn't let my kids near him, Ida. I hear it's catchy."

"That's stupid!" said Linda, Ida's daughter, who had graduated with a B.A. in psychology and no longer sat at the children's table. "You people say some of the stupidest things sometimes!" And she'd slap at the floral centerpiece on the table and spin around in her chair.

I must have dozed off because, when I woke, I suddenly realized that Quebec was behind me and my future ahead. I felt a great surge of relief. For some reason, the melody of Bach's "Sheep May Safely Graze" rolled gently through my mind. It had a compelling rhythm, like the Ontario countryside. What bliss lay ahead of me? What could I do that I had never done before? I had been to Toronto only six weeks earlier to arrange an apartment, but this was different. I was to be alone. I could throw my socks all over my room; I could put them in the *refrigerator* if I wanted to —who could say anything? I could stay up until four in the morning for no good reason and make idiotic faces and noises and lie flat across the kitchen table. I could buy skin magazines and leave them lying around on the floor — open. I could drink myself into a stupor and sleep on a park bench, or wander around the campus dorms until I found myself a girl.

That's what I especially needed to do. It had now been more than a year since I'd broken up with Mary Beth Wilkins, a beautiful girl I'd first met in grade ten, a girl I thought I'd never get over.

I sat beside her in Miss Millsap's history class and she was exquisite: long brown hair the girls behind her used to twiddle all the time; light green eyes; a perfect pink complexion; white straight teeth; small pert breasts behind immaculate sweaters; and perfectly molded legs. What caught my attention besides her appearance, though, was the routine she performed every time she came into class. She would slide into her chair; unlock her briefcase; place the text, *The Modern Era,* on the left-hand side of the desk and her notebook on the right; withdraw a sharpened pencil, a ballpoint pen, a red marker and a short plastic ruler from a zip-up Beatles pencil case and place them all in the trough at the head of her desk; clasp her briefcase locked again; place it standing on the floor beside her slim upright purse; fold her hands neatly in her lap; and await the gospel according to Miss Millsap — who, like every other teacher, of course, loved her.

More spectacular even than this routine was the one that followed. Miss Millsap would say, ''I'd like to discuss Jay's Treaty today,'' and Mary Beth would lean forward, keeping her back straight; open her notebook; flip to a clean page, write ''Jay's Treaty'' in blue, underlining it three times in red; put the date (with the month spelled out in full) at the top right, underlining that twice; mark a dash at the left of the first line; and await the first point.

It was during one of these clasping and straightening and underlining sessions that I fell in love with Mary Beth. Since I was so shy, it took me months to do anything about my yearning. I spied on her instead. I followed her to her locker, watched her delicately removing her penny loafers and pulling on her rubber boots, her white mitts, her soft wool coat. I stole around corners and followed her home, watching her until she got right into the house. Then I waited for a quarter of an hour half a block away, wondering what she must be doing inside. I imagined her trading her boots for pink furry slippers; hanging her coat on a wooden hanger (because the Wilkinses would never keep wire hangers in the front closet); kissing her mother—who was certain to look like Mrs. Ward Cleaver—lightly on the cheek; slipping inaudibly into her room and into her chair before her arborite desk with the map of the world laminated permanently into the top; taking out all her homework and completing it — neatly, underliningly — before supper.

When I finally got up the nerve to ask Mary Beth out, I hung up twice before anyone answered. Finally, the excruciating moment: one ring, two rings—WHAT SHOULD I SAY!? four rings—I'll say I caught Chief Dan George with a hatchet following Mary Beth home—

"Hello?" It was Mrs. Cleaver!

"Hello, Mrs.—um—Wilkins? This is a friend of Mary Beth's from school calling. I was just wondering if I could ask her about Jay's Treaty—you know, school work—who was Jay, and so on?"

"Certainly. May I tell her who's calling?"

"No—I mean, no, just a friend, tell her."

"Well, hold on."

Pause. I strained my ears to hear the patter of pink slippers. Nothing. Then—"Hello?"

"Hello, Mary Beth?"

"Yes?"

"This is Benjamin Beck, your classmate, calling."

"Benjamin, hello, was that you—"

"Please call me Ben."

"Ben, was that you who called before and then hung up?"

"No, this was absolutely the first time in my *life*!"

"No, I mean—"

"Maybe it was a burglar or a lunatic or something." I said.

"Oh, great!" she said.

"Yeah."

Pause.

"Was there something you wanted to talk to me about?" she asked.

"Oh, yes"—*my God, I had forgotten where it was I wanted to take her! Something historical, something cultural.* "Mary Beth, would you like to go out together to the Axelpayne Coffee House? I understand they have some superb poetry readings there—very elevating and illuminating—if you want to have a break from homework, or—"

"Sure." The word riffled past my ear through the hairs at the back of my neck, plummeted down the cliff of my spine and penetrated, fluttering through the course of my intestines until I heard, "When?"

"Pardon?"

"*When*—what day?"

"Friday—Friday night. I understand they have some very famous poets reading this Friday night."

"Sure. What time?"

"Well, I think the readings begin at eight p.m., so I'll pick you up around four."

"Four!"

"Just to get a good seat, or maybe have dinner first, or—"

"Why don't we say six?"

"My exact alternate suggestion," I said, like a complete idiot. "I'm looking forward to a grand evening," I added moronically. "See you then."

"All right. Bye."

"Right. Bye-bye, then."

I arrived at Mary Beth's on Friday night at 5:55, wearing my very coolest clothes: my light blue shirt (undone an extra couple of buttons) with French cuffs, my slightly tight gray flannels, my off-white Holt Renfrew blazer, my gray suede shoes. When I was let in by Mr. Cleaver, he smiled politely—his gray flannel sideburns twitching a bit—and said, "You must be here for Mary Beth; she'll be a couple

14

of minutes." While he said this, I noticed him staring at the few ringlets of hair my open shirt revealed. They felt suddenly like a cluster of Italian construction workers.

"Sure thing," I said, surreptitiously buttoning my shirt to the top. By the time I got to the living room, I had also buttoned up my jacket, so that I must have looked like an East European refugee when Mary Beth finally joined me.

But she was radiant. She wore her hair up and a beautiful white dress and almost no makeup. "Hi, Ben. Are you ready to go?"

"Absolutely," I said, rocking back and forth on my heels and punching my hands together. But her mother called her into the kitchen—luckily, I might add, because my rocking almost sent me flying. I nearly knocked a rack of "Silver Spoons of the Ten Canadian Provinces" off the wall. I sat down, trying in vain to make out the conversation in the kitchen. The living room was decorated much as I had expected. Beside the spoons was an old photograph of Mary Beth, her hair—beautiful even then—in pigtails, and her smile partly toothless. On the other side was a spotlessly clean fireplace over which hung a painting, called "The Hebrides," and beneath which were brass fire-poking gadgets and pewter plates and goblets. "That," Cousin Harry once said, "is the difference between the Jew and the Gentile: the Jew gives gold and silver — even if only plated sometimes—and the Gentile gives brass and pewter. What're you going to do with brass and pewter, except unload it at garage sales—and then only to other Gentiles?"

"I'm all set," said Mary Beth, floating quietly into the room. "Do you like our mantelpiece?"

"I have adored brass objects for as far back as I can remember."

We had dinner at the Café des Parques, a small French restaurant with lace tablecloths and linen napkins. "It was nice of you to ask me out," said Mary Beth, smoothing the fan of her napkin into her lap.

"It was nice of you to accept. Do you like French food?"

"Very much," she said. Her face glowed in the candlelight. "Shall we have duck à *l'orange?*"

"Sure—anything."

We ordered and spent some time staring at the candle.

"Do you know which poets are reading tonight?"

"Yes: Lord Byron and Elizabeth Barrett Browning, I believe."

"I'm *serious*," she said, and she seemed to be, but I wouldn't have been able to guess who was reading because she asked me at a point in my life when I thought Northrop Frye was a dish one cooked on a fishing trip.

"No, I'm sorry; I don't know."

"That's okay," she said. "It's exciting to go anyway. I've never been to a poetry reading."

"Neither have I," I said, as the waiter, holding our plates with napkins, placed them before us and called us "monsieur" and "mademoiselle."

I waited to see what Mary Beth would do before I began eating. I imagined myself going into Millsap's history class on Monday with a ruler, a red pen, a blue pen, a fresh notebook and a look of eagerness on my face. Just as I'd expected, Mary Beth now leaned slightly forward and with knife and fork began surgically to remove the duck meat from its bones. To play it safe, I started with the peas, dropping one into my mouth and twenty-six into my lap. Mary Beth forgave me by not looking up and I felt the desire to compliment her in some way. If only Sammy could have seen how beautiful she was as she drew small, carefully measured bits into her mouth. Two eyes were insufficient to absorb the sight. "I wish I had more eyes to watch you," I blurted out.

She finished what was in her mouth. "How many?"

"Pardon?"

"How many more?"

"Five."

"You'd be an optician's dream come true, then, wouldn't you?"

16

I smiled as I opened wide to receive a quarter-pound piece of duck into my reddened face.

But dinner turned out to be the high point of the evening. The poetry reading that followed was an unmitigated disaster. It seemed one could never be too late to get good seats, and the place was far too small to escape, if necessary. The host gave an eloquent introduction to the foremost sound poet in Canada, Barnett Cranston, who would read from his latest book, entitled *Wail of Whales*. As it happened, the word "reading" was open to interpretation: "CO-OOOAH! LUGA! LUGA! LUGA! BLOOO-OOOOAAH! LO-OOOGA! BLOOAT! BLOOAT! GAULK! GAULK! GAULK! BLO-OOOOOOOOOAAH! T! T! . . ." It went on for over a half hour. If only I'd thought to bring along a giant harpoon. When it finally ended, the dozen or so people applauded enthusiastically. The host announced that Mr. Cranston would stay on to autograph copies of the book and asked that we look forward to his next volume, to be published in the fall by Blueball Press, and to be called *Ambulance Sirens and Tractor-Trailer Honks*.

I hadn't once looked over at Mary Beth through the whole reading but, as I rose to leave, she asked if we weren't staying for the next poet. I should have known that instant that things would never work between us, but I believed at the time that innocent Mary Beth, being the devoted student she was, must have lumped the world into two categories: those in print and those not in print. If Jay had been there to sign copies of his treaty, I'm sure she would have stormed the stage to be first in line. "No, I'd really rather leave," I said.

"Don't you think we should at least get Mr. Cranston to sign a book?"

"Mary Beth, there are no recognizable human words in the entire book. Are you going to spend ten bucks to communicate with a species other than your own!?"

She looked hurt, but she came along. We walked for ten minutes down Sainte Catherine Street without exchanging a word. "Why don't we have coffee in one of these places?" I finally said.

When the waitress in the Mermaid Deli dropped our cutlery onto a paper napkin and asked, "What'll you have?" I felt more relaxed than I had at dinner. Mary Beth looked pale in the fluorescent light. "Why did we go to a literary reading, anyway," she said, "if we weren't going to stay?"

"Because it wasn't a poetry reading we witnessed."

"Barnett Cranston is an experimentalist. He's introducing a new form to poetry."

"So does that mean that anything goes? What if he was the greatest visual poet in the world and he came out on stage to demonstrate how he could make his shoulder blades touch—would that have been acceptable?"

"Don't be crude," said Mary Beth and she turned to her side to avoid looking at me.

"Listening to a guy bellow for an extended period of time is what I call crude."

We did not speak for several minutes and I wondered how I was going to redeem myself. I ordered cherry cheesecake and coffee, but Mary Beth hardly touched her cake. "I think there are limits to what an artist can do—that's all," I finally said.

"Let's just skip it, okay?" she said, as she pushed her plate away altogether.

"No, you're obviously taking this personally, so let's talk about it." Mary Beth looked up for a moment. Her green eyes were startling in the white light. "Mary Beth, I'm a musician. I know music better than poetry. If I'm to be a better musician—maybe someday even a great musician—don't you think I have some obligation to communicate with people, to make them feel what is in their souls —to arouse in them a vague sense of what it means to be alive? When I first began to take lessons, my grandfather told me that when you are in the presence of great art there are no instruments and no musical notes; there is only the music—elevating you to its peaks and dropping you into its canyons. Did you, even for a moment, feel that way during the reading this evening?''

''Was your grandfather a musician?''

''No, a tailor, but he did write some poetry.''

Mary Beth smiled and reached across the table to take my hand.

Two weeks later I took her to an organ recital of music by Frank Martin. The organist played as though he had webbed hands. I leaned over to Mary Beth and whispered, ''What do you think: maybe this guy playing and the whale poet should collaborate on an opera?'' Mary Beth rolled her eyes instead of laughing.

If looks meant anything, our parents did not like our relationship. ''Mr. Casanova, why don't you ask out Sadie Bliet?'' my mother said one morning.

''Yes, Mr. Casanova,'' said Sammy.

''Her mother says Sadie wants to go to McGill to study dentistry.''

''We could use a dentist in the family,'' my father added.

''That's a great idea!'' I said. ''I'll marry her first and then I'll ask her out on a date.''

Mary Beth's parents were not as vocal—probably not even in private—but they weren't overly friendly either. I thought, at first, that they were just that way, but I soon realized they did not express any lasting interest in me. I was invited over one evening for dinner and Mrs. Wilkins asked me what my ambitions were. ''I hope to be a musician and a composer,'' I said.

''Oh, that's nice,'' she said and Mr. Wilkins nodded, while chewing a piece of roast beef.

That's nice. Not what kind of way is that to make a living! *Not* that's a pastime—not a profession. *Not* how are you going to feed your children and our daughter? *Just* that's nice.

''Well, you don't expect them to talk to you as if you were an old friend, do you?'' Mary Beth said when I spoke to her about it later.

"No, but I don't expect to be treated like Shlomo the leper either."

"What is it with you, anyway, Ben? What do you want my parents to do: invite you to their bridge game?"

"It's because I'm Jewish, isn't it?"

"*What* is?"

"The thing with your parents."

"I thought your *thing* was with me. *You're* the one having a problem, Ben. You're the one who carries on about my Loyalist background. You're the one who turns up his nose at my father's veterans' parade—the veterans, by the way, who risked their lives to save the Jews. You're the one who speculated on the *affair* between God and Mary!"

Our parents and my paranoia aside, though, our relationship was not working out as well as I had imagined it would—however hard we both tried. We had followed the manual exactly: we had skipped through rain; we'd laughed on the ferris wheel; we'd sipped one milkshake with two straws; we'd danced without music; we'd stared soulfully into moonlight; I had serenaded her with my viola. But something was wrong. *Something.* We never talked to each other unless we were angry.

Then one day I saw her walking home with Chuck House. There seemed to be nothing to it, but I began to see him waiting around for her at her locker, and I heard her cackling a bit too loudly at some of his jokes. Chuck House: quarterback, yearbook editor. Was I in some kind of movie?

I acted hurt for a week and then I phoned her. "I have to see you tonight, Mary Beth. Let's go for coffee, or something."

"I can't."

"It's important."

"I just can't tonight. I'm busy."

"House, I suppose." (I was so subtle.)

"What are you talking about? We have exams in eight days—or haven't you heard?"

"So, you're not going to stop to drink anything between now and exams?"

"Not tonight, Ben."

"Mary Beth, how can you go out with a guy who already refers to himself as *C.A. House*? It's right there in the yearbook for all to see: *C.A. House*, Mary Beth! What does the C.A. stand for—centrally air-conditioned? You're going to spend the rest of your life as—"

Click.

Sheep were still grazing when I came back to my seat on the train with a bag of potato chips. I decided to open my presents. Sammy's carefully wrapped package contained three books: *The Catcher in the Rye*, *The Apprenticeship of Duddy Kravitz* and *Portnoy's Complaint*. There was a letter tucked under the flap of the first:

August 29, 1974

Dearest Ben,

By the time you read this letter, you'll probably have figured out what to do with the hair ball I've wrapped for you. Maybe you could attach it to your toque and tell everyone it's a pom-pom. Far be it from me to suggest the many creative ways you could use it. Attach it to your chest if you want: your very first chest hairs—with my compliments.

So you're a boy in an institute of higher learning now—am I right? Mazel tov times 2, Benny boy. Bless you for being so smart and making your family proud. How many people in Montreal will one day say, "I knew him when. . . ." Leaving us to go to another town—that I won't mention. I wouldn't want to burden you with the guilt of abandoning your family, of leaving your tiny brother a solitary child in a big room with a red carpet and a few records by J.S. Bach. A very cool guy, that J.S., and quite adept at sucking up to God.

You may also have noticed three books in the package, to return to my first topic. The guys in these books were originals, Benny. Read 'em and weep. Maybe

21

you'll grow up like one of them and make your parents cry—as you've already begun to do—all the way to an early grave.

Anyway, God bless. Feel good. Give my love. Keep in touch. Don't do anything I would do. Goodbye.

*All my love,
Sammy

(*All my love, notice, Ben. Not some. Not much. But all. None left for Aunt Goldie and Uncle Mort. None for your weeping parents. None.)

I was quite choked up over the letter and gift. What was great about Sammy was that he was as capable of being the wise man as he was of being the wise guy. If anything, he was an "original." I'll never forget once, when he was about eight and I was eleven, sitting in the kitchen having breakfast when someone rang the doorbell. My parents were in the backyard, so Sammy ran to get it. It was a couple of canvassers for the Jehovah's Witnesses. Sammy told them our parents weren't home. They asked if they could step in to talk to Sammy for a few minutes. "Who are you?" he asked. They told him. "We're Jewish, though,"said Sammy.

"Can we at least leave you some literature?" said one of the witnesses.

"No," Sammy said. "We have enough trouble believing our own stories," and he shut the door in their faces.

There were two other packages—each with its own card—from my Uncle Milt and Aunt Ida. The first card had the picture of a diploma on the front and the caption, "On your graduation day. . . ." Overcome with suspense, I opened the card to learn the rest of the cryptic message. But in case you had forgotten it by the time you turned to the inside, the caption was repeated:

On your graduation day,
With all that work and little play
Your friends will say, "But you are done!

And now it's time to have some fun!''

CONGRATULATIONS!

All Aunt Ida had written in the card was

Knock 'em dead . . .

All our love,
Uncle Milt and Aunt Ida
(xxoo)

The present was a sterling silver comb, inscribed,

Benny Beck's Graduation, 1974
Love,
Uncle Milt and Aunt Ida

I stared at the comb. Inscribed objects had a way of reminding me that time was passing. My children would one day find it in a dresser drawer and ask if I had been close to my uncle and aunt. But their children wouldn't ask, I'm sure. The comb would probably end up, in a hundred years, on some junk table in an antique store, and a young couple passing through would say, ''Maybe we can have the inscription polished off.''

''No, honey, look; here's something even better: 'Silver Spoons of the Ten Canadian Provinces'.''

The second package had the exact same card attached to it as the first, but the message, this time from Uncle Milt, was

. . . but don't knock 'em up!
All the best,
love and kisses,
Aunt Ida and Uncle Milt

The gift was my uncle's idea of a joke: a copy of *Dimento* magazine—

Publishers also of
PIMENTO
the mag for food lovers,

and
LAMENTO
the consumer's guide to funeral homes.

The magazine was unbelievable. It had articles and photos categorized under the various perversions. The centerfold fell under the "Love and Obesity" section and was a photograph of a naked woman who was so mountainous the picture was continued on p. 88.

But that was the tame part of the magazine. There were letters about bestiality with dogs, goats, pigs, cockroaches, foot fetishism (and what to do if your partner has athlete's foot), and there was a whole section of letters on urologania, otherwise known as "golden showers." One man had written in to ask other practitioners how to broach the subject on a first date. Simple, I thought. You take your date to an elegant restaurant; you order a sumptuous meal — and maybe sixteen or seventeen drinks; you light a smoke, using the candle; and, maintaining your cool and charm throughout, you lean forward to say (in a husky but delicate voice), "Would you like to come up to my place and perhaps urinate on one another?"

After the first date, though, life undoubtedly would settle down. You could find yourselves a nice apartment—three bedrooms, no bathrooms—and raise children, saving on diapers if you so desired.

There was another section on incest. *Incest.* Do people really leap on parents and aunts? . . .

"Aunt Ida, shall we step out onto the terrace for a little air?"

"Why certainly, Benjy. Isn't the Spivack Bar Mitzvah wonderful? Did you try the chopped liver? I must ask Esther where she got such delicious chopped liver."

"Aunt Ida?"

"Yes, dear?"

"Have I ever told you what wonderful hair you have?"

"Why, thank you, Benjy." (Here I would run my fingers

through her coiled, petrified ringlets.) "I must tell Stella, my hairdresser."

"Ida," I would whisper.

"Yes, Ben?"

"You've known all along, haven't you?"

"Yes, Ben?" — her fire-engine red lips glistening, her rouged cheeks reddening.

"My sal-i-vation army marches only for you, Ida!" And here I would leap at the cavernous gulch between the bobbles of her breasts, the sparkles and small coins on her dress flying in all directions, her girdle snapping, her support hose running, the needle-heels of her shoes buckling. What ecstasy!

"What are you doing?" said a young girl who had sat down opposite me.

"What!"

"What's the matter?"

"You startled me." I stashed *Dimento* between the seats.

"What magazine were you looking at?"

"I was working—doing some research for my career."

"What do you do?"

"What?"

"Can you hear okay? What is your career?"

"I'm a urologanist." I had broken out in a cold sweat.

"Kathleen, where are you?" a woman called, as she entered the car carrying two salads.

"Over here with this man. He's a yourgo—"

"Never mind!" I said.

"Why are you bothering the man?" asked the woman.

"She's not," I said, and couldn't help but stare. The woman who approached wore a loose, flowing lavender dress with a matching hat that complemented the long, luxuriant tresses of her hair and the steel-blue of her eyes. She looked like a character out of some Victorian novel and —even more peculiar—she looked almost exactly like an older version of the little girl sitting opposite me. She could easily have been the girl's older sister, but I assumed she was her mother.

The woman obviously did not want to sit with me, the entire car being empty, so she stood in the aisle holding the two salads. "I'm sorry for the disturbance. Kathleen, let's go back to our seats in the other car."

"No, I want to stay here and eat lunch with the man."

"*Kathleen*."

"I'll *scream*," said Kathleen, and I was quite sure she meant it.

The lavender lady rolled her eyes. "Excuse me," she said to me as she whisked by to occupy the window seat beside the girl. These were apparently the last words she wanted to say to me, as if all this were my fault. She did not even want to look at me, preferring instead to stare out the window or at her salad. Kathleen must have felt guilty because it was several minutes before she spoke.

I was nervous because I could feel *Dimento* at my side and I didn't want the woman to think that she and Kathleen were sitting opposite some kind of omnisexual.

I glanced back and forth at my wholesome companions eating their salad, while I munched on my potato chips. If the two had been the same size, they could have passed for twins. It was hard to believe a man had even been involved. I wondered if Mrs. Lavender had self-pollinated.

"What's your name?" Kathleen said.

"Ben."

"Are you going to Toronto?"

"Yes."

"Us too. Why are you going?"

"I'm moving there. I'm going to be a music student."

"Do you sing?"

"No, I play viola."

"*Play* something."

"Well, I can't right now here on the train."

"Do you like playing?"

"Very much."

"My Dad doesn't play a viola, but he has a lot of records

26

he plays all the time. He likes Beethoven.'' She pronounced the name perfectly. ''He always talks about Beethoven, and he took David and me to see Beethoven at the orchestra.''

''Who's David?''

''He's my stupid brother—''

''Kath*leen*.'' Lady Lavender spoke!

''He's my brother. Maybe he's only stupid sometimes.''

''Do you have a smart brother too?''

''No, just David. Have you ever seen Beethoven?''

''No, but I like his music very much.''

''My Dad says Beethoven couldn't hear the music he made. That's stupid, isn't it?''

''Well—''

''He probably wrote that kind of music because he wouldn't have to hear it.''

''No. He kind of heard it inside. He was deaf, you see; that meant he couldn't hear anything: he couldn't hear people talking to him; he couldn't hear the birds chirping; he—''

''Did God make him that way?'' I looked over at Mrs. Lavender to check how far I could go in my discussion with Kathleen, but she kept her gaze down, eating the leaves of her salad like a fawn.

''No, God didn't make him that way exactly. My theory is that, when God came to Beethoven, he had just run out of ears, so he had to give up his own to the new baby. The trouble was that God heard so much noise here on earth that the ears fell silent, listening only to the beautiful sounds within.''

Kathleen thought awhile and said, ''Do you think God's going to give away any more parts?''

''Maybe, some time.''

''I think you should eat your salad,'' said the larger version of Kathleen.

''I hate salad!'' shouted Kathleen. ''I want some potato chips.''

There were only crumbs left at the bottom of my bag. ''I'm sorry, Kathleen; I haven't got any—''

"That's very kind of you," said Mrs. Lavender. "But I'd rather she finished her salad. Besides you still have the wrapper left. I'm sure *it's* more nutritious than the contents anyway."

Evidently, I *was* being blamed for Kathleen's sitting down with me, and I began to resent it, so I joined the battle.

Kathleen said, "I want a *hamburger!*"

"Shall I bring you one from the dining car?" I asked.

"No, *thank* you," said Lady L.

"Oh, she's not allowed meat either?" I asked. "Is she permitted only to graze?" Kathleen giggled, and I immediately felt guilty for ganging up on L.

"We eat meat sometimes, but we try to avoid red meat."

"Why?" I asked. "Is it some sort of spiritual thing?" No answer. I tried to be polite: "Is it some religious thing —or philosophy, maybe?" No answer. Kathleen giggled.

"The body is the temple of the Lord," said L.

"Oh . . . well, I seem to be having trouble getting worshippers at mine," I said, and regretted that comment too, but I couldn't resist.

"Don't be so vulgar—in front of a child, too. You and your stories of God's ears. Kathleen, let's go back to our seats—*please.*"

"No. I like Ben. *You* go back."

"I'm sorry," I said. "I really am."

Silence once again descended on the car. We sat listening to the train clattering. I think Kathleen was happier when L was not talking. If I had been a gambler, I would not have bet on L to be the first to speak, but I was wrong. She was even quite civil: "Where are you going to study music?"

"At the University of Toronto."

"Granddad teaches there!" Kathleen shouted, now vying to be included in the conversation.

"What does he teach?" I asked.

"He teaches in the English Department," L said.

"Canadian literature. He's considered an important literary scholar."

"*My* grandfather was something of a poet," I said on reflex. "He used to say that literary scholars are like orthodox Jews: they're not too bright, but they keep the faith alive." I chuckled idiotically. Even Kathleen seemed to be getting tired of me. "Maybe I'll sign up for his course," I said, trying to redeem myself. "What is it called?"

No one answered. Kathleen giggled.

"Is it called 'Canadian Literature'?"

"Let's go, Kathleen." Kathleen rose. "I enjoyed our talk. Have a good time in Toronto." They were already headed down the aisle.

"I loved meeting you and your daughter," I called after them, and they erupted in laughter.

"Kathleen isn't my daughter! She's my niece! How old do you think I am?"

I laughed too. "Do you mind my asking your name, please?"

"Yes," she said, slamming the door behind her.

In grade five, one of the only ways a boy could save face and get a girl's attention at the same time was to push her or swear at her. That was not a method that was going to work any longer. I suddenly wanted very much to find L again and endear myself to her.

Maybe I would take a course with Professor Lavender.

TWO

My apartment in Toronto was located over the Blue Sky Restaurant near Queen and Parliament streets—a section that, in spite of its regal street names, had lost much of its stateliness. But the apartment was just what I needed: it had a bedroom with a large picture window overlooking Queen Street, a separate kitchen, a bathroom with a free-standing porcelain tub, and a small living room, the entire ceiling of which opened to a large wire-meshed window that brightened the whole apartment. My very first morning, before breakfast, I danced naked under my skylight.

The district, too, had a certain irresistible charm. My visiting relatives would no doubt notice the occasional bag ladies and rubbies who passed back and forth from their homes in Moss Park. But there were also hundreds of immigrant families here—Italians, Greeks, Chinese, Armenians, Russian and Polish Jews—who had long ago established businesses and despite having fled to live in the suburbs, returned morning after morning to tend their shops.

The restaurant below me buzzed every lunch hour with talk of weddings, sicknesses, break-ins, the Nixon resignation, the Patty Hearst abduction, the CBC studio that had opened on Berkeley Street, Trudeau and the latest budget, and the rookie police who wrote out parking tags.

''You see the cop writing me a ticket this very minute,'' said Mr. Stanowicz, of Queen Rebuilt Auto Parts.

"Yeah, get out there," said Mr. Katz, of Katz's Men's Wear, Clothiers to Presidents and Stars. "I think he just started. I'm sure he'll tear it up if you move the car."

"Not me, boy," said Mr. Stanowicz. "I keep a record of the tickets and sooner or later they all come into my shop. Have you ever seen prices marked on my merchandise, Sid?"

"No."

"That's because I keep them all up here," he said, pointing to his forehead, "and when they come in, I check their name on the list I keep from the tickets. If O'Driscoll comes in looking for a twenty-dollar carburetor and the tag is five dollars, he gets it for twenty-five dollars — not a penny less. If Macpherson comes in wanting a hubcap for his Chevy—and he came just this morning—the hubcap is five dollars, plus two for a tag he wrote me. 'That sounds steep,' Macpherson told me this morning. 'They don't press them any more,' I told him. 'Have it made new and it'll cost you fifteen, if a penny.' He bought it. No, Sid, I don't chase cops any more."

The owner of the Blue Sky, my landlord, was Mr. Stavro Dioskouri. "What kind of name is that?" asked my mother, when we first looked over the lease.

"It's Greek," my father said.

"It sounds Italian," she said.

"It's *Greek*! Nana Mous*kouri*, Melina Mer*couri*, Stavro Dios*kouri*."

"There's nothing wrong with Italians—"

"It's *GREEK*!"

"Don't shout. He'll hear you downstairs. There's nothing wrong with Greeks either, but you couldn't find anything in residence?"

"No, I told you; there's a waiting list and my application got in too late," I said.

"Besides, why suffer in residence when you have parents foolish enough to foot the bill for a private pad," my father said. "Let Max and Rita pay. They're old fools! No good bringing girls into a lousy room in a dorm. Why not

31

have your own place!'' And he laughed. Then he squeezed the back of my neck.

''Where are you going to do your laundry?'' my mother asked.

''There's one just around the corner. Remember? You were the one who pointed it out.''

''Well, I could come down every once in a while to do it for you.''

''Why don't you come each morning, prepare three meals, do his wash and leave right after?'' my father asked.

''I can manage, Ma.'' I called her that when I found it too adult to call her 'Mother' and too childish to call her 'Mom.' ''Besides, Mr. Dioskouri said he'd be glad to help out and that there would always be plenty of food left over for me after the dinner hour—no charge.''

''So you're going to fill yourself every night with Italian food . . . all that pasta—''

''Greek, Rita. GREEEK! Stavro is a GREEK name!''

His friends, who filled the dining room every noon hour, called him Steve. The first morning in the new apartment, as I was getting dressed to go out, Mr. Dioskouri sent up Magda, the ample Hungarian waitress, with bacon and eggs, toast, freshly squeezed orange juice, a piece of canteloupe and a glass of milk. I was embarrassed but not entirely surprised. Maybe he had sensed my mother's uncertainty.

The next afternoon, following registration at the university, I resolved to have lunch at the Blue Sky to at least give Mr. Dioskouri some extra business. The lunchtime rush had passed and only a few of the regulars remained, including a table of CBC workers (I guessed), who could be distinguished by their expensive casual wear; and a portly, aging Scottish-Canadian, who spoke without an accent, but still used ''aye'' and other such expressions. I soon came to learn his name was McConnell and he spent much of the time having the same conversation, even when he was by himself: ''Aye, if I was just a hundred pounds lighter, I could be playing in the NHL.''

I helped myself to a menu and took a table close to the window, but didn't notice Mr. Dioskouri anywhere. I did see Magda, though, who waved at me from the kitchen and indicated she'd be right over. This was the first chance I'd had to study the restaurant, which was quite a bit bigger than it looked from the outside. It was also gaudy, in its zealous attempt to bring the Mediterranean to Queen Street, but it was clean and had wonderful smells emanating from the kitchen. The ceiling was painted à la Sistine Chapel, but with goats and nymphs, centaurs and Spanish dancing girls all frolicking in a bed of clouds. The blue of the sky continued down the walls overlooking the mountain village and pasture painted all the way around the room. The artist Mr. Dioskouri had hired must have been one of those guys who gave you a good price and said, ''Leave it to me,'' thinking the more he did the more he'd be loved. Oddly enough, though, the artwork and small tables with red tablecloths gave the room a warm glow.

I ordered what turned out to be a mountainous dish of shish-kebab served with four vegetables and half a loaf of bread. Every time Magda passed me, she winked.

When I was almost through stuffing myself, I was relieved to see Mr. Dioskouri pull up in his car. I had been waiting to thank him and I didn't know how long I could keep springing into a smile for Magda. But he came in with three men—one, about my age, who headed straight into the kitchen. The other two began to inspect the restaurant and to whisper periodically to each other. Mr. Dioskouri acknowledged me with a nod and asked if I had enjoyed my meal, but turned immediately back to the men. They were speaking Greek, so I couldn't understand what the ritual was all about, but something significant was almost certainly occurring. The C B C people got up to pay and my impulse was to join them, since Mr. Dioskouri was going to the cash register anyway. But Magda emerged from the kitchen, took one look at the men, screamed, dropped her tray and ran back to the kitchen, leaving the mess on the rug. Mr. Dioskouri thanked C, B and C and ran back to see what had happened. I stared, slightly frightened, at the two men, but they hardly looked like hit men for the mafia, or even health inspectors. Both were slight, their clothing unimpressive and they mumbled to each other, seemingly as confused as I was.

"Crrezzy leddy," one said, when he caught my stare. I smiled—adding it to the hundred I had shot Magda. Mr. McConnell, the only other person left in the restaurant, merely went on eating a second lunch, not even noticing the commotion.

The young man I had first seen go into the kitchen now emerged again, stepped over the fallen tray, waved hello to Mr. McConnell, said something to the men in Greek and sat down opposite me. "My father said you're the new tenant upstairs. I'm John," he said, and offered his hand.

"I'm Ben Beck. Do you know what's going on here?"

"What do you mean?"

"I mean with these guys and the tray and Magda."

"Oh, it's nothing. She just dropped it."

"Magda doesn't strike me as the type who would drop a tray, even if there was a bus parked on it."

"Yeah, I know what you mean. Maybe she was nervous or something—well, look who's here."

I turned and, lo and behold, in through the door and up to our table came the Lavender Lady. John checked his image in the side of the napkin holder and adjusted his hair.

"Carolyn, sit down. Have you met my friend Ben?"

She looked as surprised as I was. "Yes, I believe I have. How are you again?"

"You *know* each other?" asked John.

"Yes, we met on the train," Carolyn replied. "Is Diane around, John?" She looked uncomfortable and didn't sit down. She also looked much younger in blue jeans and a sweatshirt than when I'd seen her as Tess of the d'Urbervilles.

"No," said John. "I haven't seen her since this morning. Sit *down*. Let me get you a cup of coffee."

"I'd prefer tea," she said as she sat. John adjusted his hair and went to the back. My heart raced.

"So how's Kathleen these days?"

"Oh, she's fine," said Carolyn, running her finger down the side of the napkin holder. She paused a moment. "So you're at the U. of T. now, aren't you?"

"Yes, I'm taking the music program, but I'm also enrolled in one English and one history course. Your father teaches English there, doesn't he?" My voice cracked and slid upward as I said this. "Puberty," I said, chuckling and banging my throat with a fist.

John came back through the kitchen door with a tray. "Yes," said Carolyn, as I took up her spot running my finger down the napkin holder. "But he's on a mini-sabbatical this semester. He's working on his *magnum opus.*"

"I hope it's nothing serious," said John, passing out the cups. Carolyn looked slightly stunned. "It's amazing, though, what doctors can do these days," he added.

Mr. McConnell approached us on his way out. He really was a colossus. "Aye, if I was just a couple o' hundred pounds lighter," he said, "I could be a star on the Maple Leafs."

"Look at the bright side, Mr. McConnell," John said. "At this rate you won't be a star, but you could certainly become a planet."

Carolyn giggled.

"Aye, John, aye. Where's your father, boy?"

John got up to take his money. "So we're all at the U. of T., are we?" he said from the register.

"Maybe Ben and I are," said Carolyn, "but you never go to classes."

"That's very funny," said John, joining us and checking his reflection in the napkin holder again. What would we have done without that napkin holder? "You can tell Diane for me that she should mind her own business."

Carolyn and John's mutual familiarity made me edgy. Carolyn giggled. "Well, would you tell Diane for me instead that I couldn't wait any longer for her and I'll call her later?"

John nodded.

With that, Carolyn left without touching her tea. "What a goddess, eh?" said John, as we watched her out the door.

"Diane, I gather, is your sister."

"No, she is the mouth of the family. We're not a family really—just a bunch of body parts: Diane is the mouth; my father is the arms; my mother is the heart and lungs,"—to demonstrate John sighed deeply several times—"and I, of course, am the rectum. Naturally, we have an opening for a brain."

"So, are you and Carolyn dating or something?" I asked.

"Very clever," he said. "You're interested, but you don't want to come on too strong—just in case she's *my* girlfriend." John laughed warmly and patted my arm. "No, are you kidding: Carolyn and me? Look, if you're attracted to her, I'll get you her phone number."

"Yeah, . . . sure, why not? Who knows? Right?"

"Right, right. Listen, why don't we meet at the U of T sometime and I'll show you around."

"That sounds great," I said.

"Or even better: you should come to one of our parties at my friend Bruce's place. He puts on some pretty wild parties—and once in a while Carolyn comes."

A voice in my head—my mother's—said stay away. It also said something about pasta, but I tuned it out. "Sure, let me know," I said.

Mr. Dioskouri came into the dining room, still talking with the mafioso health inspectors. "Your father's got quite a place here. Is it his own?"

John nodded as he swallowed a big gulp of coffee. He patted his hair down on one side and said, "Yeah, he owns this place and the two adjoining ones—the one with Max's Furniture Emporium and the one with Weitz's Hardware. He's also got one down the street at the corner of Sherbourne that's being rented by the Toronto Dominion Bank there."

"He's got quite an empire down here, then."

"Yeah, but he worked hard to buy those places. He lost his property during the war back in Greece, and he thought it was the coolest thing to own some slabs of concrete in a city. He has no business sense, really. It's all personality. People seemed glad to lend him money—and he's never defaulted on a payment. That's his religion: never default on a payment and things will look after themselves. And they have. I don't know why he keeps working here. We sacrificed a lot for those slabs, but they're sure paying off now."

Mr. Dioskouri finished and the men left.

"Look, I'm going to be taking off," said John, "but I'll give you a call or drop in to see you, okay?"

"Great," I said, and he, too, left, waving to his father and me without looking back.

I hadn't seen Magda since the tray incident, but I left a generous tip for her. Mr. Dioskouri wouldn't take money for the lunch, though. "I insist—please," I said.

"Doan oo-woarry," he said, but he looked more worried than I was.

"Please, really, I have plenty. My parents—"

"Nex' time," he said. "See you letterr. Come hyev deenerr letterr."

What was I to do? I would buy him a gift, I thought, or help him out in some way. "Can I do something? Can I get you something? You've been so nice."

"Mebbe sometime," he said. "Doan oo-woarry. Be a good boy. Go to school. Be frriends oo-with Dzon." There was a touch of urgency in this last request. I should have rushed out right then to buy Mr. Dioskouri a gift to repay his generosity. My better judgment told me there was too much going on here that was going to distract me from my studies.

"I forgot to ask," I said. "Is it all right if I practice my viola upstairs—during off hours, I mean?"

37

He looked puzzled. "Oo-what?" he asked, meaning, I think, "rephrase the question."

"I play music. I'm a music student."

"Ah, mooseec! Oo-what kine mooseec?"

"Viola. I play *viola*."

"Ah, play! Play! Hyeere too sometime," he said, indicating the restaurant.

"Sure—sometime," I said, hoping he'd forget he asked.

THREE

Over the next six weeks, I searched the campus high and low for Carolyn, eating lunch in a different cafeteria every day, walking through buildings I had not yet been through, hoping each time I'd catch her standing by a door talking, or sitting somewhere reading. Each time, I was convinced I had finally solved the great mystery: "Ah, the Medieval Studies Centre — that would explain her outfit on the train!" I'd go bounding up the walk and down the front hall, up a flight of steps, down another hall, into an office and out the back door. If anyone saw me, I'd head straight for a washroom to account for my hurry.

Once it was the Centre for Culture and Technology. "Of course!" I crept in the front door of what had to be nothing more than a converted old carriage house, banging my viola case against the Xerox machine by the door, and expected in an instant to see Carolyn sitting at the knee of Marshall McLuhan, imbibing his wisdom. Instead, I saw a tired-looking little man at a desk marked "Reception" with a hundred file folders scattered every which way over his desk.

"May I help you?" he asked, straightening three or four files and placing them on a pile to his right.

"Oh, no, sorry," I said. "I was just looking for my car."

I did finally run into John, though. We met during one

of his rare visits to the university and, under the great gothic ceiling of Hart House, ate baked beans and pork.

"Are you here for a class?" I asked.

"Yeah, I'm a history major and this is a compulsory course. We've got a term paper due next week and I haven't even picked up the topics yet, so I thought I'd better drop by."

John ate only a bit of his lunch, then pushed his plate aside to light a cigarette. "Do you remember you were going to give me Carolyn's number?" I asked. "I thought I'd—"

"Sure," he said. "I don't have it with me, but if you look up David Drewry—that's her father—on Heath Street you'll find it. By the way, we're having one of those parties I was telling you about and we'll probably invite her and my sister, so you should come."

"Well, give me a call," I said. He wrote my phone number on the flap of his cigarette pack, and then he fixed his hair.

On the way out, we paused at a bulletin board. There was a handwritten sign that read,

LOST
Sterling Dunhill Lighter
Inscribed "Fraser"
If found, please turn in to
Lost and Found Office.

John pulled out his pen and wrote beneath the message,

Tough luck, Fraser, I found your lighter
and I'm never giving it back.

"What did you do that for?" I asked.

"Are you kidding? I'm putting Fraser out of his misery. Do you think anyone's ever going to return his lighter?"

"Maybe not."

"Loosen up," he said. "Carolyn will love you."

I chalk it up to a new level of maturity in my life as a

result of all my independence that I did not rehearse my speech before I called Carolyn.

"Hello, Carolyn, this is Ben calling. You know: the train-Ben."

"Yes, sure; how are you?"

"Fine, fine. Would you like to see a movie with me?"

"Um, sure. When? This weekend?"

"This *weekend*? Great!" So momentous was this occasion that I somehow felt I had to make an appointment a year in advance. But I suddenly remembered my parents were coming to town this weekend. "Uh—no. How about next weekend?"

"Sounds fine," she said, her voice like a silk ribbon drawn across my ear.

Early that Saturday afternoon, I was tidying up for my family's arrival when there was a knock at the door. Expecting to see my parents, I opened it wide.

"*Carolyn*! How are you?"

"I was just downtown doing some shopping and I thought you might like to join me."

"Today? You mean right now? I would —I mean, I'd love to, but I'm expecting my family to arrive from Montreal any second."

Carolyn ignored whatever panic there might have been in my voice and stepped in. She looked positively sultry. She wore a tan leather vest and skirt that fit tightly around her shapely form. Beneath the vest was a classic white blouse. Her eyes were azure in the natural light from above, her cheeks faintly blushed, her neck a soft ivory. This was easily the most beautiful neck I had ever seen. Dangling at her side, then between her legs as she walked, was a suede purse no bigger than a pouch. "Would you like some tea?" I heard myself say.

"No, I should probably go if your folks are coming."

"My folks?" This was the first time I had heard anyone call Max and Rita Beck "folks." I could see them now: my mother wiping the flour from her hands into a big, country apron; Sammy scattering feed to the chickens; my father in a checkered shirt sitting atop his tractor and driving it in a wild zigzag through field and bush. "Honeybunch, I'd like you to meet my folks, in for the day from Omemee. Look, they've brought some berries."

A bang came at the door. "Oh," said Carolyn.

I opened it to find my father carrying two crates of records. "Let me put these bloody things down." Behind him came Sammy staggering under the weight of three boxes. Then my mother with detergents and bags of groceries. "Excuse me, dear," said my father to Carolyn as he dropped the crates from two feet up. "Let's have lunch. I'm famished."

"Oh," said my mother, as her eyes met Carolyn's.

"Folks," I said, "I'd like you to meet Carolyn."

My mother paused but a second before she said, "Intermarriage doesn't work." Then she headed for the kitchen with the bags.

"Are you as hungry as I am?" said my father to Carolyn.

"No, not really. Thanks, though," she said. "Ben, I'd better get going."

Sammy snickered.

"Are we still on for next week?" I asked. "Can I call you or whatever?"

"Call me," she said and went out the door. I watched the firm globes of her bum in the swishing leather as she ran down the stairs, her little purse leaping hysterically to the motion.

"What the hell do you mean, *intermarriage doesn't work!*" I yelled toward the kitchen.

Sammy threw himself into the easy chair.

"Don't swear, Benjy. Did she sleep here?" said my mother, wiping her hands.

"No, she *lives* here. She's homeless. I took her in."

"Ben's right," said my father. "You had no business saying that."

"So this is how our son is going to greet his family on their first visit from Montreal? With a tramp hanging out in his pad?"

"A very gorgeous tramp, though," said Sammy.

"Thanks for your support, Sammy, really."

"Okay, but that's all I have energy for after carrying those boxes," said Sammy.

"And what do you mean calling a person a tramp the second after you meet her?" I said.

"What would you call her—dressed like that?" she said.

"What the hell was wrong with the way she dressed?" My father sat down on one of the boxes.

"You call that an outfit?" said my mother. "It was a pair of shoes that didn't know when to quit."

"Great. Terrific," I said. "How would you feel if people judged you by the way you dressed?"

"Thank you very much. I enjoyed our visit. Max, get up. It's time to go back to Montreal."

"Can't we have lunch first?" said my father.

"Yeah, let's go have lunch," said Sammy.

My mother went back to the kitchen and my father followed to calm her down. He shook his head at me as he walked by.

We drove to Spadina Avenue, Toronto's garment district, where my father often ate when he came to town to do business. The two- and three-story Victorian redstones that lined the wide street were bustling with shoppers and workers. Cars and vans were double-parked. My father knew a laneway behind Moo Wong's Laundry and Maury's Furs where he always parked. Even that was crowded, though, which meant a ten-minute commotion while all three of us directed my father this way and that until he negotiated in the single tight spot that remained between two cars.

"I hope this is a kosher restaurant," said my mother, as we walked two blocks to the Red Dragon Kitchen.

"We drove on Saturday," my father said. "You don't shave your head and wear a wig. What difference does it make which rules you break once you become an outlaw?"

That my mother didn't answer was a bad sign. She didn't say, "I grew up in a kosher home; I maintain a kosher home; I'm not about to blow all that on a plate of pork hocks.'' She didn't even say, ''All right, but chicken or fish only.'' She merely hooked her arm in my father's and strolled along, looking occasionally at one window or another.

Her silence could not be interpreted as Victory by Slow and Painful Guilt either, and Sammy and I both knew it. She worked harder at inflicting guilt. She would have said, ''My stomach has been upset enough by that rodeo girl and her boyfriend for me to add to it now by eating a plate of claws.''

But guilt was exactly what I was feeling because she was not now faking hurt.

''Forget it,'' said Sammy. We passed my parents who had stopped to look at some fabrics. ''That Carolyn was unbelievable. You don't need to feel bad about it. You had good cause to yell. God knows, with your numerous defects you have enough trouble landing a date—especially with a girl that looks like that—without having your mother blow your chances.''

''You're right. I'm going to forget it.''

''Tell me something,'' said Sammy. ''Does this Carolyn have a slightly younger sister?''

''No, her sister's much older, but now that you ask, she does have a niece—her sister's daughter—that could pass as Carolyn's twin. Her name is Kathleen.''

''Oh, *really*. That's a nice name.''

''Yes, and I understand she's a recent graduate, too.''

''*Really*? Where did she study?''

''I believe it's called Forest Hill Elementary School.''

The weekend passed quickly. Neither my mother nor I spoke about Carolyn again. In fact, when I went to meet my family at their hotel on Sunday morning, my mother acted as though she had wasted too much time in silence. She wanted to come straight over to my place to give me instructions on how to survive until her next visit. Sammy asked if, next time, he could stay with me instead of with our parents, ''. . . unless, of course, you have company.

44

Or maybe even if you have company. I'm not above watching." I punched him in the shoulder. "Bless you, my son," he said.

"Huchoo."

I spent several days wondering what I would say to Carolyn. When I called, she said she had the flu. "What about next weekend?" I asked, waiting for Item Two on the excuse list.

"I've got quite a bit of school work coming up, Ben, and then" — Item Three — "I'll be going to Florida for a week."

"Oh, that must be exciting for you."

"But I understand," she said, "that John's friends are holding a party soon after that. Why don't we meet there?"

"That sounds fine," I said. "I'm looking forward to seeing you with your tan—" I was about to say "suit."

"Great. See you, Ben."

I buried myself in my studies over the next few weeks and found myself concentrating especially hard on the pieces composed in minor chords.

FOUR

I saw quite a bit of Mr. Dioskouri on my way in and out, and, although he would signal me into the restaurant and try to get me to stop to eat whenever he saw me, I would only say hello. One day he sent up a practically new couch for my living room, later explaining he had little use for it in his den. Quite often he sent up Magda with breakfast. It made me feel so uncomfortable I began to leave a tip and a thank you note on my dresser the night before in case I missed her.

On her deliveries no mention was ever made by either of us of the tray incident, and I had learned from experience with my parents' friends that it was better not to ask because you never get a simple answer. One morning, though, my curiosity got the better of me. I had never met a person as kind as Magda and yet as reluctant to attract sympathy by volunteering information about her problems. On the other hand, who was I that she should unload her worries on me? "Magda," I said, as she put down the tray, "do you remember that day those men came into the restaurant—"

"You couldn't forget about dat, could you? You vere burning to ask me, veren't you?" Aside from some switches in consonants, her accent wasn't as heavy as I'd expected. I learned later she'd come to Canada when she was ten. The accent combined with her size gave her the air of one of those great peasant women crushing the legs of the Russian invaders as they approached.

"I was just curious. I didn't mean to pry."

"It vas nutting. Don't vorry; dere vas no espionage or anyting involved." She hesitated, seemingly unsure whether or not to continue. "Dey vere just people from my past. I used to vork for Mr. Moustaki in anoder restaurant. He used to treat us all bad — da vorkers — and he cheated us, saying ve vorked tirty-two hours instead of tirty-four; and he short-changed da customers vhenever he could — not to mention da taxes department." Magda breathed here—an odd place, I thought, as if cheating the tax department was the worst deed possible. It turned out she was selecting from among Moustaki's greatest crimes. "But he vas mean—really mean. Dere vas some dogs used to come every night in da back alley looking for food and he chased dem avay and poured da soup into da sewer instead of give it to dem. Vone dog vouldn't leave, never; he vas alvays so hungry and like a skeleton. Moustaki vould kick it, but it vould come right back, crying. Den Moustaki vonce took some hot grease and he trew it at dat dog and it run avay. Next day it came back because it smelled da food, and Maria—anoder vaitress—and I started to cry: da dog vas blind, but it smelled da food. Even da cook vas crying a little and he gave da dog vone of da best sirloin steaks.

"We hated him so much, ve called dat healt inspector and ve saw Moustaki trying to give him money, but dey came—da police, everybody —and said he had to close and Moustaki said da last day he vouldn't pay us for da last two veeks and he said take him to court. Ve vere so mad ve did a terrible ting."

"What?" I asked, curious to know what cruelty they had dreamt up.

"Ve vere nice to him dat last day. Ve told him ve knew he didn't have money to pay us—vhat a liar he vas!—but ve said ve should have a goodbye lunch togeder. 'Great,' he said. Meantime Gus, da cook, took some dog shit from

47

da alley and mixed it vit his beef stew and ve vatched— togeder—all of us at a table vit da doors closed for da last time vhile he ate it—smiling and saying da food vas good, too bad it had to close, and ve smiled too.''

I made a mental note never to cross Magda. ''And you didn't see him again until he came to the Blue Sky?''

''No. And he came dat day vit his broder.''

''Well, it doesn't mean—''

''It does mean! Mr. Dioskouri told me he vas looking for partners; it vas too much vork for him.''

''Tell him not to take Moustaki.''

''I couldn't. It vas too late. Dey made some papers before Moustaki came dat day. I couldn't tell Dioskouri everyting. I love him. He is a sveet boss, very kind.''

''Maybe you should find another job then.''

''It's not so easy to find a good place and vit Mr. Dioskouri I am very very happy.''

''I'm sure it'll be all right then—with him around. But he didn't ask you why you dropped the tray?''

''I said it vas an accident.''

''Well, why don't you forget it, then? That would be the best thing.'' What I really wanted now was for Magda to leave. I was still in bed and had a pressing need to go to the bathroom. She took the hint, but before leaving turned to ask me not to tell anyone. ''I won't,'' I assured her. ''And Magda, please don't bring me breakfast anymore. I have to learn to get it myself.'' She nodded but seemed to hear nothing, preoccupied still with her dilemma.

The dog shit story was some kind of strange harbinger for the first crisis of my new independent life: I discovered I had no toilet paper. This had never happened to me before. I had assumed that somehow paper simply wound out of its holder, spun endlessly by magical toilet paper-worms. I hobbled around my apartment looking for something I could use; my spiral lecture notebook was all I could find.

The crisis did not abate even then, though. At the grocery store, I was confronted by a mountain of different toilet papers, ranging in quality, I supposed, from news-print to silk. Which do I buy? Which did my mother buy? There was a variety of bird kinds: White Swan, Dove, Downy. (Why not Pigeon?) There were fabric kinds: Silky, Velveteen, Cashmere, Cottonelle. There were flower kinds: Gardenia, Ambrosia, White Lily, Lilac. But that was not all. The best fell into the category of personality traits: Charisma. Now, it was one thing to use a bird or a bunch of flowers or a piece of cashmere to wipe your bum, but to use someone's charisma! Charisma, though, I noticed, was the "King of Toilet Papers—The Renaissance Toilet Paper." Charisma, it seems, had the sense and took the trouble to employ a person who engraved each sheet with flowers and birds and ditties of all kinds—and it was scented! Charisma it was for me!

This, then, was to be the first real accomplishment of my new life. But it was followed swiftly by yet another crisis; how was I to line up at the cash register with just toilet paper? People would say, "Is that all you have? Why don't you go ahead of me." And moments later I would be at the head of a long line of people to whom my look would say, "I'm afraid I ran out right in the middle of the deed."

I scurried about picking up carrots, a head of lettuce, meat tenderizer, dishwashing detergent, a dozen choco-late-glazed doughnuts and a pair of rubber gloves. These I piled all around my Charisma. I then lined up, a look of purpose and righteousness on my face, and paid.

As fate would have it, though, Charisma and I were not to be alone immediately, for who should be awaiting me at the top of my stairs dressed only in a nightgown, coat and slippers? Crazy Sarah.

"Sarah, how are you? How did you get here?" I said, passing what I thought was a potato on one of the upper steps.

"Fine, thank you." I backed down and picked up what was indeed a potato on one of the upper steps. "It's for the poor people," she said.

"Pardon?"

"It's for the poor people. My mother said you lived in a poor section. Put it back on the step and they won't bother us."

I placed the potato back on the step. "Does your mother know you're here?"

"No."

"How did you get here?"

"By train."

"In your slippers and nightgown?"

"It's more comfortable. Ben, I'll be staying with you a week to ten days and then I'll be going on to the States. I've brought another potato with me."

I was afraid to ask: "Another potato?"

"It's for the American poor people."

"You're going to go to the States in your nightgown with a potato?"

"Yes. Do you have a cigarette?"

"Sarah, you won't be able to get into the States."

"Why not?"

"You can't get in with potatoes. They confiscate vegetable matter."

"It's all right. I wrote to President Ford and explained that I would be bringing a potato, so there'll be a letter of permission from him waiting for me at the border. I also asked that the Coast Guard be there to escort me safely into the country."

"But the coast is not near here, Sarah."

"Then they shouldn't be very busy. Do you have a cigarette?"

I picked up my groceries and unlocked the door. "Why don't we go inside?" I took her coat and she settled, distracted, into a soft chair in the living room.

"Does the traffic helicopter fly over that?" she asked, pointing to the skylight.

"Not that I've noticed."

"Don't be so naive. They carry weapons and bombs."

"How do you know?"

"They confessed to it. I heard them on the radio."

"That was the Montreal traffic helicopter, though. The Toronto one doesn't carry weapons."

"Oh. Good." She rummaged around in her purse for her cigarettes. She pulled out her compact first and applied lipstick in the vicinity of her lips. She then lit a cigarette, looked around for an ashtray, then dropped the match back into her purse. With my luck, I thought, Carolyn will now drop in on me again.

"Would you like a chocolate doughnut, or some lettuce maybe?" I asked.

"No, I'm smoking." I brought her an ashtray. When she took a drag, her entire face was pulled forward as if it were being sucked through the cigarette.

"Sarah, I have a class this afternoon; I should go to it."

"You go. Where is the bed? I need some sleep." Moments later she was spread out on my bed, appropriately dressed for the first time that day. There was a look of trouble even on her sleeping face.

How could I go to school and leave her there? She would wake up, put on her slippers again and head for the border. What was I to do with her, though? My Great-Aunt Hazel was probably desperate, but if I called her she would instantly die of a heart attack. If I called home, my mother would be hysterical. I paced back and forth in the living room and once almost sat in the chair she had sat in, but I remembered my Aunt Ruth: what if it's catchy? I decided to wait until my father was sure to be home.

"What do you mean she's with you?" my father asked, not too surprised by the news. "Have you heard from Hazel today?" I heard him call to my mother.

I faintly heard my mother's voice saying Aunt Hazel was going out of her mind. "Why?" she asked.

"Ben has Sarah with him," he called back.

I heard a "What!" that I probably did not need a phone to hear. She picked up the extension. "What are you talking about?"

"She's here. She came by train."

"Then put her on the next train back," my father said.

"Max, you pick her up tonight," my mother said.

"You should see a doctor," said my father. "One day I get home early from work and I'm right away going to drive all the way to Toronto for the pleasure of listening to a loon all the way back?"

"All right. Ben, your father will pick up Sarah in the morning. He's right: he can't drive all night the way he drives. Sweetheart, will you be okay with Sarah one night? I'll pack some things for you."

"I'll be fine, but you don't have to pack anything. I went shopping just today."

"Good for you, dear. You hold tight until morning, okay?"

"Sure, sure. Don't worry about me." Just before we hung up, I could hear my father's grumbling voice heading toward my mother.

While Sarah slept for the rest of the day in my bed, I sank into the infected chair. I wondered how it was that Sarah could have gotten so bad she was carrying potatoes from one city to another. She was not always this way. There were times even I could remember when Sarah would appear sane all day. We'd be invited over to my great-aunt's house for dinner and Sarah would be perfectly sociable—nice even. Then you'd ask her to pass the salt and she'd overturn the table.

No one really knew where Sarah's defect came from. The relatives speculated that it came down directly through her father, my Great-Uncle Louis. *His* father had been suicidal and, as the story goes, was one day cleaning his rifle when he decided to end it all. He was sitting in the kitchen, and his wife, who was humming gaily as she cooked dinner had her back to him. He pointed the rifle to his temple, but had to hold it too far down to aim it properly so that, when it went off, it sent a large cast iron pot flying off an upper shelf and onto his wife's head, killing her instantly. Uncle Louis' father then decided he needed to stay alive for the

52

children, but Uncle Louis, who was then twelve, was needless to say never the same.

I remember only a few things about my Uncle Louis. One was that he was a dumpy little man and, probably to make himself look taller, wore his pants cut all the way up to his armpits. Consequently, when he wore a tie, only about four inches of it ever showed. As a child, I used to sit before him and trace the outline of the tie behind his pants all the way down the slope of his round belly.

Another thing I remember is that in grade four I was asked to interview an older person and to write a composition about the person's life. I asked my uncle and he seemed to be agreeable, but he always took a long time to answer. As I waited, I looked over the vast expanse of brown pant and the bald head he rubbed as he thought. He looked like a man in a rain barrel. Why, I wondered, with all that pant, did he need to buy complete shirts? Why not just dickies—with shoulders, maybe? "All right," he finally said. "But forget the interview. I'll just put together my life story and save you the trouble."

Three days later, a large brown envelope addressed to me arrived at our house. It was an essay from Uncle Louis, called "The Glove Trade in Austria: 1906–1908." In it, he named himself the inventor of colored gloves, claiming that only white gloves were in use before his innovation.

The outstanding characteristic of my uncle that lingers in my memory, though, was his extraordinarily slow speech. Someone in elementary school must have told him to pause at commas, so he spent a full minute of silence each time he came to one. He used to drive my father wild by making a forty-minute phone call to find out the postage rate for a first-class letter. During many of his calls, my father was able to leave the receiver on the table for five-minute stretches and to pick it up only to say "Yes" at each interval. I'm ashamed to admit that it was during a phone conversation with my father that Uncle Louis died and that it was easily ten minutes before my father realized it.

This was Sarah's father. By most reports, senility improved him; he had apparently been much worse when he was younger. Unlike Sarah.

At two a.m. she woke. I didn't hear her approach because I had nodded off so I jumped when her voice came out of the darkness: "Ben, do you have a teabag?"

"A teabag!"

"I would like a cup of tea."

"I'll make you one," I said, staggering into the kitchen.

"It's okay. I'll make it. You just show me where the teabag is and the cups." I found the box of teabags still packed in the larger box beneath the sink. This was a care package my mother had brought me and I had become used to simply assuming it was bottomless. (It was out of this same box I had pulled what I did not know was my last roll of toilet paper a week before.) I gave Sarah a cup with a teabag and then filled the kettle with water. As soon as I moved to plug in the kettle, she stepped up to the tap, poured water into the cup and began drinking distractedly.

She did not ask the time, did not talk about her plans for the day, nor ask about my plans, nor if I had slept at all. She merely settled back into the soft chair with her tea and asked if I had a cigarette. When I shook my head, she once again hunted through her purse, pulled out her compact, slapped a cloud of powder onto her face, found her cigarettes and lit one, flexing her face outward as she had done before. Though she seemed threatened by the world, she did not, on the whole, seem bothered by it, and this quality gave a certain kind of peace to her face—as deep as the trouble that had been there earlier.

We sat in silence until the kettle whistled. I brought my tea back and settled opposite her on my new couch.

"Ben, why are you in Toronto?"

"You mean, why am I studying here instead of Montreal?"

"Oh, you're *studying* here."

"Yes."

"What are you studying?"

"Music."

"Do you play something?"

Had we ever *met* before? "Yes, the viola. I've even played it for you."

"Play for me now, please. Play Handel's 'The Arrival of the Queen of Sheba'."

"I don't think I have the music for that and, besides, you need a whole orchestra."

"Play it, *play* it."

I took out my viola and faked what I remembered of the melody, but Sarah didn't seem to notice my mistakes. I watched her sink back into the chair and close her dark eyes, made so much darker by the powder on her face. She began to sway a bit to my poor rendition. I had barely played the last chord when she was pushing me to do the overture to Franz Lehar's "The Merry Widow." I faked the waltzy part from it and Sarah began with frenetic hands to conduct. Soon she was humming. Then, "Ben, can I sing something? Can we sing together?"

"Sure. What would you like to sing?"

As she thought, her look was passionate. It suddenly occurred to me that Sarah was famous for the long hours she sat listening to the radio, which, in fact, had come to embody her life. She must have floated between its poles like someone at once hunting and hunted—between terrifying announcements about her impending execution, or interviews with terrorist helicopter pilots, and the sweet music that calmed her. She now seemed to be drifting back to her own safe youth: we sang Chuck Berry and Buddy Holly, through which I needed quite a bit of prompting, and "Let It Be Me," by the Everly Brothers, and "Duke of Earl," and then her favorite song, for which I played the "Wim-a-way, a-wim-a-way" part on my viola:

> "In the jungle, the mighty jungle,
> The lion sleeps tonight . . .
> Hush my darling, don't fear, my darling,
> The lion sleeps tonight . . ."

Our voices crooned and faltered over Queen and Parliament streets, over the closed shops, the silent streetcar tracks, and the sleeping rubbies, until the light began to come in through the ceiling and I could hear, between verses, faint sounds in the kitchen below.

I don't know what time it was that Sarah and I dozed off. I think we simply expired simultaneously. The next thing I heard was the chorus of honks from the street, signaling the arrival of my father.

Even before unloading or seeing Sarah, who was still sleeping, my father decided he had to have lunch. Mr. Dioskouri wouldn't, of course, accept payment from him, and my father—in a rare mood—insisted he come to stay with the family in Montreal.

When everything was unloaded from the car and Sarah was loaded into it, I suddenly felt as though I had betrayed her—called the secret police while she slept and sent her back to the prison that was her home.

FIVE

In the middle of December, John finally phoned to invite me to a party the following weekend at his friend's house. He gave me directions to his house in Willowdale, a northern suburb, where I was to meet him.

The ride up seemed short, but the brief trudge through the snow from the bus seemed long. Then, suddenly — there, sprawling before me, was Oak Crescent of Willowdale, but not an oak or a willow lined the street. That is the beauty of the suburbs: they clear out the trees and name the districts and streets in memory of them. The Dioskouri house loomed in the distance. It seemed, even from a block away, to be suffering from an identity crisis: it looked Italian and aspired to be a villa complete with fountain in front and two concrete lions guarding the driveway; but the house was flanked, on the one side, by another house wanting to be a Georgian manor and, on the other, by a Texas ranch bungalow, but with Venus de Milo instead of beef herds grazing on the front lawn.

More unusual even than the architecture, though, were several small, multicolored projectiles soaring out of the snowbank in front of the house. Were these *flowers*? Some strange breed of tulips in the dead of winter? Was this Italy after all? They *were* tulips. I crunched across the lawn to examine them.

"You won't get much smell out of those!"

"What!" I was startled. It was the rancher from next door.

"You won't get much smell out of those — they're plastic."

"Oh." I felt ridiculous. Why did *I* feel ridiculous? "Thanks," I said, as if the guy had given me some valuable advice.

I had to ring the bell twice and, just as I was beginning to think John had forgotten I was meeting him here, the door opened. Before me stood a somberly dressed, unsmiling woman about a hundred pounds too large for her voice. "Hyello, hyow arre you? Come insigh," she said, the small voice coming from deep within her chest, as if she'd swallowed a little girl. "Dzon getting drress."

"Thanks," I said, as she directed me toward the living room.

"O-woould you like some pestrry?"

"Um . . . no thanks."

"Keck. *Pes*trry. Baklava."

"No, thank you, no."

"Cuffee?"

"No, nothing, thanks."

She did not budge. Maybe I had insulted her, but I became preoccupied with her appearance. She must once have been a beautiful woman: deep, brown eyes, thick, black hair folded upward in braids, a classical Greek nose, and a pale, unlined face. Everything about her was simple, with the exception of her necklace. The pendant was a large crucifix, more suitable, I thought, for a nun. "Maybe just a coffee then." She pointed me to the living room again and disappeared around a corner. From somewhere downstairs, I could hear the sounds of a TV.

The living room was immense and it was decorated like some Roman palace after the conquerors had brought back their booty. On the walls were too many prints of angels blessing lovers and lovers blessing fawns; needlepoints of Botticelli's "Birth of Venus" and of Apollo or Zeus (someone, anyway, looking muscular and righteous); photographs of village forebears in cramped suits posing painfully for the camera—all framed in gilded rococo plaster, all crowded together in the way they probably were in their villages, some smiling with that smile people fix for cameras—transparent even decades later. In one corner, beneath the photo of a young Mr. Dioskouri—proud and in uniform — was a giant grotesque Napoleonic victory clock, with sprigs of golden ivy winding around fluted decorations, embroidering leafy decorations, forming the bed of floral decorations—all whirling upward to hold a small, round, white clock face with one black hand pointing to the nine. On the other side of the room was a simple upright piano complemented on each of its sides by Florentine chairs, the backs of which were white and gold and turned upward on one end like arrogant eyebrows.

There were also lush plants all around the room; but in one corner stood a tall rubber plant held upright by a rope wound around its neck and fastened to a hook in the ceiling. The cultivation of this plant was evidently more a factor of the length of rope than the length of stalk.

I was just gazing at the dining room beyond—the chandelier with a crazed symphony of crystals, the china cabinet with more crystal, porcelain, brass, gold, silver, bronze— when Mrs. Dioskouri reappeared with a tray of coffee and pie. "Crream and ssougarr?"

"Yes, please."

We sat slurping coffee for long moments. I could still hear the faint sound of the TV and wondered if it was John who was watching it and why he wasn't coming up. Was he asleep?

"You from Moantrreul?"

"Yes, Montreal." I picked up my pie.

"Yoourr parrents?"

"My parents?"

"Yuh."

"From Montreal?"

"Yuh."

"*Een* Moantrreul?"

59

"Yes."

"Futhairr?"

"My father?"

"Yuh."

"Yes, he's in Montreal with my mother."

"Ot do futhairr?"

I repeated dumbly, "Ot . . . do?"

"Futhairr oo-work?"

"Work?"

"Yuh."

"He's in textiles! *Children's clothing*! You know, *children's* wear!" I was shouting, as if she were deaf.

"Nice, verry nice," she said in her little voice, and once again silence descended upon the palace. When it did, I realized that what I held in my hand was a lovely plate with a piece of pie, but no fork. I graciously set the plate down on the marble coffee table before me, as though I was taking a break from it. Fearful that the conversation would start up again, I peered over at my hostess, but she seemed to be somewhere else—her dark, distracted eyes reflecting the glint of her coffee. Was John the cause of all this worry? *Where* was John? "Is John asleep?" I asked.

"Excyoose me?"

"*John*. Is he asleep?"

"Yuh."

"Oh."

". . . Do you think you could wake him?"

"Yuh."

Nothing. I couldn't help but notice a very prominent vein in her neck bouncing excitedly with her pulse, sending wave after wave across the expanse of her breasts to where the crucifix rode up and down.

"You hyev no forrk," she said, finally noticing me, and she pushed forward against her girth to rise from the soft chair. When she returned, she seemed to be gathering courage, as if I'd just arrived. "You futhairr sell clothes wholesell or retell?"

60

"Wholesale. I don't think there's any such thing as retail where my father is," I said.

"Excyoose me?"

"Wholesale."

"You study at UFT?"

"U . . . of—yes!"

"Ot gonna be?"

"Um, a musician. I hope to be a musician," I said, and watched her neck.

"Nem? Ot's yoourr nem?"

"My name?"

She nodded.

"Ben Beck."

"Beck?"

"Yes."

"Eengleess?"

"No—not exactly English."

"Frrents?"

"No—closer to English. It's a German name, I think. Some of my family came from Austria and that region some time ago."

"Gairrmunn?" That was obviously the word that had registered. I checked the Richter scale of her neck.

"We're Jewish. Maybe it's a Jewish name. I'll have to find out some time."

"Dzooeess. Verry nice pipple. I like Dzooeess pipple." And here, glad that I had found something to please her, I took up my pie, but I found I couldn't get through the crust with my fork. To save the moment, I applied super-human pressure—smiling all the while—and sent a piece flying across the room into the plants somewhere. "Oh," I said feebly, rising to hunt for it.

"Doan oo-woarry. Doan oo-woarry."

If I had been asked at that moment to imagine the wildest event possible, I would never have predicted what was to come. John snuck up on us and suddenly flew stark-naked through the room, beating his chest and wailing like Tarzan. On his way out, he paused before the hall mirror to adjust his hair, then vanished somewhere into the bowels of the house.

His mother and I sat like sculpture. I looked up to check the time, but the hand on the clock hadn't moved from the nine. I looked up a second time to see Mrs. Dioskouri's vein crashing against the wall of her neck. It was clearly her move, but I felt desperate for her. If I had been in the room alone when John streaked through it, I could have passed it off as some locker room antic. If his mother had been alone, she might have regarded it as boyish foolishness. But the act had been staged for both of us: to embarrass me and to torture her. If I had left right then—decent young man from Montreal that I was, hair not too long, son of wholesale children's wear, music student, polite—I would only have added to her misery, so I sat and waited for Mrs. Dioskouri to make the first move.

Much as I had hoped they wouldn't, the floodgates finally broke and my composed hostess began muttering in Greek, at first softly and then loudly. Then she turned to me. "Ben, you come oo-with me, please." What did she want me to do? I followed her into a vast, spotless, white kitchen. "Ben, you go please oo-with Dzon to parry tonight and teck carre oth him. Doan, please, let Dzon teck the drrugs. Please. You goood boy." She pulled open a drawer out of which sprang a hundred objects—plastic bags, pens, address books, a half-used tube of toothpaste without a cap, a lighter, a watch with only half a strap, rubber bottle caps, a magazine, a bag of oregano—and withdrew a ten dollar bill.

"You teck."

"No, I couldn't—"

"Mebbe forr Dzon gonna need. Geeve to hyeem eef need, but doan tell, please. Mebbe hyee need, you geeve." I took the money. "Be goood boy, please."

"Maybe I'll check on John." She pointed the way up the stairs to his room.

I listened before I knocked. "Come in — the door's open." I was relieved to see he was dressed.

"John, I think I'm going to—"

"Hey, you look great, but mess your hair up a bit."

"What?"

"Scruff up your hair a bit. My friends are kind of freaky."

"John, you should count me out tonight."

"All I said was your hair—"

"I'm not wearing my hair as if I'd just beheld the face of God on Mount Sinai just to please your friends!"

He cracked up at this comment, partly to try to cheer me up, I think. "Come *on*; you'll have a good time anyway. Come along."

"What was all that about downstairs?"

"It was a laugh."

"I don't think your mother was amused."

"She's never amused."

"She was hurt and embarrassed."

"She's *always* hurt and she has spent her whole stinking life being embarrassed!"

"With your help?"

"Why not?"

"You're a jerk."

"Good, now that we have that out of the way, can you spot me a couple of bucks?"

"Is Carolyn going to be at the party?" I asked.

"She said she was. Maybe even my sister."

"Has she said anything to you about our meeting?"

"No, not a thing. Why?"

"Just wondering."

"Good," he said. "Now will you spot me a couple of bucks?"

"Why don't you ask your mother?"

"Because she thinks I'll spend it on drugs. She thinks you can buy a jug of hash oil for two dollars. I should arrive home one day with one of those rolling intravenous units attached to my arm and nostrils, and tell her I need to take a whole bag of heroin before I can get disconnected."

"She'll like that."

63

"Spot me a couple of bucks. I'm supposed to contribute it to the party."

"She asked me not to."

John hesitated a moment. He then went to his desk drawer, withdrew one of those desk pen-holders with the coins of the year suspended eternally in plastic and smashed it against the desk top. He pulled the coins from the crumbs of plastic and said, "Let's go."

He was *serious*. How long had I known this guy that I should put up with his lunacy? Was he *testing* me? "You're mad! Has anyone ever told you that?" I said.

"Many people. Let's go. And, Ben, loosen up, will you? Save the world tomorrow, do me a favor?"

From the vestibule, I could still hear the TV. "By the way," said John, "do you have a car? My sister took mine."

I shook my head.

"Never mind," he said. "It's a short walk."

SIX

Bruce Millgate lived in a house not unlike John's, except it was decorated downscale like a barn instead of upscale like a palace. Where the Dioskouris had marble and crystal, the Millgates used knotty pine and exposed brick. Where the Dioskouris hung Apollo and pictures of forebears, the Millgates had a giant "5" painted on their living room wall and, in the hall, a single photograph of someone who might have been Bruce's father wearing a Hawaiian shirt and a floppy straw hat, his arms around a family of emaciated black children.

"They're our foster children," said Bruce.

"You have *foster* children?"

"My family does. The Foster Parents' Plan. *You* know."

"Really?"

"They're nice like that," said John.

"Great," I said. "Really."

Before I could feel the full impact of John's sneer, I was pushed out of the entrance by someone coming in the front door. "Hi," said the new guest, offering me a firm hand. He was looking at me closely, but one of his eyes turned outward and seemed to be taking in Bruce and John at the same time.

"Just throw your coat anywhere," said Bruce. "This is John's friend, Ben."

"Hi, Ben," he said, and shook my hand again as if the

65

first time hadn't counted. "Bruce, I brought my pipe—I didn't forget."

"Great," said Bruce. The new guest instantly set to rummaging through a large Toronto Maple Leafs sports bag he had brought. The back of his leather jacket had "Haigmen Football" printed across it; below one shoulder was sewn a York University crest; and in the lapel there was a Canadian flag pin. This was apparently his global jacket. When he had finally found the pipe and shaken the snow out of his long red hair, he removed his jacket for our next entertainment: a Cat Stevens sweatshirt, with "MORNING HAS BROKEN" printed in iridescent lettering across the chest. His last adjustment was to slide a small gold crucifix embedded in the side of his neck forward and center. Now he was all set for the party.

As Bruce opened the door leading to the basement, we were struck, as if by a blast of wind, by the music from below: the Rolling Stones singing "Get Off of My Cloud." The Christian, football-playing, York University rock fan behind me was already rocking and clapping his hands as we descended.

Though John and I were an hour late, there were still only a few people at the party and no Carolyn. One was a guy lying on his back who was introduced to me as "a combined honors philosophy/biochemistry major," and whose head was wedged between the two stereo speakers. He had small sparrow eyes, which were glazed over. I noticed they were set unusually close together, as if they had migrated away from his ears.

There was also a married couple there. Nancy and Ron or Don Nash. They were in their mid-twenties. Within two minutes they had told me they were in business and then cackled incomprehensibly.

"What kind of business is it?" I asked.

"We're tobacconists," they said in unison. "That means we run a fine tobacco shop," Nancy added. "We brought some very fine cigarettes with us for people to try.

They're Balkan Sobranie cigarettes—would you like to try one?''

"Well—"

"Oh, look who has them!" Nancy shouted, sending me twenty feet in the air. When I came back down, I saw it was the speaker guy, lying unconscious, a long gray Balkan Sobranie ash curling toward his neck.

"What a waste!" said Ron or Don, jumping to his feet to retrieve the pack.

"It's okay," I said. "Maybe I'll try one later."

"Well, the funny thing is," said Nancy, while Ron or Don offered the cigarettes around, "that neither my husband nor I smoke." Cackle. I was not deeply moved by this revelation, but I think she was waiting for a reaction. "Do you know," she said, "that most of the smoke that comes from a cigarette comes from the paper?"

"No, I didn't know that."

"It's true. It'll be something if they some day invent cigarette paper that doesn't smoke, don't you think?"

"Yes."

The Christian rock fan sidled toward us, having failed to make conversation with Bruce and John. He had tried even with Speaker Man. "You getting to know the Nashes here?" he asked, smiling at me.

"Yeah, sure," I said as I watched the last guest, who was not introduced to me, pass back and forth doing some kind of research on the records.

After a period of silence during which neither the Stones nor I could get satisfaction, Nancy went back to her documentary on cigarettes and we were once again joined by Ron or Don. I was getting restless and wondering how I could make a gracious departure when, during "Under My Thumb," Mr. Speaker suddenly bolted upright, knocking over a speaker. He wailed and slapped his knee like a bronco rider. "Ooooweee, that was incredible stuff, man! Was it opium-cured or what, man?"

"Man" was Bruce, who readjusted the speakers and went back to talking to John and the record researcher.

"That was incredible stuff, man!"

"Man" was now Nancy. "Did you like the Balkan Sobranie?" she asked, feebly.

"Does anyone have a beer? I'm dying of thirst here," he said.

"Good idea," said John. "Who wants a beer?" John took orders and headed upstairs. I followed. "Having a good time?" he asked.

"Terrific. Truly terrific. Tell me, did Carolyn say definitely that she was coming?"

"Relax, will you? Maybe she'll show up yet. . . . Do you like Bruce's sister?"

"His *sister*?"

"Nancy." He was opening beers, the bottletops clattering onto the kitchen counter.

"Yes, she's nice, I guess, but—"

"You going to smoke with us?"

"Yeah, sure, maybe."

"You've never tried it, have you, you Nimbus."

"Maybe I won't this time." I remembered his mother. "I know it's nothing." *My* mother. "It's just like booze, I know." The mothers of the world.

"Have you ever once hung loose in your life? Take the lumber out of your ass for one night; you'll enjoy it."

"John, I don't like to lose all my faculties in a strange place. They have a tendency to organize against my will and report back to work one at a time."

"So go back to talking to the Nashes and have a good time." He headed back down before I could answer.

I was already in the vestibule looking for my coat when Carolyn burst in the door. "Hi, Ben," she said warmly. "Are you just getting here?"

"Yeah," I said.

"Well, come in," she said hanging up her coat and bounding down the stairs as if she owned the place. "Hi, everyone!" she said to everyone.

"Who's the straight guy?" said Mr. Speaker, confirm-

68

ing for Carolyn that I'd just arrived. His eyes swam in an oily film.

"That's John's friend, Ben," said Morning has Broken, ever on the alert for new conversation. He now sat with his beer in the corner of the room near the Nashes. The Ph.D. of Records was delicately stuffing the pipe while Bruce and John took his place hunting through the hundreds of albums. I had left a spot for Carolyn, but she sat on the other side of the Nashes to talk to Nancy.

"Have you known John very long?" asked Speaker.

"No, I'm from Montreal. We met here."

"Do you go to school here?" he asked, his voice tapering off at the end.

"Yes. The U of T."

"What are you taking?" If Speaker had only known that I'd just had this conversation a few hours before—*and with Mrs. Dioskouri, the patron saint of straighthood.*

"Metallurgy."

"Oh," said Speaker, taking a throaty swig of beer. I glanced at Carolyn at every possible opportunity, but she didn't once return my look. "Are your parents with you—here in Toronto, I mean?"

"No," I said. "I have no parents."

His eyes glubbed toward me. He combed down his mustache with his fingers. "Your parents. . . . Are you an orphan or something, man?"

"No, I never had any parents."

Speaker looked at me, then away, then down; he lit a cigarette, trying to coordinate the tip with the flame; looked down again; stared at the beer by his foot; processed the information; took another swig; floated his gaze toward me and said, "Oh, wow, . . . did you arise spontaneously in nature or something?"

Making a great display of holding his breath in, Morning has Broken now rose to pass a smoking pipe to the Nashes. Nancy muttered something about the amount of smoke coming from it—even though it was not wrapped in paper like a cigarette. Ron/Don said, "We don't smoke," and

Carolyn took this as her cue to sit between Speaker and me. John brought over the pipe and handed it to Speaker, who then passed it to Carolyn. As she inhaled deeply, her free hand rested on my knee. John handed me the pipe and I said, "I hope you don't mind: I have a mild case of cholera."

John snatched the pipe out of my hand—"*Nimbus*," he said—and passed it on to Morning has Broken. To steady herself, Carolyn placed her other hand on Speaker's knee and I got a sick feeling in my throat. Morning peered at me with an eagle eye—the one stray eye wandering to Carolyn —wondering now which club to include himself in. The club I had inadvertently joined was the Nashes'—the older sibling club, the chaperon club, the club that, while one day babbling in someone's parents' garden, tells all and gets the youngsters in trouble.

Cat Stevens sang "Tea for the Tillerman" and I studied the patch of floor between my knees. Several minutes passed as we all reflected. The Nashes sat huddled in the corner like a pair of extinguished cigarette butts.

Carolyn took the pipe again. I felt a spring form in my knees that was ever ready to propel me out of the room. Dr. Record said, "This stuff is great, but it makes me horny. Hey, Carolyn—" Carolyn held up a finger in the air before her head sank forward. "John, where's that sister of yours," he continued, "with the beautiful boobs?"

John said nothing, but he did shake his fist at Dr. Record. I'd had enough.

"Where the hell are you going?" John said to me halfway up the stairs. "Come on, *stay*. Carolyn's here. What's your problem?"

"Are you *serious*?"

"I think you're a nice guy. I'm obviously more open-minded than you are."

"Obviously, you are."

It was freezing outside and I had no idea where the hell I was. As I was bundling up more securely, a car pulled up. Another guest?

70

"Hi," I said.

The girl looked vaguely familiar. As she approached, she avoided my stare.

"*Hi!*" I tried again. "The party's really swinging. You got here just in time." She was hiding the fact that she'd been crying. "Do I know you?" I asked.

"I don't think so," she sniffled.

"Why do you look familiar?"

"I don't know? Why do I?"

"What's your name?"

"Would you mind if I went to get my brother? I have to take him home."

"You wouldn't be John's sister, would you?"

"I would, yes."

"You *are* John's sister."

"Would you mind going to get him for me? I don't think I could stand to go inside."

"Sure, I'd be glad to," I said. Halfway down the stairs I realized I was undoing my heroic exit, but I continued. The waves of the party had closed completely around me. Another pipe was going around, so I found it difficult to get John's attention. "Change your mind?" he said when I finally did.

"Your sister's here to pick you up."

"Tell her to go home."

"She's upset about something. Maybe you should talk to her.

"She's *always* upset! It's a family trademark — a goddamn career — you know: what are you going to be when you grow up? Upset." We heard the door slam upstairs. "There you go. She's even *more* upset. Why don't you go calm her down? You're the prince of peace anyway, aren't you? Go play your viola for her."

John's sister was sitting in the car with the engine running. When she saw me, she started to pull out but I ran to stop her. "I don't think John is ready to come just yet," I said when she rolled down the window.

71

"No kidding," she said, looking as if she was going to cry again.

"Carolyn's inside. Do you know that?"

She shrugged her shoulders and we paused a moment while she collected herself. The cool light of the moon illuminated her sad, brown eyes.

"Would you mind telling me how to get to the subway?" I asked.

"No, come on. I'll take you."

"What's your name?" I said, getting in. I fixed one of those subtle smiles on my face that was supposed to make me look like Paul Newman, but probably came out looking more like gas.

"Diane. . . . Are you Ben?" she asked, checking her mirror and blind spots twice before pulling out.

"Yes. How do you know?"

"My mother told me John had come to the party with some kind of Ben."

"What kind did she say? Did she say what a nice boy I was?"

"As a matter of fact she did." Diane suddenly turned toward the left. "I forgot I was taking you to the subway." With this she began to make what was supposed to be a three-point turn on the road, but she added thirteen or fourteen points, and, in spite of her navigation with mirrors and rear and side window checks, the last point was the ditch behind us. Apparently hoping I had somehow not noticed the car belly slam into the bank, she nonchalantly floored the accelerator, leaving a portion of the street sprayed on whoever's front yard. Nothing. She floored it again. "Do you know how to drive out of these? I'm never sure," she said, and hopped out of the car.

"No problem," I said. "I took a winter driving course." I slid over to the driver's side and, with expert maneuvering, carved a hole into the bank that would one day be mistaken for the Wisconsin Ice Age. As I pressed still harder on the accelerator, I believe I even spawned a fresh

72

water source—a new estuary—free of charge to the lucky owners of the property Diane and I were now shifting.

"It'll just be a minute," I said, hopping out of the car. "Look, why don't you get back in and press the accelerator when I tell you? I'll try to lift the back end out." I made this last comment with a husky voice.

I pushed and rocked and heaved the car, and felt — during the last heave—the future of my family caught in the balance. "Diane," I finally said, "I think your car is stuck."

"Shall I try it?" she asked.

"I don't think that will work."

"Well, why don't we put it in drive and both push?"

"Because, if we succeed, the car will construct a new garage in the center of that house across the street."

She smiled at me warmly, and I shot her back one of my gaseous smiles, the bits of ice and mud sliding down my cheek into my neck. "What we need is something dry for traction."

"Can we try a floormat or something? What can we use?"

"I know a guy back at the party we could use and he wouldn't even know the difference."

She laughed but just as quickly became sad. "I don't know why my brother has to hang around with those weird people."

"He likes them. They're all right, some of them."

"John's not like them, you know. You mustn't think that he is. He's just very impressionable."

I shrugged.

"I know it's hard to believe," she said, "but he really is a good person. He's just been mixed up lately."

"I believe you," I said, though I wasn't sure I did. Diane's brown hair fell in waves around her white collar. "Why don't we go back to the party and ask your brother to help push us out?"

73

"Couldn't we call my father instead? I'm sure he'd come right away."

"Your brother's only a half block away. Let's ask him."

As we trudged back to the party, our hands tucked in our pockets, I had to fight the urge to reach for Diane's hand.

SEVEN

On the train back to Montreal for the Christmas break, I was apprehensive about living at home again—even for two weeks—but I looked forward to seeing Sammy. My father greeted me at the station with his customary handshake and then took one of my bags. My mother hugged me at the door as if I'd just returned from war unharmed. "You must be hungry and exhausted."

"No, I'm fine."

"So, sit down and tell me all about school and, afterwards, if you wouldn't mind, Sammy would like you to drive to your Uncle Milt and Aunt Ida's to pick him up."

"But I'm hungry and exhausted."

"So you'll eat now, pick him up and have a nap right after. I've made up Sammy's old bedroom for you. We can negotiate getting your bedroom back when you move home again."

"What's Sammy doing at Milt's, anyway?"

"He's doing some kind of project on Milt's letter collection."

"It's the Christmas holidays. What's gotten into him?"

"Milt and Ida are going to Florida in a few days and you know Milt won't let that collection leave his house, so this is the only day they could arrange. Any more questions?"

Uncle Milt and Aunt Ida lived in the Town of Mount

Royal, an upper middle-class section of tree-lined streets and Tudor houses not far from the posh Westmount district. The collection of letters Sammy was working on was Uncle Milt's prized possession. Most of them were written by two brothers to their mother in York during the War of 1812. Several of the letters from the Pierce boys arrived after the victorious battle to capture Detroit. Others came before and after the famous Battle of Queenston Heights. The last of this group was from the younger Pierce and described the ordeal of watching his older brother shot to death just a few feet ahead of him. The most famous of Milt's letters was written by General Isaac Brock himself and described the preparations for Queenston Heights, the last place Brock ever saw. Every child related to Uncle Milt had done a project on these letters. The reason he was so proud of the collection, some of us speculated while working on our projects, was that it made him feel that his roots in Canada were eight or nine generations deep.

I rang the bell several times before Sammy answered the door. "Are you alone?" I asked.

"Welcome to my humble abode, my boy," said Sammy, taking my hand in both of his. "Come in out of the cold and rest your weary bones."

"Where is everyone?"

"They're at the store working. Come on downstairs—you won't believe what I've found."

"What? Some new letters?"

"No, just come down."

In the study, Sammy pointed to Uncle Milt's fancy film projector. "So what?" I said.

"Come over here," said Sammy. He handed me one film box after another, each labeled on the spine, "Linda's Second Birthday," "Trip to the Holy Land, 1969," "Spivack Bar Mitzvah," and so on.

"Now look at this one." He handed me a film labeled "Orno-pay."

"You're kidding."

"It's the raunchiest thing you've ever seen."

"*Sammy.*"

"Sit down for just a minute."

"Sammy, you were supposed to be working on—"

"I've finished with them. I've been here all day."

Sammy turned on the projector, which was aimed at a bare wall. There was a scene of a guy wearing nothing but cowboy boots approaching a woman hunched over a table. "That guy's hung like an onkey-day," I said.

"Imagine what he could've done with an eapon-way like at-thay in the ar-Way of eighteen-elve-tway." We laughed gutturally as the couple grunted to a climax.

"I wonder where they hid the microphones," said Sammy.

"Turn if off, Sammy. I want to get going."

"In a minute," he said.

"Sammy, someone's going to come home."

"Do you think Aunt Ida knows about this film?"

"If she doesn't, they'll have an interesting iscussion-day the day she finds out."

At home, my mother asked about school again. "Have you composed any masterpieces yet?"

"No, we don't take composition in the first year—only things like theory, harmony, the history of musical styles —that kind of thing."

"You know all that. Why don't you ask to go into the second year?"

"That's the way it's done. Everyone has to do it that way."

"But does everyone have your gift?"

"Ma," I said, kissing her on the cheek and wondering if Henny Youngman's mother had felt this way.

"Has Sammy told you who's arriving tomorrow for the holidays?"

"Oh, no. Why didn't you tell me someone was visiting? I would've—"

"Your Aunt Goldie and Uncle Mort."

Usually I was put out by long visits from relatives, but Mort and Goldie, my mother's older brother and his wife

77

from New York, I could endure. When we were younger, Sammy and I looked forward to their visits because they would bring us generous gifts like watches and electric trains and, once, a portable radio that played in stereo.

In recent years we wanted mainly to hear their stories of New York and to see Aunt Goldie and my mother in action again. They were major competitors in the Illness and Self-Denial Olympics. Sammy and I would keep score and the competition was a straightforward one. The woman who was able to make the last remark or who managed to faint for effect was the gold medalist, and Sammy and I would honor her with the appropriate national anthem.

The opening event was held beneath the beautiful Kitchen Dome the third morning of my return. This was the decathlon, which was slightly different from other events in that the first competitor who, in the shortest time, could list ten different medications she had recently taken, or ten of the world's greatest specialists she had visited, or ten different ailments (severity was taken into account here) that she had only partially recovered from, or ten reasons for not eating, or ten unshared relatives training to be the world's greatest specialists, or ten of the worst outrages her children had perpetrated against her, or ten reasons for not sleeping at night—and let me set the record straight here: these two women, at last count, had slept a total of nineteen nights since the outbreak of the second world war—or any combination of the above—was to be declared the winner.

My mother placed an assortment of bagels, lox, cream cheese, butter and cinnamon buns before my aunt. She then poured her a cup of coffee. Sammy and I consulted the Buddha clock above the sink and generally counted on it for precision timing.

"Are these Scotia lox?" asked Goldie.

"Yes, I bought them especially because I knew you were coming," said Rita.

"You know I love them." Stop the clock. The competitors have not yet warmed up. "But, . . ." said Goldie—start the clock—"I don't think I could eat a thing."

"What are you talking about! You hardly touched your dinner last night."

"What am I talking?—I was up all night—nauseous—you probably didn't hear over Mort's snoring."

"I heard his snoring, but I didn't hear you, even though—God knows—I could hear plenty from where I was sitting in the living room till 5:30 this morning."

"Funny, I took some Pepto-Bismol at five and I didn't see anyone in the living room."

"That's because at five on the dot I was in the bathroom throwing up from the extra Valium tablet I took. My specialist told me I could take an extra whenever I needed one after my gallstone operation."

"You should change specialists. I see Dr. Erwin, a pioneer in the field of internal medicine—"

"Pioneer, shmioneer—it was in Montreal that the gallstone was invented."

"What are you talking? What you had was *gall dust*. I had a gallstone the size of a grapefruit—I can show you: Mort had it bronzed."

"That's terrible." The first sympathetic remark was not to be mistaken for a concession, but merely a break the contestants usually welcomed. Here, Goldie took a bite out of a poppyseed bagel and then spread a dollop—a small dollop—of cream cheese and a sliver of lox on it. Rita did the same and the two sat nibbling and collecting their thoughts. Sammy and I avoided each other's looks for fear of exploding.

There was a time that one of these contests was decided almost before it began. My parents drove to Long Island to visit Mort and Goldie and, even before my father was able to unload the luggage, my mother staggered into Goldie's living room and collapsed in a heap on the floor. "Rita!" shouted Goldie, slapping the fallen woman's face. "Rita! Don't die in my home!" And my mother had to snap out of it or die of the pounding she was getting. Try as she did, no amount of discussion or illness or denial that weekend could have earned Goldie more than a silver and she knew it.

The two ladies polished off a bagel each. But the home side was not to be outmaneuvered. Rita said, "How's Josh these days?"

Josh was the oldest son, but—here was the clincher— not the *natural* son, of the Weisses. Mort and Goldie had also had an unnatural daughter before they were able to have a real son, "our Heshele" — destined, surely, for greatness.

Josh had once been destined for greatness: "a gorgeous boy; a male Shirley Temple." His mother had hustled him off to Hollywood to become a star. He shot two commercials, which had been shown to me forty times, but that was all. No matter: he was a brilliant student and won a Governor's scholarship to study journalism at Columbia. But then all hope vanished. "He cracked. Something happened—who knows? Someone gave him a drug—one of the stupid kids at school, maybe. And he became what? A poet." And here my Uncle Mort spat on the ground when he first told us the story on an afternoon walk through Washington Square. "And not a poet like that—what's his name?—John Keats. Not a man of vision like Ben Gurion. But a curser, a pig, a Communist. And where does he live?" he asked, pointing up to the windows of Greenwich Village. "We don't even know: in one of those hovels over there—with hepatitis for a neighbor on one side and crabs on the other."

"And he changed his name," said Aunt Goldie, staring at a couple of black children playing hopscotch in the park across the way.

"To Neptune," said Uncle Mort. "His name is now Neptune Weiss; we saw it in one of the Village papers where he published a poem with F-this and F-that every second word. Neptune F. Weiss of no fixed address—that's our wonderful son."

"Don't blame yourselves. It happens," said my mother.

"Who knows who his real parents were?" said Uncle Mort. "Who knows what was in the blood?"

"And you never see him anymore?" asked my father, participating in the conversation for the first time that afternoon.

"You know who sees him?" asked Mort. "Howard." Howard was my mother's and Mort's younger brother. "He goes to Howard and Ellie every time he runs out of money. He goes for forty dollars here, thirty dollars there. From us he wouldn't accept money, but from his uncle and aunt he accepts. I'm surprised he hasn't written you for help." My mother shook her head.

"And you know what he says when he's at Howard's place?" asked Goldie.

"He curses at them too," said Mort. "But he breaks their hearts. They saw him beautiful — a male Shirley Temple."

"And smart," said my mother.

"And smart. A straight-A student. And he breaks their hearts. Howard gives him fifty dollars and Ellie packs him chopped liver sandwiches, and he curses at them: you F-en bitch this, you F-en exploiter that, you F-en middle-class pigs—"

"Ellie told us he was so shrieking!" said Goldie.

"With his wild hair down to his ass," said Mort, "he comes to beg; then he shrieks."

"Who knows how Josh is," said Goldie. She took another half bagel, spread cream cheese on it and then licked her thumb. There was a pause filled with sighs and chomping. "Oh, Rita, a terrible thing has happened," sighed Goldie.

"What? Is it Josh? Tell me, Goldie." My mother took the other half of the bagel.

"No, it's Sheila." Sheila was the Weiss's adopted daughter and a nymphomaniac. When I was ten years old and Sheila was seventeen, she took Sammy and me into my bedroom and gave us our first full view of breasts — and what an abundant pair they were. We asked to see

81

more and Sammy asked to touch one, but she said we might get caught and packed them away. Night after night for years I would close my eyes and picture those large pink nipples before me. To this day it is that pair of breasts against which I compare all others.

"Oh, no, Goldie; not *Sheila*; tell me," said my mother, and she placed a comforting hand over her sister-in-law's. "Is she—you know—?" she said, looking over at Sammy and me.

The wonder of these conversations was that they were not confidential. The two women checked our reaction, but we looked away, pretending to be preoccupied with our own troubles.

"Are you finished your breakfasts, boys?" asked my mother.

"No," we said in unison.

The women lowered their voices to a whisper. We made ourselves look busy with our bagels and Sammy even made some remark about the Montreal Canadiens to reassure the ladies that, indeed, here we were: two boys, interested only in hockey and breakfast, and not even curious about the best pair of knockers that ever pointed at Montreal.

"Oh, Rita, Rita. You remember how I got some kind of bug when Mort and I were in Florida last March?"

"This is something you've kept from me since *last March?*"

"I couldn't tell you; I just couldn't. I've told no one."

My mother squeezed Aunt Goldie's hands. "Yes, I remember," she said.

"So we came back a couple days early—remember?"

"Yes, yes, I remember."

"We thought we would surprise Sheila and not trouble her she should come to the airport to pick us up."

"Where was Heshele?"

"Heshy was away for a couple of days on some kind of field trip to Pittsburgh—*you* remember, I wrote you."

"Yes, I remember now."

"And of course Josh—excuse me, Neptune—was no

longer with us." My mother nodded. "So we walk in and yell, 'Sheila, surprise!' and we hear a lot of moving around, like a lot of people hurrying. Morty thinks something's wrong, so he runs up to the bedrooms to see."

"Oh no."

"Yes. You know what he sees?" Goldie lowered her voice still more. My mother shook her head and leaned in. Sammy and I were practically lip-reading. "He found Sheila there on her back, and *six*—count 'em,"—she held up six fingers—"*six schwarzes* stone naked with Sheila!"

"Oh, my God, no—"

"*Six of them*, Rita," and she held up the fingers again, "in varying degrees of darkness—you'd think she went to the United Nations to recruit."

I jammed three-quarters of a bagel into my mouth. Sammy held up a napkin to his face, but his chair shook violently.

"Maybe they broke in," said my mother.

"No, that's what we thought. No, these kids are honest these days. They just tell you straight out. They don't think they've done anything wrong—that's what hurts. I've got a son who thinks he's god of the sea—you ask yourself, 'What have I done wrong?'—maybe I fed him too much tuna fish—who knows? Then I have a daughter—one single gorgeous daughter—and I suggest to her in passing now and again to please try to find yourself a nice Jewish boy—not even necessarily a doctor—just a decent young man of Jewish extraction maybe; and we come home one fine day and what does she have there to welcome us? Three-quarters of the population of the Dominican Republic in our bedroom with our lovely daughter standing in the middle —her *tsitsels* and *shmanya* taking in the breeze. What did I do to deserve this, Rita? Tell me, *what*?"

Sammy left the kitchen and waited to catch my attention outside the door before he held up six fingers and began whistling "The Star-Spangled Banner."

This was not the right day for my father to rib Aunt Goldie about her various political positions. He and Uncle

Mort came back from a visit to my father's factory and Mort said that my father had nearly run down an old Hassidic Jew who was crossing the street.

"Why didn't you offer to drive our car when you went, Mort, you know. . . ." said Goldie, pointing with her head at my father and raising her eyebrows.

My father said, "The old fool walked in front of the car with his hundred-pound coat and that beard and hat—"

"He was crossing at a green light," said Mort.

"He *started* on a green light. It was red when he was half way across."

"So you were going to run him down?" said Goldie.

"What do you know? . . . Anyway, you're right. I should be more careful. In Montreal, they've just raised the fine to five dollars for running down a Hassidic Jew."

"Max!" shouted my mother.

"Do they have a similar penalty in New York for such a thing, or—"

"Max! Enough!"

"Don't talk about my people that way!" said Goldie.

"They're my people, too," said my father, "or have you forgotten?"

"It's not me who forgot!" said Goldie.

"Tell me, do you have to be Jewish twenty-four hours a day?"

"Well, between you and me, that makes an average of twelve each."

"You should have your head examined!"

"And you're an anti-semite!"

"Like FDR.?"

"Worse!"

My father was fond of ribbing Goldie about Roosevelt because she maintained he turned his back on the European Jews. In the war years, Aunt Goldie fought his administration to open the gates to refugees. There was even a front-page picture in the *Washington Post* of a young Goldie chained to the White House fence. "You never lift a finger to help Israel," said Goldie.

"I've given plenty."

"That's not enough! You should campaign to win Israel friends! You should fight to free some of those still caught behind the Iron Curtain." During the Czechoslovakian uprising in 1968, Goldie flew to Eastern Europe to rescue a cousin of hers, Noah, and his family. She pestered the authorities so much that they finally let the family go — with all their belongings and even a friend and his wife and their belongings. There was a photograph of Goldie in the *New York Times* kissing the tarmack at Kennedy Airport, her Czechoslovakian relatives and friends behind her —smiles, after the long flight, now sewn onto their faces.

That evening the camps were quiet. Mort went to bed early; my father read the newspaper in the den; Sammy and I joined my mother and aunt in the living room for a cup of tea. For ten minutes not a word was said. Jews, FDR, refugees, children, sickness and lack of sleep did not come up at all. My mother mentioned something about looking for a new house, but no one wanted to pick up the topic. For a time, my mother came to sit between Sammy and me on the couch and intermittently put a hand on his knee or mine. Although I had no real evidence for it, I was convinced that my mother was more optimistic than most of our relatives. She believed Sammy and I would be successful and she pushed us, but never too hard. What was sad about Goldie was that she saw the fate of Neptune and Sheila as a reflection on her, and she never understood her fate as being separate from theirs.

Powerful though she appeared to be, unwavering in her ideals and unrelenting in the pursuit of those ideals, Aunt Goldie, on rare occasions, allowed her vulnerability to show. As we sat across from her, waiting for her to say something, she suddenly burst into tears. "What did I do to deserve this, Rita? Tell me, what?"

My mother comforted Aunt Goldie, and Sammy and I slipped downstairs to his bedroom. I threw myself on his bed and he swiveled opposite me in his desk chair, putting his feet up on the end of the bed. I could barely recognize the room. He had painted and polished and recarpeted. Where once had hung my Deutsche Grammophon poster of Herbert von Karajan conducting the Berlin Philharmonic in Beethoven's Ninth Symphony now hung a photo of Sammy playing Cornelius in his school's production of *The Matchmaker*. The blank spaces in the photo were covered with signatures. On the opposite wall, where I had displayed my two framed Kiwanis Music Festival Awards and the charcoal drawing of Mary Beth Wilkins that I'd had her sit patiently for one summer night in the Old City, Sammy had hung the pennant and banner of his new school, Lower Canada College, the school for privileged boys on their way to the Ivy League. The books were all different—as were the bookcases—and whatever books I'd left behind were packed in boxes by the door with my red rug, rolled up and tied. All that remained of my legacy were my night-lamp and the two plants on the windowsill, my Jade and Wandering Jew.

"Like it?" Sammy asked.

"Sure I do. It's nice the way you've redecorated."

He tickled me under the knee with his foot the way he always used to do to pester me, and I swatted at him.

"Well, you said I could have the room, so—"

"I meant it. I'm glad, Sammy, really."

"That was too bad upstairs about Aunt Goldie, wasn't it?"

"Yeah, it was."

Sammy shook his foot rapidly on the edge of the bed. "Did you have a chance to read any of the books I got you?" he asked.

I nodded. "All of them—the Philip Roth twice. I loved them. The Salinger is a classic without a doubt, but Roth is the proof that you can laugh your head off even though it may be the end of the world."

"If it *is* the end of the world," said Sammy, "you might as well laugh your head off." Then he said, "What happened with Carolyn? Are you still seeing her?"

"Not that I'm aware of."

"Too bad. She was dynamite."

"I think I found someone I like better."

"A tramp also?"

"*Sammy.*"

"Sorry, sorry."

This time I tickled him under the knee, and he swatted at me as he laughed.

My mother insisted I call Sarah while I was home, since Sarah had spoken so highly of her visit to Toronto. When I did, Great-Aunt Hazel invited Sammy and me for lunch the day before I was to leave. I quickly discovered, though, that living in a timeless state the way Sarah did, it would not have made any difference if I had visited her that day or two years from that day. Before we stepped into the door of their apartment, Sarah said, "Play 'The Lion Sleeps Tonight'."

"Sorry, Sarah, I didn't bring my viola."

"Come in," she said. The apartment was neat but smelled medicinal.

"Where's Aunt Hazel?" asked Sammy, on the verge of cracking up.

"She went to buy you some pop for lunch. I'm having my lunch ahead of time because I want only soup. Come, keep me company in the kitchen while I make it." We followed her. She seemed a bit wan and more doped up now than when I'd seen her in Toronto. Although it was foolish, for a moment I felt responsible for her state. What if I'd helped her go on to the U.S.? Would she have managed? But would she have gotten by the authorities at the border in her nightgown?

Sammy and I watched from the kitchen table as Sarah warmed up a skillet, opened a can of Campbell's oxtail soup and dumped the contents into the pan. The glob soon began to sizzle. Sammy tore out of the kitchen, laughing uncontrollaby. Sarah paid no attention, so I joined him.

We were wiping tears from our eyes when she brought the pan into the living room, placed it on a folded newspaper in her lap and began cutting the half-burnt hunk of soup into smaller pieces with her spoon.

"We're in trouble," she said, looking at no one.

"Who?" I said. She took a piece of soup into her mouth and ignored us. "Who? You and I?" She said nothing. "Sammy and I . . . ? You and Sammy . . . ? Canada? The Jews? The solar system . . . ? *Who?*" She finished her soup, sat back and asked if we had a cigarette. "No. *Who's* in trouble!"

"I'm pregnant, Ben. I missed my period and I think you're the father." It was easily ten minutes before Sammy collected himself and returned from the washroom. He held up six fingers and then it was my turn to bolt for it.

When I returned, Sammy was discussing parental arrangements with Sarah and saying what a good father he thought I'd make. "Ben," she said, the second she saw me, "don't get too attached to the idea of having the child. I don't feel ready to be a mother, so I've decided to get an abortion."

"Do you think that's a wise choice?" asked Sammy.

"*Sammy*," I said, and he turned the other way in his chair.

Luckily, Aunt Hazel walked in just as Sarah put the skillet on the coffee table and wiped her mouth with a piece of newspaper. "You keeping Sarah good company, boys?"

"Well . . ." I said, and she nodded knowingly. Sarah stood up without acknowledging her mother and left for the bedroom. "Aunt Hazel, is Sarah—"

"What Ben is trying to ask," said Sammy, "is, is Sarah big with child?"

"What!"

"No, what Sammy means is—"

"Has she been saying that nonsense again?"

"She said she'd missed her—"

"She often does with these drugs. Do you know how many grandchildren I'd have if she'd been pregnant every time her cycle was off?"

The next day, as I was packing my suitcase—my clothes

all neatly laundered and ironed—my departure came over me like a flood, as if this time I'd just been a visitor. I wandered into my parents' bedroom and gazed at the pictures of my grandparents and of my parents on their wedding day. On the dresser were the photographs of Sammy and me on our bar mitzvah days, both of us pointing solemnly at the heavens, even though the pictures had been taken at our rehearsals. How different our bar mitzvahs were. Sammy went to lessons for months and studied Hebrew every night until he was utterly rabbinical. I went to old Rabbi Galinsky only a year before his death, and he was practising for eternal rest during my lessons. "Read for me," he'd say and, while I stumbled over the first letter of the first word, he'd nod off. As the day of my confirmation approached, I began to cough loudly to rouse him because I was getting nervous about my lack of knowledge. "Leave it to me, Solomon," he'd say, and start to nod off again.

"Benjamin," I'd say.

"Leave it to me, Benjamin."

On the day before my bar mitzvah, Galinsky handed me a copy of the service written out in English letters. "Now read this," he said.

I read: "Baruch attah adonai elohaynoo. . . ."

"You're a talmudic scholar, Sol," he said as he slapped the back of my neck.

"Ben," I said.

"I'm going to tape those sheets into the Torah for you."

"But what if one of my relatives comes up to read!"

"Leave it to me, my boy. Just leave it to me."

I sweated through the entire service, though when I looked up periodically from my recitation I noticed my parents smiling proudly and the congregation bobbing dutifully. When I finished, my blood chilled as Uncle Mort rose from his seat and walked toward Galinsky and me. The Rabbi, his eyelids half closed in reverence, bumped me gently out of the way, rolled up the Torah and packed it in its silver casing before Mort arrived.

I said my good-byes to Sammy and my mother at the door. As I hugged my mother again, I wondered how long it would be before I could do this sort of thing with ease. "Come down to Toronto some weekend," I told Sammy.

"I will. I plan to." He hugged me too. "Oh," he said as he pounded my back, "my brother, the pioneer, go forth, go forth. Bless you."

"Huchoo."

In Toronto, I lumbered up the stairs with my suitcase and the part of my stereo my father had forgotten to bring the time before and found a gift wrapped in Christmas paper waiting for me outside my door. The card read,

Dear Ben,

Thank you for helping
Diane with her car and
for being John's friend.
Have a good holiday
with your family.

Merry Christmas,
The Dioskouris.

I quickly reasoned that neither John nor his parents could have written the card and my heart soared. Leaving my belongings at the door and wearing my new black angora scarf, I ran downstairs to wish Mr. Dioskouri a happy New Year. But it was Mr. Moustaki who brought me a cup of coffee, and the only other customers were his young son and daughter. Moustaki stroked his daughter's hair as she sipped through a straw on a Shirley Temple, the round glass filled so that it looked like a red balloon. The boy was eating a chocolate doughnut. Moustaki wasn't particularly friendly to me nor unfriendly, but he had no cause to be either.

EIGHT

Although it was John who phoned to ask me to see a movie with him, it was Diane I found myself preparing to meet. I took an extra long shower, put on my brand new flares and flapped around the apartment looking for a shirt and socks, sprays and ointments and my silver comb. I styled my hair seven different ways, parting it on the left, the way I usually do; then on the right; in the center; horizontally from ear to ear; diagonally; not at all; left and right; and settled for the original left. I sprayed my underarms until something resembling Saran Wrap formed on them. I flexed my muscles in the mirror, brushed my teeth and practiced various kinds of smiles. To add a touch of cool, I raised first one eyebrow, then the other, then the first again, until I suffered a facial spasm and quickly readjusted myself for fear of going out looking like Madame Butterfly. I went so far as to stuff a pair of rolled-up socks down the front of my pants to add bulge, but the bulge shifted to the back, making the wrong impression. So I stuffed a whole T-shirt down but reasoned that, if I went out like that, Diane could come to one of only two conclusions about me: either that I was holding a genital convention in my pants, or that I had contracted a case of gigantism. I was more anxious than I thought I'd be, so I picked up my viola and played along with the cello part of a recording of Beethoven's Triple Concerto. I finished fifteen minutes before the record did.

Maybe Diane wouldn't be home anyway. I hadn't even thought of that. Maybe she was visiting an aunt in Winnipeg. Maybe she was out for the evening with her *boyfriend*, a tall, oiled and curly-haired Adonis who drove a Porsche and studied business administration.

When I arrived at the Dioskouri house, I was delighted and relieved to see Diane.

"Hi, Ben," she said. She was dressed in sweats, her hair in a ponytail. "I didn't know you were coming over tonight."

"That figures," I chuckled.

"Hyi, Ben, hyow arre you?" said Mrs. Dioskouri as Diane skipped up the stairs to her bedroom. "Dzon downstairrs. You oo-want cuffee?"

"No, thank you," I replied.

John and his father were downstairs watching the Miss Universe Pageant on TV. A life-size procelain Lassie guarded the den. Mr. Dioskouri, still in his suit and tie, stood to greet me warmly. "Seet down, seet down," he said, offering me his own chair. Then he headed upstairs.

"Where do you want to go?" asked John.

Mrs. Dioskouri arrived with coffee and cake. "Eat," she said. "Eat something."

I smiled and nodded, and turned to John. "I noticed in the paper that *Play It Again, Sam* is showing again. I wouldn't mind seeing that."

"Sure. You haven't seen it yet?"

"I have, but I could see it again."

"Sure, why not. I didn't catch it the first time around. It's pretty good, is it? Look at that goddess," he said, pointing to Miss Argentina in a bathing suit.

I nodded. "What's Diane doing tonight?"

"Who knows?" he said. "I think she has a friend coming over—Carolyn, as a matter of fact."

"*Carolyn?*"

"Yup." Miss USA came strutting out in a leopard-print

swimsuit. "Look at those legs!" said John. "There's a mile of leg there."

"She looks exactly like a blonde leopard," I said. "It's uncanny: I went to the zoo the other day and saw this leopard wearing a Miss USA sash — *twins,* I swear. *Identical.*"

"Piss off," said John.

I heard the doorbell ring and broke into a sweat. It was several minutes, though, before Carolyn came down with Diane.

"Oh, hi, Ben," said Carolyn, "how have you been keeping?"

"Great," I said, but my eyes were riveted on Diane. This, surely, was what Praxiteles and Phidias had imagined when they sculpted feminine grace out of marble slabs. Diane had done almost nothing to herself: let her hair down, put on a blouse and a white lambswool sweater, a pair of jeans. But I was overcome by the glow of her chestnut eyes, the artistry of her classical nose, the damp redness of her lips, the curves of her body. Beside Diane, Carolyn was suddenly pale and ordinary. I don't know what came over me. Diane caught my stare several times as she tried to look over at the TV, and I noticed her toes curl in her wool socks. She then put her hands on her shoulders in a peculiar way, as if she were singing "Alouette."

"Is this the Miss Universe Pageant?" asked Carolyn, settling on a cushion on the floor beside Diane.

"Yup," said John, adjusting his hair on the side with one hand and then lighting up a cigarette.

"Terrific," said Diane, lowering her hands.

Mrs. Dioskouri brought Carolyn coffee and cake and I quickly became busy with mine. "No, thank you, Mrs. D.," she said.

"Oo-why?"

"Later, maybe." Mrs. Dioskouri went upstairs with the tray.

A former Miss Universe who was now a grandmother

held up a jar of face cream and purred, "See how you can keep you skin soft and supple."

"I wonder who's going to win," said John.

"Miss Pluto," said Diane. "It's strange the way the Miss Universe judges always pick someone from Earth, don't you think, Carolyn? I have a feeling they're biased."

"Would you and Carolyn like to come with us to see a movie?" I asked.

John looked over at me, surprised. Carolyn looked unwilling. "With you and John?" asked Diane.

I nodded.

"Which one? What are you going to see?"

"*Play It Again, Sam.*"

"That sounds good," she replied, her beautiful eyes lighting up. "What do you think, Carolyn?"

I waited for John to object, but he didn't.

Carolyn hesitated. "I don't know. I've got some stuff to do later on."

"Oh, come on," said Diane. "We won't be home late."

John said, "I don't think Diane and I have been to a movie together since *One Hundred and One Dalmations*."

"You haven't been to a movie without being stoned since *One Hundred and One Dalmations*," replied Diane.

"Up yours," said John.

"Come on," repeated Diane to Carolyn.

Carolyn shrugged her shoulders and rose.

Mrs. Dioskouri was obviously delighted that her children were going out together—and with Carolyn and me to boot. She was throwing ten-dollar bills at us as she hustled us out the door.

John drove and the girls whispered and giggled in the back seat, so I kept fixing my hair. When we stopped at a red light, John checked the rear-view mirror and fixed his hair too.

Though I laughed as much the second time as the others did their first, I was overcome with sadness the minute the movie ended—sadness at Allan Felix's unresolved loneliness. The four of us stood out in the cool February lights of Yonge Street trying to decide what else to do, while Toronto was closing down around us and, inexplicably, all I could think of was my bed in the old bedroom in Montreal.

Diane was still humming "As Times Goes By" from the film and Carolyn was bobbing up and down to stay warm, as we waited for John to make some kind of decision. The doors of the movie theatre kept opening and closing and we were struck intermittently by a warm popcorn breeze. I caught Carolyn making a gesture to Diane to go off on their own, and Diane was about to say something when John made up his mind. "Let's go to the doughnut shop just up ahead."

Carolyn agreed grudgingly, and the two girls locked arms and headed up the street. I caught up with them when they paused to look at a pottery store window. "Diane, I've been meaning to thank you for this beautiful scarf."

"Oh, do you like it?" she said. "My mother picked it out." This I took to be my cue to wrap the scarf more snugly around my neck and tie one end to the nearest lamppost. John took it as his cue to begin some kind of competition. "Carolyn," he said, "tell me honestly: what did you notice first about me—my mind or my body?"

"Your body," said Carolyn, and the two girls giggled all the way to the doughnut shop.

Inside, Carolyn asked the tired-looking woman at the counter if they served fresh fruit salad.

"Just coffee and doughnuts," the woman replied.

"Do you have tea, then?"

When we sat down, I turned to Carolyn. "How's Kathleen these days?"

"You met on the train, didn't you?" said Diane. John was uninterested. He was concentrating on his chocolate doughnut.

"Yes," said Carolyn, "when I was bringing Kathleen home from Kingston, remember?" Diane nodded. "He thought I was her mother." More giggles. "So how are you making out at the U of T?"

"Fine, fine. I'm in the music program, as you probably remember."

"Yes, Ben is one of Canada's most promising triangle players," said John. "It all started when he was a young lad, watching 'Sesame Street.' They showed a square first, then a rectangle and then a triangle. Benny's eyes lit up at the beautiful shape before him. 'If only such a thing could make music,' said the young prodigy. The rest, naturally, is history."

"Ignore him," said Diane. "He would have been fifteen or something anyway when 'Sesame Street' was invented."

Carolyn turned to look at me again. "You play cello or something, don't you?"

"Viola."

"Kathleen still tells your stories to people. She told her father we met Beethoven's brother on the train and that you were a yodeler."

"Yodel something for us," said John, licking chocolate off his thumb.

"Music is wonderful, isn't it?" Diane smiled at me.

"So what are you going to do with that?" asked John. "You going to play rock viola with a band, or something?"

"What are *you* going to do?" said Diane to her brother.

"I'm going to be a fireman," he said.

"I plan to be a diplomat and travel the world," said Carolyn, sounding vaguely like Kathleen. "I have an uncle in the foreign service."

"She's being modest," said Diane. "Her uncle is Canada's Consul General in New York."

"Oh, really? I have an aunt in New York who almost became American Ambassador to Czechoslovakia a few years ago. You could follow in her footsteps."

"*Really*? What's her name? Maybe my uncle knows her."

"It's Goldie Konigsberger. K-O-N-I-G-S-berger."

"I'll ask him."

"What about you?" I said to Diane. "You talk about everyone but yourself."

"She looks after the world's great unwashed," said John.

"What do you do?" I asked.

"She washes them," said John.

"I work as a social worker's aid in a home for juvenile delinquents. I want to go on to university to get a degree in social work, but I thought I'd take a little time off first to see if I enjoyed this kind of thing."

"And do you?" I asked.

Diane's eyes glistened in the fluorescent light. "She did until some kid slugged her in the head," John put in.

"What a shiner you had!" said Carolyn.

"You're kidding. What happened?" I asked.

"This kid about fifteen, but a big guy, came into the office while I was doing some paperwork. I'm usually not nervous with these kids because I've gotten to know them all, but this one stared at me a lot in kind of a blank way and it worried me a bit. He'd had a violent past and—"

"He'd set fire to his house," said John, "with his family inside."

"They got out," said Diane, "but only just, because he did it in the middle of the night and with gasoline."

"My God," I said.

"I didn't know that part," said Carolyn, "about the gasoline and in the middle of the night."

"Anyway, so the kid comes into the office and he's got that awful blank look again, and I say 'Would you like something, Mikey?' and he said, 'Don't call me that. My mother always calls me that.' 'Your mother calls you that,' I told him, 'because she loves you.' 'Like hell she does!' he yelled, approaching me. I had my hand on the stapler on my desk and I was trembling. 'I should have killed them all,' he said. 'I should have used a gun.' I started to say, 'Mike, your family is—' and he shouted, 'You're all the same!' and he lunged at me, grabbed my collar and slugged me across the face."

"What did you *do*?" I asked.

"I broke his nose with the stapler, and he ran out of the office. He's in a tight-security place now."

"And this is what she does to dabble in the field," said John.

"Well, it's not that bad usually, and not all the kids are violent."

"What do you do with them on a regular basis?" I asked. "Do you bake muffins or throw around a ball or what?"

"That's not far from the truth, actually. We have activities with them; we talk to them; we look for their talents and skills; they go to counseling—that sort of thing."

Outside, the girls walked ahead of us again. John said, "Are you ready to make your move?"

"*What?*"

"Do you want to go parking or something?"

"Are you crazy?"

"Don't act so surprised, Nimbus. You've been flirting with Diane all evening."

"Maybe I have, but I don't feel good about parking right now—I mean it, John."

"Then sit in the back with Diane and watch."

"You won't even get Carolyn to sit in the front with you, let alone—"

"*Watch.*"

John caught up with the girls and began chatting up a storm with Carolyn. He had a serious expression on his face that was supposed to look cool. But it's one thing to be a hero in your bathroom and quite another to translate that into cool on a date. Diane fell back from the Pounce Brigade to join the Chaperon Squad. I'm not sure what was going through her mind—maybe that John was better off spending his time with Carolyn than with Bruce and Dr. Record—but, without a word passing between them, John seemed to win Diane's cooperation.

When we got to the car, John rushed to open the front

door for Carolyn. That left the back seat for Diane and me. On the way, John said, ''Carolyn, are you tired?''

''*Very*,'' she said.

I spread my arms casually across the back of the seat and felt the doughnut, which had only just left my throat, get zapped by a thousand volts of stomach acid. I could sense Diane's embarrassment growing with mine and, by the time John pulled over on a dead-end street a few blocks from Carolyn's place, our hearts racing, my numb arms suspended over the back of the seat, Diane and I had frozen over completely.

But it turned out to be Carolyn who was in control. Diane was looking out her window into the dark when her friend said, ''This is not where I live, John.''

''Carolyn,'' he said, ''have I ever told you what beautiful eyes you have?''

''No, this will be the first time.''

''You do. You have beautiful eyes.''

''Thank you. I have found up until now, though, that my eyes are more functional than decorative.''

''Great,'' he said, laughing hoarsely. ''May I kiss you?''

''I don't think so, but thank you for asking.''

''My pleasure,'' he said, starting up the engine.

After Carolyn got out, John asked me to come back to their house for a drink, saying he would drive me home afterwards. I had become convinced I was going to need surgery to free my arms from the back of the seat. ''I'm sorry, John,'' said Diane.

''It's not your fault. Can you help it if you have a friend with functional eyes?'' Diane laughed. I realized I had concealed my designs on her so successfully that I was being included in their confidence, like another brother.

When we arrived at their house, Diane said good night to me, then put her hand on my shoulder and whispered, ''Thank you,'' before heading off to her bedroom.

John and I sat in the den not talking for several minutes. ''So when are you having another party?'' I asked.

''Not very soon,'' he said, pulling a cigarette from a

pack his father had left on the table. "What do you care, anyway?"

"Just asking," I said. A minute or two passed.

"My friends at the last party were not too fond of you, by the way," he said.

"*None* of them?"

"Well, some of them."

"I think I can live with that."

"I have to admit I've been having some problems myself with those guys lately."

"Why?"

"They're getting into some pretty heavy stuff: acid and speed." John fixed his hair and pulled heavily on his cigarette until the flame burned into the filter. He took another one from the pack. "Do you want one?" he asked.

"Sure," I said. This was to be only the second cigarette I had ever smoked. The first had been when I was twelve and the experience had been so traumatic I'd never tried it again. I was visiting Steve Brady, a school friend of mine, at his cottage and, while his sister fell asleep roasting on the dock, Steve stole her cigarettes out of her purse. We smoked a whole cigarette each in forty seconds flat and then—our tongues burning—rushed to the local store to buy triple-scoop ice-cream cones. The problem then was to steal back to the dock and replace the cigarettes before Steve's sister noticed. Steve was just unzipping her purse with one hand—why he had ever zipped it back up in the first place was beyond me—and balancing his cone with the other when the three scoops dropped smack onto her belly. She leapt up so violently that Steve, his sister, the purse, the cigarettes, everything, went flying into the lake. She told her parents and they told us that, even if we eventually went to heaven, our tongues would go to hell.

I was trying to smoke this second cigarette more calmly when Mrs. Dioskouri suddenly appeared in the den, having decided that this moment—1:30 a.m., February the 16th, 1975—was the ideal moment to dust off Lassie.

John ignored her. "You boys not slip?" she said.

"No, I'm leaving soon, Mrs. Dioskouri."

"You smoke, Ben?" she asked.

"Just recently, yes."

She left as quickly as she had come, muttering something in Greek.

"Has she gone back to bed?" I asked.

"Only for a few minutes. Soon she'll have a bath."

"She has her baths at this hour?"

"Only when I have company." John dragged heavily on his cigarette and let out the smoke with a sigh. "I really blew it tonight."

"I wouldn't worry about it," I said.

"And you weren't much of a help."

"What was I supposed to do?"

"You could have said *something* to contribute to the atmosphere. At least you had the advantage of knowing Diane likes you."

"She does?" I was thrilled.

"Yes, Nimbus. Boy, are you dense. But I'm never going to make it with a white woman. And neither will you," he added, when I laughed. "Don't kid yourself. They can never get adjusted to us wild Mediterranean types."

"What do you mean?"

"You're Jewish, aren't you?"

"Yes, but I'm asking what you mean by 'they can never get adjusted to us Mediterranean types'?" I thought immediately of Mary Beth.

"I mean white people come home and they say, 'I'm not very hungry this evening.' And what they mean is 'I'm not very hungry this evening.' An off-white person—a Jew or a Greek, say—comes home and says, 'I'm not very hungry this evening,' and what he means is 'You never loved me as a child. You neglected me.' "

"It's not always like that," I said.

"No, not always. When I was a child, I would come home to our little apartment—the one you're living in right now, by the way—with my family, an aunt, an uncle and my grandparents, and there'd be so much commotion all

101

the time. I'd say I'm not very hungry and fifteen people would be at my throat—one wanting to know what poison I'd eaten on the way home; another thinking I ought to be whipped; a third feeling my forehead and shouting over the chaos for me to open my mouth so she can look down my throat, while—to help out—her husband is holding a naked light bulb a sixty-fourth of an inch from my forehead and inadvertently inflicting second-degree burns; and all this time my mother—my own mother—is trying to pour chamomile tea down the thumb of my aunt, who's holding my mouth open, and into my throat. Then, one fine day I visit the house of a friend from school and I'm invited to stay for dinner. The roast is going around and I begin to sweat, so I take a giant helping to make sure no one attacks me. Then the platter comes around to my friend and he says, 'No, thanks, Mom; I'm not very hungry.' And I hear —though I'm not sure my ears are not deceiving me—I hear, in a voice like Tinker Bell's, his mother saying, 'All right, dear, maybe later.' *And that's my friend's mother talking.* I still don't believe it. I'm still expecting my friend's father to make a belly-flop over the dining room table to rip out a clump of my friend's hair, but it doesn't happen. Do you know what I'm talking about?'' As he said this, John pointed to the ceiling. ''Listen.'' We heard the bath water being drawn. ''Do you think Carolyn's mother would be taking a bath right now, Ben?''

''I think you're rationalizing, John. White people have problems, too.''

''I'm not saying they don't, but they express themselves differently. They get up in the morning and they say, 'Good morning' to each other, as they load up bowls with Wheaties. 'Good morning.' That's what they say and mean. We grunt. We remember the night before, the *years* before. When we pinch each other's cheeks, we leave a bruise. When we kiss good-bye, all of the love in the world weighs on the kiss. It's different—that's all I'm saying.''

''It all sounds pretty simple.''

''Well, it is. We're *different*. We're strange.'' John paused to listen to his mother shifting in the bathtub above our heads. ''You grow up thinking you're weird and, whether or not it's true, you *think* you're weird and that's what counts. Do you know what it's like going into your first grade class thinking you're the most popular kid in the Show and Tell hour because you're getting all the laughs —and realizing only years later that what they were really laughing at was the way you spoke, not what you said? You'd walk into the room with a red balloon the day after a nice picnic with your parents and you'd begin to explain how you got your *kokino balloni* and there'd be a tidal wave of laughter, so you'd bounce the balloon around a bit—on your head and so on—thinking you're a real hit. What a humiliation!''

''But you didn't realize it until years later.''

''Believe me: retroactive humiliation is even worse than the regular kind. What you realize is that you're weird. It hits you one day and you never recover from it. Do you know what I'm talking about?''

''I guess I do, yes.'' We listened to the bath water being drained. I couldn't get Diane out of my mind. A minute later the vacuum cleaner was switched on in the living room. ''Were you born in Greece?''

''Yup.''

''What about Diane?''

''No, she was born here, but only just—and it really makes no difference. She *handles* her sense of weirdness differently from me. She doesn't like herself—plain and simple—and she thinks no one else does, so she'll do anything to please everyone. All of it's to be loved. She's just like my mother—don't kid yourself. When she has kids, she'll be doing the spring cleaning in the middle of the night, too.''

''I find that hard to believe.''

''Suit yourself.''

''Has it occurred to you she's just trying to do what she thinks is right?''

''Now who's over-simplifying?''

103

"Has it occurred to you that she's protecting your parents because she loves them and knows how much you upset them?"

"Look, everything has occurred to me. She also works with kids who want to barbecue their families. Let's not talk about her. I love my sister, but she gets on my nerves."

The vacuum cleaner was switched off and Mrs. Dioskouri came down again. "Go to bed, please, boys, please. I gonna get seeck rright away. You gonna keel me, boys. Slip hyerre, Ben, please. I make bed forr you?" I nodded and she went straight to it.

"I like Diane very much, John."

"So marry her and we'll be brothers-in-law. Then you'll really *keel* my mother."

"I'm *serious*."

"I'm serious, too. Take her out sometime; you're just her type."

Assured that Mrs. Dioskouri had finally come to a resting position, I fell asleep that night full of the possibility of becoming—if not Diane's Greek god—then at least her Hebrew godling.

NINE

It was almost Easter before I managed to see Diane for more than a few minutes at a time. Generally, just as I arrived she would be leaving and when she arrived John and I would be heading somewhere else. I was beginning to wonder if John had said something to her and if she was avoiding me.

I was trying to muster the courage to call her directly to set up a date—I could always say it was John I wanted to speak to if my courage failed me. If her mother answered, I would *have* to say it was John I wanted.

I felt a surge of adrenaline when I thought of Diane one day during my String Harmony I class, which met in the old, wheezing office of Professor Roget, the course director. The office was located in a wing of University College, an eighteenth-century Gothic structure that would not have been out of place in Cambridge. The room was spacious and had a ceiling that sloped down into the oak paneling of the walls, which met in a great oak door. "This office is itself a musical instrument," Roget had said at our first meeting, "and we are merely its bows and strings."

Roget was a teacher for whom music was everything. When we played a Brahms *Andante*, his face sagged with the minor chords. When we played a Mozart *Allegro*, his cheeks and the lines around his eyes burst into the smile of a child opening a birthday gift. When a false note sounded, he cocked his head and pointed to the very string of the very instrument that was out of tune. He had sent hundreds of graduates to the major orchestras of the continent, and he had promised each one of us the same glory if we followed his direction exactly as it was proffered.

The afternoon I decided I had to call Diane, we were playing a piece by Max Bruch when Roget waved us to a stop. "Mr. Beck," he said in a gentle voice, "are you unhappy in the low registers?"

"No, sir; not at all."

"Have you ever wondered if you'd be more comfortable with the viola's soprano cousin?"

"It depends," I said. "Is she better-looking?"

"She is for some, Mr. Beck. You think it over. In the meantime, let's call it quits for today. For next week, can we practice the Bruch and reread our Adam Carse?" This was another habit of Roget's: he had forgotten the word "read". He always said "reread," as though we had already read everything there was to know about music.

Martin Stitzky, who always walked me to the library after class, asked me if I wanted to have lunch before we hit the books. "Sure," I said, "but I have to make a call right after lunch."

"So, call," he said, as we walked across the grass-covered quad to the Women's College cafeteria.

We got our lunch and sat at one of the many tables in the bright hall. "Is she beautiful?" asked Martin.

"Who?"

"The call you have to make?"

"Oh, yeah . . . yes, she's beautiful."

"Is she Jewish?"

"*What*? Why does that matter? Two Jewish guys from a music class sit down to have lunch, and instantly they form a ghetto. What does it possibly matter if she's Jewish?"

"Okay, okay. I was just asking. Why so defensive all of a sudden?"

We ate quietly and then I excused myself to make the call.

"Good luck," said Martin.

I became more and more nervous as I searched for a pay phone in a quiet spot. I was worried I would never get beyond the dialing-for-a-date stage of a relationship. I would end up like one of the bums I passed every day who sat at the corner of Queen and Berkeley streets saying, "Susan . . . Susan." That was his whole vocabulary: "Susan."

My knees were knocking and I had to go to the washroom, but I forged ahead. Please answer, Diane. She did.

"Diane, there's something important I want to talk to you about."

"Is everything all right?"

"Oh, sure. I just need to talk to you in person."

"Well," her voice broke, "do you want to come up here? John might be home soon—"

"No, I thought just us. I thought maybe we could meet somewhere out later this afternoon—maybe at one of the Greek restaurants on the Danforth."

"No."

"You mean you won't meet me?"

"No, I mean not on the Danforth. Why don't I come down to the Blue Sky?" She might as well have said meet me at home, but I was so happy I agreed.

I rushed home, skipping my next class, to wash and change and spray my underwarms with Saran Wrap again. I was seated by the window in the restaurant a half hour before the appointed time. Diane arrived a half hour after it. Meanwhile, I wondered how Mr. Dioskouri would react to our meeting.

When he saw me, he brought over two drinks and sat down. "Everrything okay? School okay?"

"Yes, fine. Just about finished my first year."

"Verry nice. Goood boy." Magda waved hello. "Everrything okay oo-with Dzon? Goood boy?"

"Oh, yes, John and I have become close friends. . . . Your daughter is nice, too."

He sat looking out the window awhile and said, "Eef

107

all pipple in these oo-worrld like Ty-ane, everrything — everrybody—gonna be byooteefool."

"That's for sure," I said. "But, if one of those people were John, there would be perpetual war." And I chuckled —alone.

"Oo-what'rre you gonna eat, boy? Oo-what can I brring you?"

"Nothing, really."

"A steck — I hyev beautiful stecks, freesh these morrning."

"Just a sandwich. Say, a grilled cheese sandwich." This had become a staple with me. I had mastered the grilled cheese sandwich in my own kitchen and had made 571 of them since I'd acquired my home. The first few, I confess, were a little touch and go. I ruined a toaster trying to squash my as yet ungrilled sandwich into one of the slots. Later, after I watched Mrs. Dioskouri grilling one up, I graduated to the frying pan. But even the first few of these I made into grilled Teflon sandwiches, until I discovered that butter was no mere spread, but also a lubricant. This revelation did not mean I became instantly proficient in my technique. One morning, in a rush to make it to my first class, I forgot I was making one of these delicacies and came home to discover that I had grilled twenty-five percent of the kitchen and that the original sandwich was nowhere to be seen.

Be that as it may, eventually I became something of a master of the grilled cheese sandwich, and the ingredients I combined to make my little meals—the bread, the Kraft Pimento Slices, the butter—were just about the only ones in my kitchen that didn't hide in the back corner of the refrigerator until they turned into fur-bearing animals.

It was my sandwich that I now wanted to compare to Mr. Dioskouri's. But, as he passed Magda on his way to the bar, Mr. Dioskouri asked her to bring out a "byooteefool filet steck oo-with all the extras forr my frriend." Magda smiled and waved again from afar. She had not spoken to me very much since the time she'd told me about

Moustaki, so I assumed she had resigned herself to working with him.

An old bum staggered through the door of the restaurant and narrowly missed having his legs walk him straight back out again. Mr. Dioskouri quickly met him to escort him out I thought, and I rose to lend a hand. Instead I watched in disbelief as Mr. Dioskouri led the man into a nearly full restaurant and helped him to a table by the bar. "Seet down, seet down, Meesterr Seymourr, rrelax."

"Thanks, Mr. D. Thanks a million."

"Oo-one meenoot," said Mr. Dioskouri and he brought the man a cup of coffee and a muffin and sat opposite him for a few minutes until the man steadied himself and sat quite upright.

This was only the first surprise. Mr. Dioskouri then rose to empty the cash register of all its cash and credit-card vouchers, arranged everything into envelopes with rubber bands around them, placed them carefully into a canvas bag and returned to the table to hand the bag to Mr. Seymour. "You hyev to hourry leetle beet, Meesterr Seymour. Benk close een feefteen meenoots." Mr. Dioskouri pressed an extra couple of dollar bills into the man's hand.

"Thank you, Mr. D. You're a great soul." He gulped down his coffee and rose from the table.

Mr. Dioskouri stood by my table and we watched Mr. Seymour make his way slowly but steadily past the front window and down the street toward the bank.

I was half way through my after-dinner brandy and having a smoke with Mr. Dioskouri when his daughter walked by the front window. My stomach jumped.

"Oh, Thy-ane," beamed Mr. Dioskouri, rising from the table.

"Oh, *Diane*. What a *surprise*!" I said, rising too.

"*Pardon*?" she said.

"Seet down, seet down," her father said, offering her his chair and kissing her as she settled.

My stomach returned to its resting position and readmitted the steak it had briefly propelled throatward. Mr. Dioskouri hustled off to order Diane dinner.

"Diane," I said, but she didn't look up at me. "Do you know that your father just sent a man with highly questionable credentials down the street with the entire bankroll?"

"Who? Mr. Seymour?" she said, still not looking up. "Oh, he always does that."

"How could he?"

"Mr. Seymour's a decent man—just down on his luck. He was once some kind of lawyer or accountant, but he gave up his family, his job, everything for the bottle. It's quite sad, really."

"Has he been coming here long?"

"Oh, some years, I guess. My father once gave him a cup of coffee and heard his life story." As she spoke, I stared at the reflection of the front window bending in her eyes. "Do you know," she said, looking down again, "that John has had a big fight with Bruce and they've decided to part company?"

"No. John hasn't told me a thing. Do you know what it was about?"

"I was hoping you could tell me. It happened only yesterday and John's taking it hard. He left with the car this morning to go up north by himself."

"I'm sure he'll be all right, Diane."

"You've been a good influence on John," she said. "I'm sure that had a lot to do with it."

"Well, who knows?"

"You know, it means a great deal to my family."

"I know. I know."

"Does that bother you?" She looked up for the first time.

"Not in the slightest."

A table of familiar customers stopped to greet Diane on their way out. Crazy Mr. McConnell patted Diane's shoulder as he went out the door.

"How's Mrs. Stanowicz coming along since her operation?" asked Diane, as Mr. Stanowicz kissed her.

"Oh, I wouldn't worry about her," said Mr. Katz. "She'll outlive us all."

"Who's the new flame?" asked Stanowicz, winking at Diane, and she sank, blushing, into her chair.

"Oh, he's—"

"We've met; don't worry," said Katz. "He's becoming a regular around here, too." And now he winked at me. They filed out, and Diane and I watched until they were out of sight down Queen Street. Diane put her hands on her shoulders as she had done the night we went out to the movie.

"They really don't mean any—"

"It's all right, Diane. I'm sure they didn't." Mr. Dioskouri now brought his daughter the same meal I had eaten and returned to the bar. He stood in his spring suit—one hand on the counter, his back straight—and gazed over his restaurant like a lord surveying his empire.

Diane had not yet picked up her fork. "Ben, was there something you wanted to talk to me about?"

"As a matter of fact there was." My mind rifled through the possibilities: Diane, when I was hardly much older than I am now—Diane, I am struck by your beauty and kindness —Diane, should you ever feel the desire to go parking again, in a ditch, say—Diane, if you agree to date me just once, I shall wipe from my mind the vision of my cousin Sheila's pink—Diane, I have a great fondness for you only my viola can describe—

"Ben, is everything okay?"

"Diane, I have a great viola for you." And with this I gulped my glass of brandy so that some of it splashed as far back as my ears. The rest I coughed through my nose.

Diane gently slapped my back. "Ben, have you been seeing my brother's friends?" she asked.

"No, honestly. I've just been meaning to ask you out," I coughed. "I'd like it very much if we could go out together one night."

111

She stopped slapping my back. Her eyes darted straight to her father, who was mixing drinks, and she slid back into her chair. My face must have changed from green to red like a traffic signal. "No, Ben, I don't think so, but thank you for asking me."

"No?"

"No, thank you."

"May I ask why not?"

"No."

"Do you plan to have a terrific headache for the next—"

"No. I just thought Carolyn was more your type."

"*Carolyn?*"

"*Drewry*. The girl whose number you once got from John. The girl you once asked out."

"So what? I'm not interested in Carolyn Drewry. I asked *you* out. I find you far more attractive than—"

"I'm not at all like Carolyn, you know. We're friends, but—"

"I know you're not like Carolyn. I *know* that. I think you're beautiful and sweet," I said.

"How can you say that to me? Has John put you up to this—you know, because he did mention something."

"I asked John if he thought you would be interested in seeing me. Tell me, honestly, would John put me up to this? What would he gain by doing that? Say yes, *please*."

"Yes, please."

TEN

In the weeks before I was to return to Montreal for the summer, I became more popular than I had expected. On the very evening I was taking Diane to a concert, Carolyn phoned to ask me to a party her parents were having the following Saturday. "My Uncle Bruce, the Consul from New York, will be staying with us and I thought, since your aunt is also in the diplomatic service, you might like to meet him."

"Carolyn, my aunt is a terribly incognito type because, you know, it's an Iron Curtain country and—"

"Never mind. I'm sure you'll enjoy it. Please come."

"I really don't know at this point, Carolyn. Honestly, I—"

"You'll have a good time, I promise."

I agreed, but felt guilty. My way of compensating for such feelings was to order a taxi instead of taking a bus to pick up Diane, as I had originally planned. Nature's way of compensating me was to provide me with a taxi driver who had a doctorate in philosophy so that I would be lucky enough to have my very first teleological car ride. "I believe in the *empirical* as opposed to the *abstract*."

"I'm not sure what you mean."

"I mean the *experiential* rather than the *theoretical*."

"You mean like *contracting* gonorrhea as opposed to *watching* a documentary on it?"

"Not exactly. I mean *event* as opposed to *hypothesis*."

"You mean like *arriving* in Willowdale as opposed to circling Ann Arbor, Michigan, before you *head* for it?"

"Yes, I suppose so. . . . Did you know that Hegel, the German philosopher, believed that truth could be apprehended only through contraries."

"Oh, I have some relatives who believe the same thing."

The driver did not speak to me for ten minutes. Then he said, "Where did you say? Oak Crescent?"

"Yes, that's right."

"Ah . . . Oak Crescent." He said it as if I'd asked for the Via Dolorosa. "Are you doing something interesting on Oak Crescent?"

"I'm picking someone up. We're going to a concert."

"O-o-h?" He gave the word two extra syllables. "Which one?"

"The Bob Dylan concert."

"Bob Dylan! How did you manage to get tickets? I called the day they announced he was coming to town and I couldn't get any."

"I had to buy them from a scalper. They cost me a bundle, too."

"*Bob Dylan*." His look was ethereal. "Bob Dylan, I believe, holds the key to heaven."

"Yes, but I think they've only recently changed the lock," I said, hoping to lighten up the atmosphere a bit. I was wrong. Not another word passed between us and he did not even turn onto his beloved Oak Crescent, but asked me to get off at the corner. It was just as well—I don't think I could possibly have ridden with him all the way downtown again.

Diane and her mother had apparently had a quarrel just before I'd arrived because they were pleasant toward me but not to each other. "Are we all set to go?" asked Diane.

"Well, I was going to phone for a taxi."

"Let's take a bus. It's a beautiful evening."

"Hyev a nice time, Ben," said Mrs. Dioskouri, turning on her heel toward the kitchen.

"What's the matter? What happened in there?" I asked at the bus stop.

"She's worried about John."

"I thought he'd broken off with his freaky friends."

"Yes, but he's been very strange lately. He's short with everyone and he takes off who knows where for whole days at a time. It upsets my parents."

"I think he needs some time to himself. He feels pestered at home."

"I *agree* with you. That's what my mother and I were fighting about. I think they should let him be."

The bus came and we found ourselves a seat in the back. "Did Carolyn call you?" she asked.

"You *know* about that?"

"Well, where do you think she got your number? She knew where you lived, but she didn't even know your last name."

"I'm going to a party her parents are giving next weekend—to meet her uncle."

"Good, I'm glad." Her tone, which was anything but glad, gave me the courage to reach for her hand, and she held mine tightly. "I love Bob Dylan—I really do," she said. "His music makes me feel there's someone looking after the world."

"I know at least one person who would agree with you."

"Who's that?"

"Well, it's not my Aunt Goldie."

"The diplomat?"

"She's not a diplomat."

"I know."

"You *do*?"

"You were just being silly—the way John always is."

"Does Carolyn know?"

"No, I think she believed you."

"How can you be sure I was just being silly?"

115

The bus soon pulled into the subway station. "Tell me, instead, why your Aunt Goldie doesn't like Bob Dylan."

Though it became problematical, Diane did not let go of my hand as we got off the bus, rode the escalator and stood on the platform. "Where have you been practicing your grip?" I asked, and she dropped my hand and blushed. "I didn't *mean* anything by it. You're so touchy." I had to chase her hand all around her body before I could get hold of it again. "Well?"

"Well, what?"

"Where did you learn your grip?"

"I once went out with a football player friend of my brother's and he held my hand like that. I thought that's the way people held hands."

Without thinking, I hugged Diane for a moment, but she pushed me away gently. "Please, Ben, not yet."

The subway screeched to a stop. We found a seat and I took her hand again; she held mine lifelessly. "What happened?"

"Well, you don't want me to hold your hand like a vice and you don't—"

"What else is the matter?"

"That's the other thing my mother and I were discussing: you."

"Me? I'm not a nice Greek boy—is that it?"

"*You* talk about being touchy."

"But it's true, though, isn't it?"

She caressed my hand. "Well, can you blame her? How do your parents feel when you go out with a Gentile girl? Do they mind?"

"Mind?" I remembered my mother's subtle remark when she first saw Carolyn. "I don't know if they would."

"They *would*."

"Look, let's forget about all that now and enjoy ourselves, okay?" She nodded, but I knew we were not finished with this subject. A few minutes passed. I watched her eyes flutter from side to side as we whooshed into a station:

YORKMILLSYORKMILLSYORKMILLS-YORK-MILL-YORK-MILLS

YORK MILLS.

A guy wearing army fatigues covered with camouflage blobs sat down opposite us and began instantly to read the ads above our heads. The camouflage did not work well. Diane tugged at my arm. "Now tell me about your Aunt Goldie and Bob Dylan."

"My Aunt Goldie claims to have met Bob Dylan's mother—claims even to have *known* her for a short time." The trooper looked down from his ads, but only for a second, until my eyes met his. "Is it true?" asked Diane.

"It's definitely possible. You really have to know my Aunt Goldie to realize that almost anything's possible with her."

"And?"

"And she says she met Mrs. Zimmerman—because that's Bob Dylan's maiden name, not *Dylan*—and it was quite a long time ago, just before he became a big star. He had just dropped out of college then, I think."

"Did she say it was exciting?"

"She didn't say, but it wouldn't have been too exciting back then."

"Are you telling me the truth?"

"I swear," I said, holding up six fingers. This had become Sammy's and my universal symbol.

"What does that mean?"

"It means *six*," I said.

"You're so silly. How will I ever know when you're telling the truth?"

I was thrilled by her use of the word "ever" because it meant we would see each other at least one more time. "I thought you already knew when I was telling the truth."

"I need some more practice. Now, *what about Mrs. Zimmerman?*"

"Apparently, Mrs. Zimmerman wanted her son to make something of his life out in the Mid-West—that's where they're from. And, odds are, that part of the story is true. Of course, my Aunt Goldie identified with her right away and talked about her children a bit, though they were very young then.''

''How many children does your aunt have?''

''She's not too sure any more, but she started out with three.''

''You're so silly.''

''Anyway, Mrs. Zimmerman told my aunt that Bobby wanted to become a singer and 'I didn't have the heart to tell him,' she said. 'He had the lousiest voice I ever heard. And *nobody* ever told him. Not to mention that he comes home from college and he's got a harmonica—but does he know how to play? Maybe he knows the notes, but you'd never know it the way he blows here and there during his songs whenever it strikes his fancy. So my husband and I told him: Bubbeleh, write your songs—you're a great song-writer—maybe someone else will sing them. Send one or two to Doris Day—she'll buy one, I'm sure. But does he listen? No, he goes down to the basement when I have friends over playing canasta and he's singing his songs—it sounds like a cat with some kind of abdominal condition. So I go downstairs to ask him to pipe down a little, and he's playing his guitar, ignoring me, and he's got this harmonica on a contraption wired up to his face somehow—all through his childhood I couldn't get him to smile with braces, but to walk around with a harmonica wired to his beautiful face—that's okay.''

It was wonderful to watch Diane unstiffen as she laughed. ''I find that story a bit hard to swallow.''

''My Aunt Goldie swears to it.''

''I think this problem must run in your family.''

The subway was filling up as it approached Maple Leaf Gardens. Two more people sat in our seat and Diane was crowded against me. I felt once again—as I had when I'd first met her — that I had known her a long time. We watched the people standing over us swing perilously to and fro. One of the swingers was an older Bob Dylan fan.

She wore a headband, a breezy floral dress and, with great chomps, she ate an apple with the McIntosh label still stuck on it. As she rocked, I watched her gnarled and painted toes jockey for position at the front of her sandals. Diane gave my arm a tug just in time for me to see the apple label disappear into the woman's mouth, and I had to stand up and look away or burst. Diane followed and we squeezed toward the door. "There is one distinct advantage to growing up that I can think of," I whispered to Diane, as we huddled together.

"What's that?"

"You become tall enough that, when you get on buses and subways, you don't have to stand wedged beneath a person and feel those two jets of warm air from the person's nose constantly coming at your head."

The subway, the parking lots, the streets all emptied into Maple Leaf Gardens. Into this great arena, where Johnny Bower and Terry Sawchuk had seen more pucks shot at them than bullets fired in a battle, came the unimposing figure of Bob Dylan. With short, throaty lyrics, with the incessant strum of guitars, and the plaintive call of the harmonica, he sat not far below the great clock with "Leafs" on one side and "Visitors" on the other, and quietly dismantled the machinery of depression and war and of the great societies that had assembled the machinery. And there were "long, lonesome highways" and "highways gettin' filled" and "streets gettin' empty" and roads leading every which way, but never back. In spite of myself, I was transported to my childhood, to a simple time in my life, when the songs Mrs. Zimmerman was talking about were being written:

"It's hard and it's hard and it's hard and it's hard—
It's a hard ra-a-ain gonna fall."

When his guitar wandered into the opening strains of "Blowin' in the Wind," he stopped my breath and the breath of all those around me. Here was a song so fundamental—it must have seemed to all of us—that it could never have come into being, but always just was. It was sung on Saturday morning by the Friendly Giant and around campfires and in the back seats of cars as we drove to visit our grandparents.

"How many times must a man look up
Before he can see-ee the sky?

Yes and how many ears must one man have
Before he can hear people cry?"

Out on the street the world looked different, as it always does when people are moved in this way. I could hear Diane's voice and my own—feeble even beside Bob Dylan's —still humming the last melody, humming it even in the dim light of the Café Marika as we looked at the menu.

"Ben, thank you for taking me to the concert." Diane warmed herself by crossing her arms and rubbing her shoulders. I stared and she lifted her hands as if to sing "Alouette" again.

"I enjoyed seeing it with you," I said.

"I hope we didn't go just because you thought I wouldn't like the symphony because—"

"No, I like all kinds of music. I really do."

"I envy you your ability to make music," Diane said wistfully, and she moved her hands from her shoulders to rub the sides of her neck. "Music speaks to us in a place where language is helpless. It takes us beyond the edge— do you know what I mean?"

"Yes, I do."

"We're oafs when we speak," she continued. "We pretend we can figure out just what is going on every day in our little lives. But when we sing we are birds. We, well . . . you know what I mean." Diane pulled out of her trance and glanced up at me as though I might be judging her.

I ate a piece of apple strudel and half of hers. As I brushed flakes of pastry off the upper half of my body, I said, "Tell me about yourself. I know hardly anything about you."

120

"What do you want to know?" she said, looking down as she put down her cup of tea.

"Everything."

"Believe me, you don't want to know everything."

"*Anything*, then."

"I was born on March 7th, 1957, at Mount Sinai Hospital in Toronto, the second—and likely *last*—child of Stavro and Cassandra Dioskouri, an immigrant couple from Northern Greece." Diane started giggling.

"Go on, go on; I'm enjoying this."

"Ben, it's so boring—"

"*Go on!*"

"My grandparents on my mother's side and my aunt and uncle, who also belong to my mother, came with them and they settled into a tiny place. My parents started a snack bar, and my aunt and uncle worked at Primrose Bakery. John and I were the only children in the family because my aunt was barren, so we got a lot of attention."

"Why did your family come to Canada?"

"My father ran away from home when he was very young, and my mother's house in a small village was burned to the ground twice: the first time during the second world war and the second time during the civil war between the Communists and Nationalists. They'd had enough, I guess, and my mother especially hated village life—she hated farming and hated the way everyone in the village knew everyone else's business. She always wanted to be a big city lady and my father wanted a clean start."

"So your grandparents and aunt and uncle eventually got places of their own here?"

"No, they went back. Life was hard here in those first years. No one knew the language and they worked hard just to make ends meet."

"Well, they obviously made ends meet."

"Not at first—hardly. My father wanted to buy property right away—and he did—and cheaply, by today's standards. But it kept us on the brink of ruin. It was hard—especially for my aunt. She's not at all like my mother—

the opposite, in fact. She thought everything in Canada was backward; even the climate, she used to say, had an inferiority complex — making everyone take notice both winter and summer. Anyway, they went back, and my grandparents both died in Greece soon afterwards. I was there when my grandfather died."

"I thought you said it was hard to make ends meet."

"Oh, it was, but I was living there."

"*Living* there! Your family—"

"No, just me. My aunt couldn't have children, I told you, and that was the cruelest fate nature could have handed her. Every night after she came home from Primrose Bakery, she'd ask my mother if she could take me back with her. She wouldn't even wash when she got home; she'd go straight to my mother to talk about it. I'm told she'd get so excited during those conversations that clouds of flour would fly all over the room. My father would come home and he'd get into the argument. My uncle never said very much about it, and my grandmother always tried to calm her daughters down."

"But they finally gave you away."

"No, they didn't *give me away*. I was only two or two and a half and my aunt argued it would be good for me and they'd bring me back when I was old enough to go to school. My parents never actually agreed to it; they just gave up fighting, so my aunt practically kidnapped me. When we got back to Greece, my aunt must have told the entire village she'd given birth to me while they were in Canada. This made giving me back even harder, but here I am."

"I can't understand how your parents could have given you away."

"I *told* you—they didn't. But I did come along at an inconvenient time and they both had to work so, with my other relatives leaving, who was going to look after me? Better my aunt and uncle, who were like parents to John and me anyway, than some stranger. My aunt and uncle are kind of crazy—they're villagers through and through, you know—but they loved us dearly.''

Out in the cool spring evening, Diane and I walked arm in arm toward the subway. ''Diane, I've enjoyed this evening very much.''

''Me, too, Ben.''

''Will I be able to see you again? Can we go out together somewhere else?''

''I guess we can.''

''It's not going to create a serious problem?''

''You don't understand. My parents like you very much. They *really* do. It's not that.''

''I understand. It's like the empirical as opposed to the abstract.''

''What's that?''

''An important philosophical concept I learned this evening.''

''I see,'' she said. ''You're really very silly.''

It cannot be said that I am a veteran kisser, but Diane's kiss was much like her hand-holding. She clamped her eyes shut and pressed her lips hard against mine. Soon, our neck muscles tired. ''The football player?'' I asked, ''or Mikey, the pyromaniac?''

''The footall player.'' She kissed me again, but this time it was as if she was born to it. Her lips became soft and warm and our bodies throbbed together.

''Whatever happened to the football player?'' I said, not letting go.

''I don't know. I went out with him only a couple of times.''

''He didn't ask you out again?''

''No, he did, but I didn't accept. He was just feeling sorry for me.''

''Diane, you're a hopeless case. How can you not see how beautiful you are? What did your aunt *do* to you in Greece?''

We arrived at Diane's house at 1:30 a.m. As we walked

between the lions guarding the path, the living room lights went out and the curtains fell shut. She did not kiss me again at the door.

It was almost 2:30 when I got home, so I couldn't help but notice Moustaki's lime-green car still parked on Queen Street. The lights of the Blue Sky, though, were out.

ELEVEN

Only *I* would have agreed to do what I did at Carolyn's place. "Come into my room, Ben, please," she said, before I'd even gotten in the door of their penthouse. "Ben, everything's a disaster. The couple my parents usually hire to be the hostess and bartender were called out of town unexpectedly—somebody's dying in their family, I think—and now there's no one to tend bar. Will you do it?"

"You want me to be the bartender?"

"There's really no one else coming to the party except for my parents' friends and we can't very well ask one of them to do it."

"And your parents want *me* to do it?"

"No, they don't even know. It's my idea—Daddy is having a fit."

"Why don't people just get their own drinks? I mean, I'd like to help you out, but I'm having trouble understanding the disaster exactly."

"You can't have people get their own drinks. It's not that kind of party—I mean, my uncle and his friends are going to be here."

"And you can't explain this to your uncle?"

"Ben, *please*."

"Carolyn, you don't know what you're asking. I've never *tended* bar before. I wouldn't know the difference

125

between a gin and tonic and hair tonic. Do you understand?"

"No one asks for unusual drinks, really. And, if someone does, there's a manual we have right underneath the bar. Ben, my parents will be glad to pay you, I'm sure."

"I don't want to be *paid*. I'll tell you what: if you'll be the hostess, I'll be the bartender."

"I think my mother has already called someone else to be hostess. Please, Ben; I'll be forever grateful."

I nodded and Carolyn leapt at me, throwing her arms around my neck and kissing me dead on the lips. "Let me bring you something else to put on."

"*Carolyn*, what's wrong with what I'm wearing?" I said, still woozy from the kiss.

"I'll bring you a bow tie. You'll be so cute!" And she dashed off.

I stood in a fairy-tale room with stuffed animals, puffy down bedding and pink walls. There was a giant wristwatch clock on the wall with floor-to-ceiling red straps. I wondered if the pink of the walls was selected to complete the wrist motif. In came Carolyn with the bow tie, followed by her parents. "Ben, I'd like you to meet my parents, Professor and Mrs. David Drewry."

"Oh, that's convenient: you both go by *David*."

Carolyn's parents tittered politely. Professor Drewry stepped forward. "Ben, I am very grateful. Carolyn told me you'd offered to tend bar for us this evening." Carolyn looked away. "I hope you'll allow me to pay you for your services."

"No, forget it, please."

"Well, if there's ever anything I can do—"

"Who knows? Maybe sometime you can tamper with the computer at school to raise my grades." They tittered again and filed out.

"I'll just leave you alone to put on the tie," said Carolyn, as if I needed to undress to do it.

From my vantage point behind the bar, I was able to survey the entire colonial living room, from grandfather clock to glass and oak bookcases, to coach lights with dim flickering light bulbs over pine wainscoting—all precisely the way a pioneer family would have decorated a penthouse.

The first guest—after *me*—and quickly to become my first customer was a woman beneath whose platinum hair was a yellow dress cut so low in the front and back and so high up her thighs that in any other surroundings she would have passed for a tramp. In these surroundings she was a colonial tramp. I soon learned she was the good professor's "administrative assistant."

"May I have a Harvey Wallbanger, please?" she said.

"Absolutely," I said, hunting for the manual beneath the bar. "Old Harv was a little hard up, was he?" I said.

"Pardon me?"

"Oh, nothing; just a little bartender's joke."

"Oh."

I found the drink in the index and stood to mix it. "Harvey Wallbanger, Harvey Wallbanger, Harvey Wallbanger," I said idiotically.

"Oh, look! It's Ben Beethoven!" shouted Kathleen, coming in the door with her parents and brother. She ran over to give me a hug. "Aunt Carolyn said she met you, but I thought I would absolutely *never* see you again!"

"You're very pretty, Kathleen," I said, thinking she looked even more like Carolyn now with a frilly white dress and her hair up.

"And this is stupid David." She whispered the "stupid" and stood aside to let me shake the hand of a handsome blond boy dressed in a navy blazer and gray flannel pants. He looked tired already.

A second of Carolyn's sisters came through the door with her husband and a daughter about David's age. This was apparently the chubby wing of the family.

When the hostess came in from the kitchen with a tray of hors d'oeuvres, the children swarmed around her and stuffed their cheeks two and three delicacies at a time.

"Oooooo!" squealed Kathleen. "This one tastes like snot!"

"That's an oyster, dear," said her mother, stepping in. She was yet an older clone of Kathleen and Carolyn. "And don't say those nasty words. Besides, how do you know what sn—you know—tastes like?"

Carolyn's father directed the hostess toward me, and I, too, helped myself to three hors d'oeuvres. Carolyn glanced over at me and winked. I must say here that I consider this form of communication patronizing, unless there is a fifty-year age difference between the winker and winkee. I am willing to concede, though, that wearing a bow tie and being the winkee at the same time might have made me overly sensitive.

People were now filing through the door with some regularity, and a man with a pipe came straight to me to ask for a Scotch and water. "How much water?" I said, though what I should have asked was "how much Scotch?"

"Just a splash."

I took a good look below the bar to discover an assortment of glasses that rivaled even the Dioskouris' collection. What, *really*, were all these different shapes for? Globular ones? Tubular ones? Conical ones? The father of the cup invented it so he wouldn't have to pour liquids into his hands any longer. "Was there any particular kind of glass you wanted your drink in?" I asked.

"An old-fashioned one," he said. A man after my own heart, thought I. He wants a regular glass. So I took a twelve-ounce tumbler, filled it nearly to the top with Scotch and splashed it.

"Enjoy your drink," I said, beginning to like the job, and the man walked away with a peculiar look on his face.

The man turned out to be Uncle Bruce, the diplomat. He returned moments later to ask for a dry martini "with a hint of lemon" for his wife. I didn't mean to become resentful, but I was a stand-in bartender and it was difficult enough to concoct a dry martini—which looked to me just about as damp as any other drink—but to have to add a *hint of lemon* was more than I could bear. I mixed the drink, whispered ''lemon'' at it, and handed it over.

He carried it to a white-haired woman with a diamond necklace who was too busy showing off her dog to pay any attention. It took some showing off, too, because the dog was no bigger than a small rodent. ''Did you see Aunt Gladys's Chihuahua, Ben?'' Kathleen called to me from the couch. I beheld an animal wearing a pullover no bigger than a glove.

''Say hello to Ben,'' said Aunt Gladys. But the little thing was extremely agitated. It was shaking up a storm on the living room rug. ''Say *hello*, Mindy.'' The dog barked hysterically. I thought it was on the verge of a nervous breakdown. It leapt on little David's foot and he pulled both legs up. ''Oh, don't worry, dear,'' said Aunt Gladys. ''Mindy's been spayed.'' That bit of news came as a relief because, if Mindy had decided to mate with anything other than an insect, she would have been crushed.

Kathleen took Mindy into a bedroom to calm her down and David followed. Their place on the couch was taken by the Wallaces, Carolyn's heavy sister and her heavy husband and daughter. I stared in disbelief as Mrs. Wallace opened her purse, withdrew a nursing bottle filled with milk and administered it to their large child, who sprawled across their laps. Carolyn came over to the bar to pour herself a glass of juice. ''Ben, you've been very sweet.''

''Carolyn, how old is that child drinking milk over there?''

''Who? Suzy? She's seven or eight, I think.''

''Isn't that a bit old to be drinking from a bottle?''

''I guess she's never broken the habit. It calms her down. My sister Nora says it's better than having her suck her thumb.''

''That may be, but if this goes on much longer she'll be finishing her bottle and having a smoke afterwards.''

The Mindy entourage returned to the room. ''Look at

129

Suzy," shouted Kathleen, stopping the party. "She's drinking from a bottle!"

"*Kathleen!*" shouted Carolyn and Mrs. Drewry, in unison.

But Kathleen wouldn't listen. She leaned on the back of the couch and said, "Suzy, you drink plenty of milk and, when you grow up, you'll have big boobs just like your parents."

A half-dozen people descended upon Kathleen and it was decided unanimously that the children should be put to bed. As these things go, though, Kathleen was allowed to stay up, probably because she would have made the loudest noise if they'd tried to banish her, and she would have no one else to bother if the others went to bed.

The party began to scatter into pockets around the room: one pocket contained whatever was left of the Drewry descendents; another contained the university and diplomacy types, all solemnly repairing the world; a third was led by Mrs. Drewry and Aunt Gladys on some kind of mission to the kitchen; a fourth held Kathleen and Mindy; and, in a final pocket, the one the dry cleaners always have to empty for you, sat the woman in the yellow dress, holding her third Wallbanger and leaning heavily on the grandfather clock.

Kathleen wandered over to me with Mindy, who started yelping uncontrollably again the second she saw me. "Ben, could you give Mindy a bowl of water? Aunt Gladys said she should have some."

"If you bring me a bowl, I will." Kathleen left, and Mindy barked and barked in a way that it would certainly not have if it had looked in a mirror.

I was on the verge of crushing out its little life when Kathleen returned. She was carefully carrying a bowl with the water already in it. Mindy rushed at the bowl. "Maybe you should loosen its pullover a bit," I said.

"I'll bring over my chair and we can watch her," Kathleen said. Mindy drank rapidly, her little tongue shifting the water as if a stream of droplets were falling into the bowl. But she was not barking and I wanted to keep her drinking, so I topped up her bowl with Scotch.

"Ben," said Kathleen, pulling up her chair beside me. "What is it like to be dead?"

"It's like having a job picking out clothes for the Queen Mother."

"Oh."

"Kathleen, why do you want to know?"

"I just *do*."

"Well, do you remember what it was like before you were born?" She shook her head. "It's exactly like that when you're dead."

As they walked by us, I heard Carolyn's father tell his administrative assistant, the woman in the yellow dress, that he would escort her down to the parking lot, and the two left quietly. Mindy finished nearly the whole bowl and settled by our feet. "Ben, why do skeletons always smile?"

"When have you ever seen a skeleton?"

"My dad has one in his office."

"Is that some kind of decoration?"

"No, he's a doctor. Have you ever seen a skeleton?"

"Well, my father has one in his office too, but that's his partner. My father calls him Mr. Levinson."

"How does your father work with a skeleton?"

"He wonders the same thing."

"Does Mr. Levinson always smile?"

"Only when my father's not talking to him."

"Does he have skin?"

"Oh, yes, he's got more than enough skin."

"My father's skeleton hasn't got any skin."

"Maybe that's why it's always smiling. I guess you need skin to frown."

"Yeah, I guess so, too." Kathleen was rubbing her eyes. The kitchen party returned and joined Carolyn's. Kathleen's mother came over to her at the bar. "Honey, let's collect David and go home. It's long past your bedtime."

131

"Mommy, couldn't I stay a while longer? I want to help Ben mix drinks and I want to look after Mindy."

Kathleen's mother smiled at me. "I don't think so, dear. Ben is doing fine by himself and, look, Mindy's fast asleep." Mindy was lying on her back gazing at God.

The mothers went off to gather up their sleeping children. "Ben, will you marry Aunt Carolyn and become my uncle?" said Kathleen.

"I think I stand a better chance with Mindy—but look at the bright side: we'll still be related."

"Okay," said Kathleen, and she put up her arms to hug me again.

Within moments, Carolyn's sisters and their families were gone. Mrs. Drewry asked Carolyn if she knew where David Sr. was. Carolyn shrugged her shoulders. Aunt Gladys came looking for Mindy and, when she couldn't wake her, carried off my little lump of bride to a bedroom. Carolyn sat on my bar stool. "These parties are deadly, aren't they?" said Carolyn.

"Speak for yourself. I think this is wonderful," I said.

"I'm sorry, Ben. I didn't mean to be so self-centered."

David Sr. came quietly through the front door and joined his friends. He went over to his wife and Gladys to ask if they wanted a drink. "A dry martini for Gladys," he said. "And Scotch and water for Mrs. Drewry and me." Carolyn helped me get the drinks.

When he left, Carolyn said, "Ben, will you stay for a little while after everyone leaves?"

"Sure," I said. I could feel the blood rise behind my bow tie.

Carolyn's father and uncle strode toward the bar. "I'll have another Scotch and water, please," said her uncle. "And you can go a bit heavier on the water this time. So, David," he said, turning toward Carolyn's father, "what's new and exciting at the university? I understand your famous literary treatise is almost finished."

"Yes, Betsy, my assistant, just brought over the typescript this evening." That would explain his extended trip to the parking lot. Proofreading.

"What is it about?" asked Uncle Bruce. Carolyn nudged me to listen. Her uncle took a hearty swig of his drink, spilling a little down his chin.

"It's about artistic responsibility. The idea came to me quite accidentally—in one of my classes, actually. We were discussing Shakespeare's influence on modern writers, and one of my students said, in passing, 'It's crazy, isn't it? Shakespeare retired seven or eight years before his death. Imagine having Shakespeare's brain and lying on a beach or something, knowing you could be at home writing more of the greatest plays in English.' It was a provocative point."

"Maybe he was finished writing whatever he had to write," said Uncle Bruce.

"Maybe he was, but even if he'd written a new play based on themes and circumstances he'd already explored, wouldn't it make for better reading than most other literature? And—don't forget—there's still the possibility that he *wasn't* finished."

"That's true," said Bruce. A rivulet of Scotch now worked its way down his neck toward his collar.

"And there are better examples," said the professor. "Rossini was so successful with his music that he spent the second half of his life in retirement. Now, to repeat my student's question: how can you be Rossini and know the pleasure of your music and the power of its influence—and *stop composing*? How can you be Hemingway and put an end to your life—even if you feel you are written out? Isn't it worth the effort to try to produce more?"

"I suppose it is," said Bruce. "So what was your conclusion?"

"My conclusion was sophormic, really, but it was the opposite of what I'd anticipated. At first I thought my student was correct, but I quickly realized that the world had no right to expect its creative people to keep producing."

"Why not?" I asked, as Uncle Bruce seemed to be losing interest.

"Because Rossini didn't compose music to fulfill a need the world had. He did it because he felt like it; he wanted to—maybe he *needed* to. And, when he didn't feel like doing it any more, he quit."

"Don't you think that's a little bit self-centered?" I asked.

"No, self-centeredness has nothing to do with it. It's nice that Rossini and Shakespeare and Hemingway contributed to the world, but they were compelled to contribute to it because of circumstances that they themselves— and not the world—had created."

"I'm not sure I agree," I said, and Carolyn and her uncle smiled at me. "If they had such gifts, don't you think they were *obliged* to share them? If you are a research scientist and one day in your lab you come up with a cure for a certain kind of cancer, are you not obliged to share your discovery?"

"No, you're not. You share your discovery because many of the circumstances you've created for yourself throughout your life have led you to your little lab where you mix your miraculous cure. You do it because *you* need to. You take chemistry courses because *you* need to. The world can't make you do it because you *ought* to or because you feel guilty when you don't do it. It's your own obsession that drives you. Shakespeare and Einstein were following their own hearts and, when they were finished, no amount of global need could make them do more. You come from the school that says you ought to suffer when you work and keep your nose to the grindstone no matter what. Those things have nothing to do with creativity. They have to do with guilt and responsibility—the Protestant work ethic."

Carolyn and I sat on the couch after everyone had left and her parents had gone to bed. "He's like an orthodox Jew, right?" she said.

"What? Oh, yes, they keep the faith alive. You remembered."

She took off my bow tie for me and we put up our feet on the coffee table. In the flickering light of the coach lamps, Carolyn's blue eyes darkened to purple and, without a word of warning, she kissed me passionately.

TWELVE

I spent the summer in Montreal doing what John had predicted: playing with a band—except that this troupe did the wedding/bar mitzvah circuit. Benny Altar's Band of Renown had played at two occasions my family had attended, and Cousin Harry had mentioned my name to the bandleader both times. One thing led to another and I found myself sitting opposite Mr. Altar on his pool deck at his house near Westmount. What I thought was going to be an audition turned out to be an interview—if it could be called even that.

"So you're Benny—I'm Benny—you can't be all bad. Why do you want to be a musician? You think you want to live in Westmount?—*Forget it*. This house was already in my wife's family and I hardly make enough to pay the bills for upkeep."

"Well, all I thought for this summer was—"

"Of course, excuse me. Summer only, am I right? You're *studying* music. That's what crazy kids do these days. They study everything—they think it's going to help. They don't want to play in a band. They want to become J.S. Bach— am I right?" He was lying on a lounge chair dressed only in his bathing trunks. During the conversation, I kept having to look at the squashed bulbs of his toes, and I wondered how many pairs of lacquered shoes they had been crammed into. "You want to know about J.S. Bach?—He had twenty-one children and had to write up a storm just to keep body and soul together. All those hymns?—You'd write hymns, too, if you had to feed twenty-one children. And—don't kid yourself—you know why he wore a wig? Because he ripped his hair out trying to compose those ten thousand canticles—that's why." Benny Altar rubbed his own bald head. "So what d'you play?" he asked.

"Well, I play a viola best—"

"I can't use a viola. What am I going to do with a viola in a four-piece band? Freddie, my piano player—another *mishugeneh*—is off to Israel this summer to find himself."

"I play piano, too, and violin."

"Violin's even better. It breaks them up every time. The violin is the Jewish heart singing—am I right?"

"Well, it appeals to—"

"You know what I think?" I had the feeling I was about to find out. "I was a handsome young dreamer like yourself when I first thought up this scheme." He rubbed his head again. "Matter of fact, it was long before my hairline receded back to my ass. Just when I was starting up the band, it came to me like a vision. I thought, why not have a special country—you know, like the Vatican—just for special ceremonies: weddings, funerals, bar mitzvahs, like that? It could be created somewhere in the Laurentians, say, or the Catskills. The only residents allowed would be caterers, photographers, musicians, ministers of every denomination, florists, like that—do you follow?"

I nodded.

He leaned forward in his chair and put his feet down, popping his right testicle out of his trunks. "It would be wonderful! There would be no taxes—maybe just a small team of managers, like plaza managers, with a small service charge paid to them, some kind of percentage — do you follow? And anytime someone wanted to get married or mourn their dearly departed, a team could be in place to arrange everything. The only consideration would be to move the dead afterwards to their respective lawns."

He leaned forward still more until I thought the testicle

137

would burst. "It would be a *country*—do you follow?—with its own flag with a cake and candle design and maybe a national anthem: 'Those Were the Days'—something like that." He leaned back in his chair again, his trunks sucking up his testicle. "But I'm too old now—you do it. I'm giving you the idea free—just throw me a couple of pennies in my old age."

That summer I played 'Those Were the Days' a thousand times. I played it on the piano, adapted it to the viola, sang it with Benny Altar and played it on the Jewish heart. People requested it twice, three times, and, when they didn't request it, let out an "aahhhh" of recognition each time we played it anyway. And, each time we played it, Benny Altar's eyebrows slanted upward and his eyes closed, and I thought of the nation of Ceremonia, which is what Sammy dubbed it in a story he and I began to write together one night on some napkins. It was called "Canticles and Testicles: The Rise and Fall of the Ceremonian Empire." We were right in the middle of the story—Ceremonia had just invaded Diamonda and was firing violin bows at an army of jewelers—when my mother's hand, like a chicken head, came out of nowhere, plucked up our napkins and threw them in the garbage. "Don't write obscenities all over my napkins, please. Now I know who's responsible for all that disgusting graffiti I see in the subway and phone booths."

Sammy and I saw quite a few movies that summer and, occasionally, I met with some of my old friends from high school, but I was usually busy on weekends when they weren't and, gradually, I felt my hold on Montreal weakening. It was a mixed feeling I experienced—a feeling I can compare only to those last days in June each year in elementary school when I looked forward to the summer coming, but lamented the fact that I would never see my class together again. Whatever happened to Elizabeth White, who communicated cooties to all of us in my grade five class and answered every question in Arithmetic? Or to Sandy Teschler in grade eight, who always rubbed his crotch with a ruler under his desk and kept himself in a permanent state of excitement? Or to Tommy Wilty, who had to write "I shall not be late for Mr. Blackstock's class ever again" five hundred times at least once a week in the detention room and who rigged himself up a set of ten pens bolted together in a line so that he could write ten lines simultaneously?

Many nights I would like awake in bed pining away for Diane and worrying that Carolyn had told her about our evening together. Though we had dated only once officially, Diane had a quality about her that made even the slightest indiscretion feel like disloyalty. It won't matter, I told myself. Surely Diane will understand what I went through—turning, the way I did, from a gnome to the Great White Prince. But it was a fleeting moment, I will tell her. I didn't even have a chance to develop a rash where my leotards rubbed against the saddle of my white steed.

I wanted Diane to know how I felt about her. Why hadn't I called her before I left Toronto? I wanted to take her to another concert—to feel her grip as we waited for the subway. I wanted her to see me play for Benny Altar. I wanted to call her. I *did* try to call her—one afternoon before work—but the phone rang fifty times before I gave up. I wrote her a postcard one evening when I was downtown, but when a couple of weeks passed and I realized she wasn't going to answer me, I became certain she had spoken to Carolyn. To drown my sorrow, I drank my first Scotch and water at a wedding one evening, but it was my only one because it tasted like disinfectant.

I told Sammy about Diane. "Is she beautiful?" he asked. This time it was Sammy lying back on his bed, and I with my feet up. He was smoking one of my cigarettes because our parents were out. Elton John was playing on his stereo.

"Yes, she's really beautiful," I said.

"Has she got a great ody-bay?"

"Sammy, she's beautiful—let's leave it at that—and she's sweet and kind. I've been out with her once, and I miss her like crazy."

He sat up. "Is she J—I dare not utter the word—J—J."

"Sammy—"

"Just kidding, Ben," and he rose to make the rare gesture of putting his hand on my shoulder. "Have you spoken to her since you came home?"

I shook my head. "I've written to her, but she hasn't answered.

"Why would she? Were you asking her a question?"

"No, but she could write me back something — anything."

"Maybe she's shy, Ben. That's all. She's probably just shy—or maybe she's just busy with something. Maybe she has her mind on something else. You know what it's like. Two people can have a perfect relationship, but at times they may just not be connecting. You may be upstairs putting the finishing touches on a romantic dinner while your husband's downstairs pretending to be watching 'Trip to the Holy Land' when he's really watching a cowboy putting it to Miss Nude Texas of 1961 or something. People can't connect all the time or they'd suffer from static cling, or whatever."

"Thanks, Sammy, really."

"Don't mention it," he said. "Feel free to consult your more experienced brother anytime, Benny boy."

Then one morning I thought news was at hand. John called me. "Where are you?" I said.

"Here in Montreal—at the train station."

"What are you doing here? When—"

"I ran away from home. Now, are you going to come and pick me up?"

"Sure. Of course I am."

At the station, John told me he was having problems at home. "I bombed my school year; do you know that?" he said.

"Were you surprised?"

"Not really. But you know how it is: you just hope these things will work themselves out, and they didn't this time.

140

My parents were crushed. Their doctor-lawyer-engineer-*violist* was a failure.''

''Very funny.''

''Well, you know what I mean. Jews don't have a monopoly on ambition for their children.''

''*Did I say they did!* I'm not the one who blames your parents.''

''Okay. Calm down. Sure I blame them. Wouldn't you? I go into the restaurant to help out and my father says I'm dressed like a bum. I get into a fight with that asshole my father took in as a partner and *I* get thrown out.''

''Moustaki?'' He nodded. ''You got into a fight with him?''

He nodded again. ''I sat down to have a beer, and Moustaki told me liquor was expensive—if I planned to have another one, I should pay for it. *Me.* My father builds up a business for over two decades, lets a jerk become a full partner *on credit*, and I should pay for a beer. Do you know what he did one day?''

''What?''

''He told McConnell he ate too slowly. He should go have his lunch somewhere else next time. So McConnell walks out—followed by Katz, Stanowicz and a few other people. It's a community down there—a *family.* You can't kick people out. The guy chases away customers and then robs my father blind for good measure.''

''Hasn't your father noticed?''

''Sure he has, but he never talks about it. He's never been taken advantage of in this way and he still doesn't know how to react.''

''So, what are you going to do?'' I said, as we stood on the platform of the Metro. ''Are you going to keep working there?''

''I've been thinking of going to Greece for awhile—just to clear my head. At least I won't have anyone bugging me over there. I'll stay with my mother's sister. She'll be so happy to have me she'll stay off my back. I'm going nuts here—I'm not kidding.''

"And your parents don't mind sending you to Greece?"

"Are you kidding? Greece is lotus land; it's the land of the virgins—even the mothers are virgins. All Greeks were immaculately conceived; didn't you know that? Virgin Marys with their Joseph sidekicks. Poor shmucks. My father forgets about the life he had in Greece. He was a policeman—can you believe that?—and he was making peanuts. And my mother forgets she was more miserable there than she is here. Just ask her relatives sometime. She thinks Canada ruined us—ruined *me*. *Willowdale*. That's what did it. But if we'd stayed downtown it would have been *Toronto* itself. Toronto the good. And she forgets she was miserable downtown and that's why we moved in the first place."

We got on the subway train and a girl of fifteen or sixteen in bobby socks sat down opposite us. She took a book out of a plastic bag and began to read immediately. It was Mordecai Richler's *Cocksure*. A baleful look came over John's face. He whispered, "Watch this," and he mussed his hair a bit.

"John, she's a child."

"I know that," he said. "What do you take me for?" He got up and strode across the car to her. "Do you have a pen?" he said.

"Pardon me?" she said, barely looking up.

"I'd be glad to sign that for you."

"*Sure* I do! Are you? . . . But I thought, you know, that you were much, you know—"

"Older? I hold my age very well, but I'll take that as a compliment." She scrambled around in her purse and pulled out a pencil case. I cringed. "Now, what's your name?" asked John, opening the book and waving the pen over it like a magic wand.

"It's Cynthia Appleby."

John spoke as he wrote. "To Cynthia Appleby. Have a good read! The best of luck to you. Mordecai. August 12th, 1975." He blew on the ink and handed her back her book.

"I'd be curious to know your reaction," he said. "Why don't you write to me and let me know."

"What's your address?" she asked.

"You can write directly to my publisher. You'll find the address on the first page. Have a good summer, now." He picked up his bag and waved to me to get off. I was about to protest, but he cut me off with another godly wave.

We got off the train two stops early. I saw Cynthia madly checking the covers for a photo. "Do you not drive?" asked John.

"I do but my father has the car right now, if you have no objections."

"Oh," he said. "I thought of bringing my car, but I didn't want to overly excite anybody."

"John, I can't believe you. Why did you do that to that poor girl in there?"

"Are you kidding? I made her day. There's no picture of Richler in that book and, when she finds one, she'll forget completely what I looked like. Now, where the hell do you live?"

"Let's take a cab, come on," I said, picking up his bag.

My mother greeted us with tuna salad sandwiches and chicken soup. "How's your family?" she said immediately to John.

"Oh, they're fine," said John. "My father has a bit of a heart condition, but it's under control." My mother smiled warmly. "And my mother's putting on a lot of weight and that can't be good for her." I was impressed by John's ability to make small talk. "The doctor told her, if she couldn't eat diet foods, she should at least cut down. And she's progressing: the first day for breakfast, instead of two pieces of cake, she ate one piece and a grapefruit; the second day she ate one piece and only half a grapefruit; and the third day she cut out the grapefruit altogether."

My mother jumped right in. "Well, she can't be putting on weight at the rate I am." She put her hand on her hip.

"Oh, I'm sure she is," said John. "When she walks

143

around outside now, astronomers are starting to pick her up on their telescopes.''

That big my mother decided she was not going to get, so she put on her rayon jacket and said she was going shopping with my Aunt Ida. ''Do you want me to pick up your suit from the cleaners?'' she asked at the door. There was a honk from outside.

''Yes, please. Benny will kill me if I work again without my suit on.''

John ate ravenously. ''Your mother makes a great tuna salad and I haven't eaten since yesterday.''

''You're kidding. Didn't you eat breakfast?''

''No, I spent the night at Union Station and took the first train out.''

''You must have left in quite a huff.''

''Not really. My mother had just polished Lassie and gone to bed. So I went to my room and decided only after I'd gotten ready for bed that I was leaving. I took a small bag and snuck out.''

''You mean they don't know you're here?''

''If I'd announced I was leaving, what would that have accomplished? We'd have had a fight; my father would've left home to open the restaurant eight hours early; and my mother and Diane would've had a bird.''

''But they're probably having a bird now.''

''But I'm not there to see it.''

''What if they call the police in desperation?''

''My parents won't call the police for awhile because my mother is afraid they'll find me in some kind of opium den and that'll bring untold shame upon her head forever more. And, besides, I'm twenty years old, Ben; I think I'm mature enough to make this kind of decision without anyone's permission.''

''But you're not mature enough to move out of your parents' house—is that it? Look, why don't you call them at least?''

He finished off his sandwich and I gave him half of mine. ''If you want to call them,'' he said with his mouth full, "you go right ahead, but leave me out of it." He cleaned up his plate. "I'd really like to lie down. Would that cause much of a problem?"

We took his things into Sammy's old bedroom, which I had once again taken over. "May I ask you a couple of questions, though, before you go to sleep?"

"No, I'd really rather you didn't."

So I left him. Another lunatic napping, leaving me to guess what he was going to do next. I pictured Mrs. Dioskouri's vein heaving against her neck as she condemned another plant to death by hanging in her living room. What would Diane be doing? What was she thinking? If I called and she answered, maybe she could handle it better. Surely they would be relieved to find out John was with me. I resolved to call the restaurant in the hope of catching Mr. Dioskouri, but not until John woke up and I had a chance to discuss it with him.

"So what did they say?" he asked an hour later.

"Who?"

"My parents. You mean you didn't call them?" I refused to answer. "Listen, do you have any cigarettes?"

"No."

"Let's go buy some. Is there a store around here?"

Outside, John said, "Look, are you going to be resenting me for the rest of the day?"

"All I'm trying to understand, John, is why you are making me responsible for your family's sanity."

"I'm not making you responsible, you jerk. If you want to feel guilty, that's your business."

"It's not a question of feeling guilty. You came to Montreal to have your little rebellion and to transfer to me the responsibility of keeping your family happy at the same time. If that wasn't your plan, you would have stayed in Toronto and hidden away in a flea bag somewhere."

"That's guilt. I came to Montreal because you're a friend of mine and I don't care if my family knows."

"What the hell difference does it make what it is! If your

parents die of a heart attack tomorrow, isn't it your responsibility?''

''No! That's what I'm trying to tell you. *If my parents link their well-being to my becoming a doctor or a supreme court justice or the prime minister, it's their problem, not mine!* If they want to invest all their pride in me, it's *their* risk—not mine! Why don't *they* become supreme court justices! I'll tell you why. Because they're afraid. They feel unworthy. They want me to fly their flag for them. I am their child. They want people to say, 'Oh, loook hyow smarrt these Thioskourri child ees.' And I refuse. Do you understand?''

''I can't be that cynical, John. Many people want their children to succeed. They can't be blamed for that.''

''But that's your little Jewish gut talking. You think that if parents lean on you and drive you and push you to play your viola ten hours a day, you'll play Carnegie Hall when you're ten.''

''There *are* ten-year-olds who have played Carnegie Hall because their parents stood by them day after day.''

''But parents like that have destroyed more George Gershwins and John Stuart Mills than they've created. How many children have collapsed under the burden? *Them* we don't hear about.''

And, as if John had willed it to happen, a man with a life-sized crucifix on his shoulder appeared out of nowhere and crossed Monkland Avenue. The cross rested on a wagonwheel. We both started laughing.

''You see?'' John said. ''Loon city. His mother probably wanted him to become a priest. But why stop there, he must have thought. Why not go all out and become the Messiah?''

I bought us a pack of cigarettes and we smoked heartily. As we walked, the shadows of the leaves rolled over John's face like film.

''John, how's Diane these days?''

''Same as always.''

''What's she doing this summer? I wrote her a card, but never heard.''

146

"Oh, she'd never answer your card. That would be like phoning a guy and asking him out. Are you kidding? Anyway, she's still working at the home for delinquents. She's decided to go on to university in the fall, as she was telling you, to study social work. She spent her life coming to *that* decision—can you believe it?"

"Has she said anything about me?"

"Of course. She said she liked the way you comb your hair."

"Come *on.*"

"I don't know. Yeah, she says the odd thing. I think she likes you a lot."

"Why, what has she said?"

"I don't know. I don't remember. But she read your stupid card about fifty times, and she asked me once if I knew when you were coming back."

"Did you tell her?"

"How was I supposed to know! *You* call her and tell her."

"I think I will."

"Good—but just beware. She's just like my mother, you know."

"I don't believe that. Diane *laughs.* She gets a kick out of things."

"Well, maybe you can save her from certain misery. You're the saving type. Who knows?"

That night John ate well and turned into a regular Eddie Haskel. "It's a lovely house you have here, Mrs. Beck."

"Not really, John, but thank you. We've been talking about moving."

'You've been talking about it for quite a long time," I said.

"I think they're serious now, though," said Sammy.

"Why would you move?" I said.

"*You,* now. Do you hear, Max? No more *we,*" said my mother.

"The area's getting a little run down," said my father. "The Jews are moving elsewhere."

147

"You're not in Israel," I said. "You don't always have to move where the Jews are."

"You see that, Rita? One year in university and he's already Dr. Martin Luther King. Have you been following the political climate here since you left, smart aleck? Do you know that in a year from now your wonderful province could have a separatist government? Put that in your pipe. And many people—never mind Jews—are talking about leaving Quebec altogether."

"How about us?" asked Sammy. John didn't look too worried either way, but went on eating.

"We have the business. What am I going to do? Drop everything? No, we'll look in T.M.R., if we can afford it."

"What's T.M.R.?" asked John, not looking interested.

"The Town of Mount Royal," my mother said—slowly, as if to a foreigner.

My father said, "Not that I'm going to have sons over there any better than I do here to whom it would occur once in a blue moon to mow the lawn." And with that he rose from the table to do just that. My mother shook her head at us, partly because he was right and partly because my father mowed lawns with much the same skill he used to drive cars. There was no pattern to his mowing. He went in a kind of spiral and then in circles, leaving tufts of lawn everywhere, not looking, and running over anything in his path. One morning last summer, when my mother asked us to clean up the lawn after him, Sammy and I found the pieces of a squirrel all over the garden—a claw in one corner, a bit of tail in another. When we told him that he had distributed a squirrel over most of the yard, but that after careful analysis we were confident that the mowing was not the immediate cause of death, but that the squirrel had likely gone to its maker at least a day before its body had been processed, he said, "That's all you two can do: criticize. To do the mowing yourselves would be too much to ask, but to comment—that you have time for."

After dinner, Sammy took John downstairs to show him

148

his record collection and I told John I would call his family. "All right, call them, if it makes you happy," he said.

"I don't see how it could hurt," I said, trying to keep my voice down so that I wouldn't attract my mother's attention.

"All right, call, call. But I don't want to speak to anyone."

I went into my parents' bedroom and called the Blue Sky, but Magda told me she thought Mr. Dioskouri had left for home. Without hesitation, I called John's house. Diane answered and my heart raced. "How *are* you?" I said.

"Is this Ben?"

"Yes, it's Ben. I'm calling from Montreal."

"How is your summer going?" she asked. I heard her mother asking questions in the background and Diane's "Shh."

"Fine. I'm playing in a band and it's been good practice."

"I know. You told me in your card." Her voice was quiet and warm. "Thank you for sending it. That was very thoughtful."

"Diane, try to control yourself when I tell you this — especially with your mother standing there—"

"Is everything all right?"

"Yes, there's nothing to get upset about—"

"If you don't want my mother to hear, you'd better hurry because she's gone to pick up the extension."

I sped up. "Diane, John's here with me and he's fine. I'll send him home just as soon as he—" the extension was lifted — "calms down. Hello? Mrs. Dioskouri, how are you?"

There was a silence. Then Diane said something angrily in Greek.

"Hyellone, Ben, hyow arre you?" said a little voice.

"Just fine, Mrs. Dioskouri. Break it to them calmly, Diane, and I'll try to have him call."

"Ots?" said her mother.

"Nothing," said Diane. "Thank you, Ben. Thank you again." And she hung up.

A few days later, John had a call from home. He said no more than "Hello" and the call lasted only a few seconds. "What happened?" I asked, when he hung up.

"Do you want a direct translation?" he said. "Dzon, you come hyome rright away. You futhairr gonna die oth a harrd attuck rright away you doan come hyome."

That night John seemed more dejected than when he'd arrived. "John, do you want to go to a movie? Woody Allen's *Love and Death* is in town and I hear it's even better than *Play It Again, Sam*. Why don't we ask Sammy and the three of us will go?"

"My parents should never have had a family. They're desperate. They don't know what to do to keep it together. They should never have had a family really."

"Why don't you forget it now? We'll go out and have some laughs."

John followed me to Sammy's room. Sammy was clipping his toenails.

"Do you know what my father does when he goes to a beach in Greece?" John continued. "He stands by the sea in his suit and tie and hat. And when he gets tired of my aunt's place, he hails the only taxi in her village, gets in and says, 'Thessaloniki.' That's a four-hour car ride." Sammy waited for a cue from me to laugh. "And my mother — that's another story. She won't go to Greece unless someone is deathly ill—and last time she wouldn't go even then until my aunt installed an indoor toilet. She hates the goats and pigs and rabbits. Hates the neighbors asking her personal questions. She hates the reminders of her youth—her period of uselessness. And they came here. The lady and the gentleman. To this most civilized of British worlds — because their civilization had faded. Aristotle, Pericles, Plato — how long can heroes like that be worshipped?" Sammy took advantage of a pause to leave the room. "Do you know what Diane and I used to do when we were young—where our parents used to take us in our first car? We'd go to other restaurants owned by Greeks and we could have whatever we wanted—roast beef, chocolate doughnuts, whatever—and we felt good, felt taken care of wherever we went. Sometimes, if we went in the evening, we'd wait until closing time and the men would play poker until all hours and our mothers would sit together and gossip—though this was not something my mother did happily. She almost never talked. Her idea of a good time was to take Diane and me to department stores — to Simpson's and Eaton's especially — or *Seempsone-Eatone*, as she calls them—to study the racks and racks of clothes. To this day, my mother knows every rack by heart, knows when new articles have arrived — knows every price.

"But when we got older we didn't always go with them — not even Diane. We got tired of the circuit. They lost control of us. They were never really sure enough of themselves to lead by example, so they led by fear or guilt. This will happen if you don't do that. That will happen if you don't do this. Go out with the guys and you'll kill your father instantly. Go for a beer and—*bang*—a bullet straight through our temples. And Diane was pretty good to them—she still is—but I gave them their money's worth of anxiety. Do you know what I once did?"

"John, why don't we get Sammy and go to a movie?"

"Do you know what I once did—and they don't even know it to this day? They had these gold coins — British sovereigns—that they'd had since the war, and my mother hid them away in an old leather glove until our wedding day. It's an old tradition: you give coins to your children on their wedding day. And I stole them, Ben—one at a time. I sold them to my grade eight homeroom teacher."

"Why did you do that?"

"To have money to do what I wanted—to buy dope—anything."

"But they buy you whatever you want. They bought you a car—"

151

"That was to go to school with. Everything has a purpose."

"Well, it seems to me you've put them in that position, John. You were the one who told me about guilt and control. Why don't you make a move to get control of your own life? You really are strange."

Woody Allen, in two hours, was able to extract not a single giggle—not even a smile—from John. He sat nibbling his popcorn, the kernels making a trail down his chest, and staring blankly at the screen. In the Metro, when the subway came, he wanted to finish his smoke before leaving the bench. Sammy and I stood at the edge of the platform and Sammy whispered, "He knows our address. If he doesn't want to get on the next one, let's go. Maybe he wants to be alone for a while."

That John had a penchant for the unpredictable did not surprise me—or even Sammy, since I had spoken to him about the Dioskouris. But we both soon learned that *knowing* a person is unpredictable does not necessarily prepare you for the *form* that unpredictability is going to take. John walked right by us and, with a casual wave, leapt down onto the tracks. "See you later, guys," he said.

"Are you out of your mind!" I yelled.

"Get out of there!" shouted Sammy.

"No," said John. "I've made up my mind." And he crossed his arms as he stood in the middle of the tracks. The people from the other end of the platform began to gather around us.

"But, John," said Sammy, "the trains come at least ten minutes apart at this hour."

"What do you mean?" said John, dropping his hands.

"I mean you may have to stand there for seven or eight more minutes," said Sammy.

"Isn't this just my fate," said John. "I'm committing the most embarrassing suicide in history." And he sat down and cupped his face in his hands.

"Get the hell out of there!" I said. "You're going to get electrocuted or something."

"Where?" he said, as he stood up and looked around. Sammy and I climbed down to help him back onto the platform. The crowd was muttering as we headed toward the exit.

"Let's go get a drink," I said.

"I have to go to the washroom first," said John, unable to look Sammy or me in the eyes. But he was quickly back to normal. "Either of you guys got a comb?" he asked, examining a pimple in the mirror.

Sammy cracked up.

"You want a *comb*," I said.

John was already parting his hair with his fingers.

"You find that to be particularly deviant, do you?" he said.

"John, five minutes ago you were prepared to have the subway part your hair."

"All right, so give me a comb."

"I don't have one!"

"I have one," said Sammy. "But I wouldn't give it to you. I don't want your greebies all over it."

John grabbed Sammy and rubbed his knuckles into his temple. "You little smart aleck," John said, as they laughed. "You guys are such smart alecks."

"Next time you want to kill yourself," Sammy said, breaking free and still laughing, "take a bottle of aspirins —one a day until they're finished." John chased Sammy out of the washroom.

But a sickly pallor hung over the evening. Long after Sammy had gone to bed, John and I sat in the backyard smoking and looking up at the stars. I wondered if this was the most outrageous thing John had ever done. Or was that the point? Did he prefer the outrage he could see to the mourning he would not see? I was suddenly angry. "So what were you trying to accomplish, John? Were you trying to make me responsible? Were Sammy and I supposed to feel guilty?"

"Sammy's a great kid; do you know that? You're really lucky to have a brother like that. He's a sharp kid."

"I know."

"Play something on your viola for me," he said, blowing perfect rings of smoke up at the heavens. "Go get your viola and play one of your credenzas."

"*Cadenzas*. It's two in the morning."

"Then sing something."

"How about 'Those Were the Days'?"

"Great. Sing that."

"John, I want you to call home in the morning."

"No, I'll go home instead."

THIRTEEN

Toronto. Saturday, September 14, 1975. One thing I do not know about this day is that it is Mr. Dioskouri's name day. Stavro Day. One thing I do know is that seven a.m. is an unseemly hour to be answering the phone, no matter how persistent the caller. "What!" I answer.

"Ben?" says a quiet voice.

"Diane?"

"Ben, did you hear the crash sometime in the middle of the night?"

"The crash?"

"The window of the restaurant was smashed. Someone broke in last night and made away with nearly two thousand dollars. My father thought you might have heard some noise. I'm sure the police will ask you."

"No. I heard nothing. Hold on." I went to the window to look down. Two policemen were crunching through some glass, and Mr. McConnell stood pointing at the bits of "Blue Sky" lettering in the rubble.

I went back to the phone. "I don't know how I could have missed it, Diane, but the window sure is broken. I don't see your father anywhere, though."

"He's on his way down. Could you go down, please, Ben? He'll be so upset."

"Sure I'll go down. I'll call you back."

Downstairs, a few of the locals had gathered to see what

155

was happening. Mr. Dioskouri was just arriving in his giant New Yorker. He had on his best light gray summer suit and his matching fedora. "Oo-what hyappun hyerre? Ooh-what hyappun?"

"Looks like someone broke in here," said Mr. McConnell.

"It sure does," said one of the officers, who was writing notes.

"Or maybe someone broke out," said McConnell, chuckling.

The other policeman looked at him. "What do you mean *out*?"

"All the glass is outside on the sidewalk. You can put together all the letters right here." He pointed with his foot. "There's hardly a speck of glass on the inside." He chuckled again.

All of us leaned over the window frame to look inside. Mr. Dioskouri nodded solemnly. "Whoever it was," said the policeman with the notebook, "he wasn't too experienced—smashing the window like that. He could easily have cut a bit out of the door near the lock."

I was asked a few questions and the police left. Mr. McConnell stepped through the window frame and took a seat inside. The restaurant staff had begun to arrive and, after some muttering, began to sweep up the sidewalk. Soon, except for a few of the neighborhood children passing by, interest in the window waned. Mr. Dioskouri asked me in for breakfast though the restaurant did not open on Saturdays until lunchtime. If he had a suspicion about the break-in, he was sharing it with no one. Instead, he stood behind his bar, with the posture of a soldier, and made calls on his red telephone to get the window replaced and the business moving. Just as I was leaving, Moustaki roared up in his green Javelin.

I slipped upstairs to call Diane. John answered. "What are you doing up so early?" I asked.

"It's early for you maybe, but I've been in bed since yesterday morning."

"Aren't you feeling well?"

"I'm fine. Just tired."

"May I speak to Diane, John?"

"No."

"Is she not there?"

"She probably is. Don't you want to speak to me?"

"Sure, but put Diane on first and I'll speak to you after."

"No. Just call back and I'll let it ring."

I slammed down the receiver and waited a few seconds before calling again. Diane answered this time. "So, what happened?" she asked.

"The money was definitely stolen, but there was no other damage. Does anyone have any idea who might have done this?"

"No, but it had to be someone who was watching the place fairly closely because they hide undeposited cash in a secret place under the counter. The weird thing is that my father never leaves that much money in the place over the weekend and he's mad at Mr. Moustaki because he was too lazy to make a deposit yesterday as he was supposed to."

"Was your father here working last night?"

"No, he hasn't been feeling that well lately, so he hasn't been there since Wednesday."

"Well, there's something very strange going on around here."

"What do you think it is?"

"I don't know, but this was no ordinary robbery."

"My poor dad has had so many problems lately, and now he's got this to deal with, too."

"Yeah, poor guy."

"Ben?" Diane's voice got quieter.

"Yes?"

"Are you coming today? Did John invite you?"

"To what? No."

"To my father's party. We're having a party to celebrate his name day."

"No. No one invited me."

157

"You can come if you want to. You'd be welcome to join us."

"Sure I'll come. I'd love to." As I hung up I realized I'd forgotten to ask her what one buys for a name day — or even what a name day is.

I returned to the restaurant to eat breakfast and Mr. Dioskouri sat with me, drinking coffee and smoking. Mr. Seymour joined us. Moustaki had his hands on his hips and was studying the broken window. He was wearing white pants and a powder blue polo shirt, which exaggerated his growing ponch. "Ben," said Mr. Dioskouri, "you come to parry at my hyouse today." This was a statement, not a question. "And you too, Meestairr Seymourr. You both come buck hyerre thrree o'clock I gonna drrive you hyome. Come buck thrree o'clock."

I went from store to store hunting for something with "Stavro" written on it, but all I could find was a bronze statuette of "St. Stephen, the Just Martyr," whoever that was, with his palms out, standing on a reclining dog of some kind. I wondered if the dog thought him as "Just" as everyone else. I had made my way to Danforth Avenue, the part of Toronto known as "little Greece," but one that tried even harder than big Greece. Beside Pallas Athena Bakery was Mount Olympus Travel; then Parthenon Leather Goods; then Zeus Grill; then Mesopotamia Beauty Salon; then Socrates Tavern (where I stopped to have the house special: "Hemlock Cocktail"); then Dionysos Groceteria, which overflowed onto the sidewalk almost to the road with crates of ripe melons, tomatoes, red peppers, eggplants, celery, carrots, black olives, grapes, plums and peaches that were worthy of the old country; then Nick's Shoes — Nick was apparently in it only for himself; then Salonika Shish Kebab, whose fiery grill could be heard sputtering even from the street; then Apollo Sweets, where I stopped to buy a box of soft jellied fruits sprinkled with icing sugar. But I was becoming frustrated about the Stavro gift. I thought of buying him a bottle of liquor, but he owned a bar with a thousand bottles. I looked at clothes:

shoes, hats, ties, everything. I was flipping through records of the Russian Army Chorus—having decided I could never buy a Greek record I was sure he didn't own—when I realized it was almost 2:30 and I hadn't even done my Saran Wrap routine yet. I rushed back to the icon store, bought St. Stephen and headed home.

At the best of times, I have difficulty wrapping even a plain box, and St. Stephen didn't come in one, so he ended up looking like a small mummy, which I held in my lap as we drove up the Don Valley Parkway. Mr. Seymour sat in the back. "Thank you verry muts you loook ufterr Dzon these summerr," said Mr. Dioskouri.

"It was only a week."

"Thenk you I doan forrget."

"Well, you know, he's been having some troubles."

"I know," he said.

"Mr. Dioskouri, your partner Moustaki—"

"I know—please, I doan talk now about these. I gonna feex. Doan oo-woarry, please." He put his hand on my shoulder.

The highway that followed the path of the Don River from Lake Ontario to the northern suburbs wound through dense deciduous forest, which might have looked from an aerial view like a country forest were it not for the houses and the few apartment buildings and factories spotting the slopes. Lush though they were, these were city trees with gray leathery leaves and hardy stalks that gave one the impression they would outlast the people living here.

"You hut?" asked Mr. Dioskouri, removing his hat and placing it between us on the seat. "Toorrn on airr-conditione."

"Are you hot, Mr. Seymour?" I asked, turning to find him asleep in the back. I wasn't hot, but I studied the panel anyway. There was a "Climate Control Center" with a hundred buttons. I tried a few in the hope of switching on the Equatorial Rain Forest. But nothing happened. Mr. Dioskouri pushed a single button, and Arctic winds howled through the vents.

"It's a nice car," I said. "Like a Cadillac."

"Only time I gonna rride een a Cadeellac gonna be when I dead."

It was clear Mrs. Dioskouri wanted everything to be perfect for the party and those things over which she had control *were* perfect. She and Diane had obviously worked themselves to a lather to get the house ready and the food out. But John sat in the den in his underwear, flipping channels with the remote converter from one football game to another. It was not until his father spoke to him—a short swift yelp — that John dragged himself upstairs. Diane bounced down the stairs and kissed her "*baba*." She wore a plain white linen dress which complemented her dark eyes. "Hi, Mr. Seymour, Ben. It's nice to see you both. Would you like a drink?" She took my box of sweets and the mummy and put them on the mantel.

"A wrapping service," I said. "It's a new technique." Diane giggled.

Three glasses of brandy arrived aboard a silver tray. "*Steeni Yassou*," said Mr. Dioskouri, holding up his glass.

Mr. Seymour downed his drink with a throaty gulp. "Congratulations, Steve," he said.

"Many happy returns of the day," I said, wondering immediately if Stavro Day came once a year or once a century. I was safe, though, because the worst I could have been wishing him was a four-thousand-year life.

"Come upsterrs," said Mr. Dioskouri.

"Right away," said Mr. Seymour. "If you don't mind, I'll tidy myself up a bit first." And he headed for the washroom.

In the living room, I sat before the same marble coffee table I had the first time I'd come to this house. But there was a difference. The tulips I had first seen jutting out of the snowbank in front of the house had been harvested and placed in a crystal vase at the center of the table.

Mrs. Dioskouri rushed by us, pausing to say hello on her way up to the bedrooms with a suit for John. Little did I know that, sitting in that living room, I would be in the

160

direct line of fire: other guests soon began to arrive and filed by Mr. Dioskouri and me. "Mr. and Mrs. Christopoulos, this is Ben Beck, John's friend," said Diane, leaving to bring people things to eat. The Christopouloses kissed me, leaving a cool spot of saliva on my cheek.

I have never been fond of people touching me; it is a trait I inherited from my father, who shook my hand to say good night from the time I was five. I endured my mother's kisses, but as a rule preferred not to have my Aunt Ida keep her hand on my knee as she spoke, or to have Cousin Harry grab my chin and shake my face just because I had grown a little since the last time he had seen me. And at absolutely no time would I allow lips behind which were bits of herring caught in dentures to come within a half-foot of my lips.

So, when Mrs. Ioannou, who had spilled a bottle of Chanel No. 5 on herself before she came, kissed me, I cringed. But, when Mr. Ioannou—two tablespoons of five-year-old Brut — stepped up and kissed me too, I nearly gagged. Then came Elizabeth Ardenopoulos and her husband, Mr. Old Spicis, whose saliva burned a hole in one of my cheeks. Then Mr. and Mrs. Mothball and their three little moths, who fluttered unwillingly up to this complete stranger called "John's friend" and then flew away to a light bulb somewhere. I was in a reception line. I had saliva forming a crust on my cheeks. Then came Uncle Musk and Aunt Musk Ox, both of whom, after kissing me, crushed my hand to powder. Then Aunt and Uncle Garlic and their little cloves. I was desperate. There was only one person in the entire house I would gladly have kissed—passionately—and she was the one person I could not kiss because the whole room would have dropped dead on the spot— one of *us* kissing one of *them, and meaning it*—the Man from Mount Sinai ravaging the White Virgin from Mount Olympus.

I ran into the kitchen to find Diane. "What's the matter?" she said. "You look pale."

"Diane, do you think it would be all right if I had a shower?"

"Now? Didn't you have one before you came?"

"I did have one this morning, but—"

"Well, don't be silly. You don't need to take a shower twice a day."

"Diane, a hundred people kissed me and shook my hands. I don't feel right."

"That's *mean*, Ben. It really is. Come with me and I'll give you a towel and some Javex."

"I didn't mean what you think. Honestly, I didn't."

"What did you do the night we kissed?" she whispered. "Did you walk through a car wash afterwards?"

"How can you say that?"

"Don't raise your voice."

"How can you say that?" I whispered. "I *loved* kissing you. I'd do it again right now."

She blushed. "Don't you dare!" She was walking away from me holding a tray. I took the tray away from her and kissed her, as I'd been waiting to do all summer.

"Then, why would you want to wash?" she said, pulling away.

"I don't. I was only joking. Why do you keep introducing me as *John's friend*?"

"Don't change the subject."

"Why not as your boyfriend—your *friend* at least?"

"Right here? Now? I have to make a production out of it in front of all these people?"

"Have you told even your parents?"

"Have you told yours?"

"No, I haven't. I'm sorry."

"Ben, my parents know we went out. What should I tell them? They like you. They'll never forget what you did for John and neither will I. You saved his life."

"I didn't really, you know."

"It doesn't matter. You were there when he needed someone. You're the best friend he's ever had—even if you only half care about him."

162

"My liking John makes a big difference with us, doesn't it?"

"No, but it's important. It says a great deal about you."

"Will you see me one night this week?"

Diane's mother came down and Diane snatched up the tray as she reddened. "I have to help out now."

"Will you, though?" I said.

"Yes, of course I will." And she rushed up the stairs.

"Come, Ben," said Mrs. Dioskouri. "Too munny nice pipple hyerre. I oo-want you oth them."

The party had swelled since I'd left the room. John was now there. He wore only the white shirt and gray slacks his mother had taken him. He was holding forth to some people and they kept smiling painfully. I sat beside him and he seemed glad to see me, but I could do little else while he talked and pointed at me than smile. I quickly discovered that kissing a room full of people does not make it any easier to talk to those people—nor any easier to be more than a fragment of myself: the straight man at one party, the help at another, the musician at a third, the Jew at a fourth. "My doaterr-low ees Dzew, you know thut? See ees byooteefool girrl. Byooteefool." "I hoo-was een Eesrrael oo-once. Byootteefool. Those Syrians they gonna theenk twice nex' time they uttuck Eesrrael—thut's forr ssoorre. Byooteefool. Grreat pipple." "The thrree grreatest pipple een the oo-worrld een my opeenione arre the Grricks frrom Asia Minoarr, the Grricks frrom Mucedonia and the Dzews—thut's my opeenione."

I was introduced to the Poltzers, a Jewish family I had kissed but had not yet met, and we quickly established a ghetto on the couch. Debbie Poltzer was my age and said she would "never go to Israel if you paid me."

"Why not?" I asked, only because Mrs. Poltzer was standing by. For the record, I would not have *paid* to send Debbie Poltzer to Israel, but I would have contributed to a fund to launch her to Mars.

"I have many reasons: (a) Israeli men think they're God's gift—they're always coming on to women; (b) they drive like maniacs over there; (c) I can't stand the food; (d) it's dangerous—I wouldn't want to get my head blown off; and (e) Israel's just bizarre—that's all."

"What do you do, Ben?" asked Mrs. Poltzer. "Do you go to school?"

"Yes. U of T pre-med. I hope to specialize in podiatry."

"Feet?"

"Yes, feet."

"God knows, we could use a podiatrist with my bunions and Mr. Poltzer's misshapen toes."

Now that was a prospect to relish: the Poltzers' bunions and misshapen toes. "I look forward to having you as my first patients."

"Have you been reading about the Jamieson baby?" asked Debbie.

"The Jamieson baby?"

"Yes, you know, the one that drowned in the backyard pool. Really bizarre. I knew the Jamiesons, you know, and I used to babysit for that baby."

"Oh, I'm—"

"It's hard for me to imagine how it could have happened. Maybe you can help with your feet thing: (a) it could have slipped while someone—Mr. or Mrs. or both—was not watching—the story was not clear; or (b) the grandmother was over babysitting, and God knows, she's blind as a bat, and besides (c) what could she have done anyway —jump in after it? and (d) what are they doing leaving the grandmother *at the pool* babysitting anyway? really bizarre; or (e) maybe there was some deep psychological reason they didn't want to keep the child; or (f) they were trying to teach the child independence at that age — can you believe that?"

Mr. Katz saved my life. "What are you two discussing so seriously?"

"We're just reviewing the alphabet," I said. Debbie laughed a throaty, goofy laugh and I escaped to the other side of the room where Mr. Seymour sat in one of the eyebrow chairs with a glass of brandy, and John stood talking to a man I recognized from the CBC.

"You know," John was saying, "someone once said— an American journalist, I think it was—that the only real difference between Canada and the United States is the CBC."

"Oh, I don't know about that. Do you think there's much difference between the CBC and the other networks?"

John thought a moment. "To tell you the truth," he said, "I don't. The only difference, as far as I can tell, is that the other networks give away concert tickets that no one can get, and the CBC gives away tickets no one wants."

John and the man laughed—John a bit harder—but he stopped abruptly just as I felt a tug on my elbow and we both turned to find Carolyn standing behind us. She winked at me. I blushed and could not look at John. "Have you tried one of these?" she said. "They're little cabbage rolls made with grape leaves instead of cabbage."

"Try the moussaka, too," John said. "It's very good. It's made with eggplant." And, as we turned to search for some, I looked over my shoulder and John winked at me.

Carolyn and I wandered into the kitchen where several of the men huddled around the table. They were kibbitzing as Mr. Dioskouri and Mr. Christopoulos flung down the dice in a game of backgammon. Mr. Christopoulos's large diamond ring clattered against the table. "It's called *Tavli*," said Diane, and she put her arm around Carolyn's waist.

Mr. Christopoulos held up his empty glass until Diane took it from him to refill it. "Ben," said Carolyn, "would you like to spend Thanksgiving weekend with us on our boat? My parents think you're nice and they'd like to return the favor you did at the party."

So Carolyn and Diane had not spoken about me. "Look, tell them it was nothing," I said. "I enjoyed being there."

Diane leaned in to give Mr. Christopoulos his drink.

"I'm sure they'll insist," said Carolyn. "Why don't you come, Ben? I'd like it if you did."

Diane left for the living room with a tray. "We'll see, okay, Carolyn?" I said. "It's still a month away."

"Please say you will so I can make arrangements." She reminded me again of Kathleen, the way she asked.

"Well . . . are you asking anyone else? Diane or—"

"There really isn't room for that many extra people and Diane's been on the boat several times. You'll love it, Ben, and the water may still be warm enough for swimming. We'll have a wonderful weekend!"

"I don't know about swimming in October, Carolyn."

A chorus of cheers went up around the table as Mr. Dioskouri won the game. A couple of the women who were drying dishes joined their husbands at the table to help pick the new opponent. Mrs. Dioskouri put her wet hands around our shoulders and asked if we'd had enough to eat. Her cheeks were red and she had a look of satisfaction on her face. "You play *Tavli*?" she asked me. I shook my head. "You play oo-one time oo-with my hyusband and Dzon. You gonna like."

"Sure," I said.

"This is a nice party, Mrs. Dioskouri," said Carolyn.

In the living room again, I saw Debbie Poltzer talking to Mr. Seymour and she was counting off with her fingers. I found myself a conversation that turned politely into English as I sat down. John was being offered a job in a lab by Mr. Gambros, a thin man who had white hair and smoked a pipe. "Mr. Gambros is a pharmacist," said John, turning to me. Mr. Gambros nodded and had a serious look. "Can you imagine?" John whispered. "I'd be dropping DNA tablets all day long."

"Doan luff, Dzon," said Mr. Gambros. "Eet's a rre-searrts lub. You coould do muts oo-worrse."

"Why would you laugh?" asked Mr. Seymour, leaning forward from his chair. He was sinking rapidly into a familiar stupor. "This gentleman comes from Greece—probably without money, without the language—and gets himself educated as a pharmacist. Then he offers you a job—you, who had every possibility—and you laugh that you can't do it. It's not right, John. It's not; believe me.'' Mr. Seymour leaned back and placed his glass down, carefully negotiating the table beside him.

Mrs. Gambros shared the chair with her husband, but she was facing the other way, talking to a lady named Mrs. Leftani, who sat squeaking on the piano bench. Mr. Gambros left to get himself another drink. ''Do you know the Leftanis?'' whispered John. ''They're the richest family in the entire Greek community.'' I looked over at Mrs. Leftani, whose cleavage was deepened by a snug sequin dress. ''The last time she wore a dress like that,'' said John, ''a member of the Winter Olympic Committee tried to sign up her cleavage as a site for the giant slalom event.''

On the other side of us, the conversation was heating up. I heard the tail-end of a remark Mr. Poltzer was making about the wisdom of American foreign policy. Mr. Gambros leapt to his feet, so that his watch-chain clattered against his vest. ''Amerrica ees the oo-worrst. Theenk only of the self.''

''Whho doesn't?'' said Mr. Leftani, coming in from the kitchen.

Doug Lucas of the CBC was eating a *kourombiethe*, a shortbread cookie covered in icing sugar, and he sneezed, blowing a cloud of white powder all around him.

''They eenstalled a puppet een Grreece and they geeve all the supporrt—all the arms, all the money, all the trrade —to Toorrkey. That ees the frriend Amerrica ees. Eef the Grreeks oo-woould elect a Coammyooneest goaverrn-ment, therre oo-woould be no puppet!'' said Gambros.

''Then oo-we oo-would be Soviet puppets,''said Leftani. ''You always come oo-weeth yoourr Coammyoo-neests. Eef you coould hyev keeled all the parrteesans, you *oo-woould* hyev!''

''Oo-ee *soould* hyev!'' And Gambros threw his pipe into an ashtray as he left for the kitchen.

''Do they do this often?'' I whispered to John.

"Always," he said. "It's a good thing the guys in the kitchen aren't in here. Full scale civil war breaks out when they're not slapping down cards or dice."

"How does it usually end?"

"It never does. These guys love each other. They would die for each other, but don't mention politics or breathe the word 'America' or 'capitalism' or 'communism,' if you know what's good for you."

"That was really bizarre," said Debbie Poltzer, holding her hand up beside her mouth to conceal her words. "Excuse me—I'm going to the Ladies' Room," she said and swept by us.

"Oh, feel free," said John. "It's just next to the Hat Check."

Mrs. Dioskouri summoned all the guests into the living room, and Diane and Carolyn helped to bring in the gifts. Mr. Gambros sat down again beside John. "Thank you for the job offer, but I'll be going to Greece soon," John told him.

"What did you get your father?" I asked John.

"Nothing. I forgot. I wouldn't want to ruin a perfect record. What did you get?"

"St. Stephen, the Just—in bronze."

"That's certainly something he doesn't have yet. If we hurry, I can still add my name to your card."

"Well, I didn't have a chance to find something better. If you'd invited me when you were supposed to, I might have—"

"Okay, Nimrod. Don't worry about it. He'll love it."

When they opened it, Mr. and Mrs. Dioskouri kissed me and placed St. Stephen on a doily on top of the piano. Even after the other gifts were opened—including one that had to be brought in from outside and contained a lively beagle puppy—I sat with a mystical air as the guests and I tried to figure out what the statuette was.

FOURTEEN

A couple of days later, Carolyn phoned to ask again about Thanksgiving weekend. "Well?" she said in a tone that made me wonder if she would simply hang up and call someone else if I said no. I pictured her when she first dropped in to my apartment unannounced and then dropped out of my life just as quickly when she sensed the slightest complication. I thought, too, of the way she had kissed me at her parents' party and then seemed unconcerned when I didn't see her again for several months, picking up in September the way she was now doing as if the moment had contained the kiss and nothing more. She was easy-going and yet sensuous, but her sensuousness was unconnected to passion or even emotion. It seemed to me—though I could not have pretended to know her—that affection for Carolyn—like a good film or concert—was little more than an amusement.

So I agreed to go. I forgot, momentarily, how I had yearned for Diane day and night all summer, and I thought how good it would be to feel as fanciful for a single weekend as did Carolyn all the time.

"So go," said Sammy when I called to tell him. "You've already said you would, haven't you?"

"Yes, I have. . . ."

"Look, if you're that worried about it, I'll go in your place. I have seen uglier in my day."

"You've seen nothing but uglier, Sammy. That Suzy you took out—"

"Never mind Suzy," he said. "Look, you're young, you're stupid. *Enjoy* yourself. People have had worse problems than to have to pick between two beautiful girls to date."

"But they're not the same. Diane—"

"Diane, you're going to love, right?"

"Well—"

"Big deal: you'll spend a weekend with Carolyn and the next hundred weekends with Diane. Benny boy, I'm holding up six fingers: do you get my drift?"

"No, not really, Sammy boy."

"Then bless you—"

"Huchoo—"

"And Godspeed—"

"Good-*bye*, Sammy."

"My best to you and yours—"

"*Bye*, Sammy."

"My love to all."

In the weeks that followed, I could think of no one else but Diane. When we weren't speaking for hours at a time on the phone, we were out together.

One night I took her to see *Swan Lake* performed by the National Ballet. We sat in the front orchestra section, and Diane glowed with excitement as we waited for the show to begin. I squeezed her hand in her lap and she brushed her cheek against my shoulder. A light but consistent scent of perfume flowed by us as if emitted in small puffs by the polite conversation buzzing throughout the theater. I was distracted for a moment by a guy sitting to the left of me who, I knew from the start, thought he owned the armrest we shared. He was a person who believed that holding a ticket entitled him to a chair and two armrests. The gesture was not intentional, but its very unintentionality spoke of his egocentricity. I leaned forward slightly to peer over at him and his parents sitting beside him. Because I already hated him, I decided they embodied the very culture we

170

lived in and reminded me that the rebellion of the sixties had now slipped quietly into the establishment of the seventies, and the establishment itself had scattered into altogether different time warps. Here, beside me, were the year's winners of the Duke and Duchess of Windsor Look-Alike Contest together with their son, Frank Zappa, Jr. The mother, who knew better than to try to share the other armrest with her son, sat in a pair of elbow-length gloves. I felt like saying to her, "Where would you be with those gloves if my Uncle Louis hadn't been loon enough to have invented them for you?"

"What are you doing?" asked Diane, tugging at my elbow.

I leaned back. "Nothing."

"What have you been thinking?"

"Nothing, really."

"Are you always going to do that: say 'nothing' when I ask what you're thinking?"

"No, of course not."

"Do you want me to do that? Do you want me to think things and say nothing?"

"Let's try it. Go ahead: think something and I'll watch."

I stared at her and we cracked up laughing.

"Do you regret having made this date tonight?" she asked.

"Absolutely. Did I ever tell you you had the most extraordinary brown eyes I've ever seen?"

"No, and it's not true."

"I love the way you're dressed," I said. "In fact, I love the way we're both dressed: simple but elegant. It's not calculated overdress or calculated underdress. Just simple but elegant. *Invisible*, really, except to each other."

"May I ask what you're talking about?"

"You said you wanted to know what I was thinking, and I'm telling you."

"That's what you were thinking?"

"Exactly." She turned up her lip on one side, which carved a dimple into her cheek. I wanted to ask her if she'd mind my devouring her right there in her seat in Toronto's stately O'Keefe Centre, but I opted for a slightly more discreet question: "Do you know what the story of *Swan Lake* is?"

"Is there a story?"

"Yup. I had to learn it for my Music History exam."

"Then you have to tell me."

"It's the story of Prince Siegfried, who is told by his mother on his twenty-first birthday that he has to find a bride. He gets depressed because he's about to lose his freedom, so he goes off to hunt swans. This is a real hero, this Ziggy. Anyway, just as he is taking aim at one of these swans, they all turn into beautiful women. He falls in love with the queen, whose name is Odette, and the rest is history."

'What do you mean?" asked Diane. "Do they run away together?"

"Well, he has a bit of difficulty explaining to his mother that he has fallen in love with a girl who, five minutes before, was a swan. It would present a problem having the new in-laws over for dinner, don't you think?"

"I guess it would," she said, as the lights dimmed.

"The other major difficulty—"

"Shh," she said.

"The other major difficulty," I whispered, "is that it's one thing to turn into a beautiful woman, but what if, one fine day, the reverse happens? Try to file divorce papers on *that* basis."

The overture was played, the lights glittered in Diane's eyes and, in spite of my efforts—and those of Zappa Jr. beside me—the ballet's net of enchantment fell over us. If not for conscious resistance on my part, I too would have plunged after Siegfried and Odette and Diane into the Lake of Tears.

Birds became the theme of that weekend for us. The next day, Sunday, we went to Ontario Place, the provincial exhibit that was meant to be a showpiece for Ontario but was designed to look more like a lunar landing station, complete with a giant white ball in which movies were shown, and great saucers that stood on steel girders and loomed over the lake.

It was Italian Day at Ontario Place, which meant that pasta was being served everywhere except the die-hard hamburger and chip places, that gondolas replaced the customary paddleboats and that Mario Del Monaco was singing that night with the Toronto Symphony. Twice Diane and I were stopped by Italian families and asked a question in Italian. No second thoughts. No hesitation on the off-chance we were not Italian. Both times I pointed the direction, though I had no idea what they were looking for, and both times everyone smiled warmly, thanked us and seemed to be wishing us well.

Diane and I stopped at the Forum, the outdoor theatre, to watch a spectacular dance show staged by a Sicilian troupe. Then we sat by the water to have lunch. Diane ate spaghetti out of a plastic tub and I had french fries with gravy. On the bank beside us were two gondoliers eating hamburgers. "Would you like one?" I asked Diane, extending my plate toward her.

"No, thanks. I'm out of my french fry period."

"What was that?"

"I always hated to eat—all my life, really—so because my parents were worried I'd starve to death they fed me anything I asked for. There was a time I ate nothing but Boston cream doughnuts and drank strawberry milkshakes."

"How long did that go on?"

"At least a year. Then I went through my cheese omelette and Coke period, and that one lasted until I discovered the baconburger. Then Caesar salad. Two years of Caesar salad. I hate Caesar salad now," she said, taking part of a meatball into her mouth. While I watched her, she stopped chewing.

"And now you're in your spaghetti and meatball phase."

"No, my repertory has expanded a bit. Would you like some?" she said.

"Maybe I'll try a meatball."

"Have it all," she said. "I'm not really hungry."

One of the gondoliers was throwing bits of his hamburger and bun to the ducks that swarmed all around us. The other gondolier was smoking. "Oh, look, Mom," said a young girl, who ran to the other side of us. She was wearing a sweatshirt with Princeton University lettering on it. "Look at the ducks!" she said and slung half a box of Cracker Jacks into the water. The ducks became hysterical and we had to move back from the bank or get wet. The gondolier who had been smoking threw his butt into the water and one of the ducks chewed it before spitting it out. I threw in several french fries and a meatball, which were snatched up almost before they landed.

"Look at those things," I said when the surface of the water had settled and the ducks were merely patrolling the shore. "They're just hunks of turd with beaks."

"What does that make us, then?" asked Diane.

"Hunks of turd without beaks."

"That's mean," said Diane. "Maybe *we* are, but those ducks have no place to go. They have their wings clipped and are stuck here to perform for the tourists."

"I'm sorry," I said, and I put my arm around her as we continued to stare into the water. "I wonder what happens to them in the winter."

"Who knows?" she said. "Let's go; do you mind?"

"But we haven't seen the exhibits yet."

"Another time. Please?"

The following Saturday, Diane and I took out one of the delinquents she used to work with. He called her frequently, but this was the first time she was taking him out. "I appreciate your coming, Ben," said Diane, as we drove toward the Hopkins Centre in the east end.

"What do you mean? Do you mean you would have taken this kid out alone if I hadn't come?"

"Oh, this kid isn't dangerous like the other one—just

174

lonely mostly. He's spent most of his life in foster homes and I'm kind of a mother-figure for him, that's all. His name is Bart and he knows you're coming, so please be nice."

We drove through the Beaches section of Toronto, a quaint neighborhood of tall trees and converted old cottages on winding streets that led to the lake. On the main street there were small antique shops, cafés and old-fashioned candy stores. "What did Bart do to get into the Hopkins Centre?" I asked.

"Just break-and-enter convictions mostly — and one armed robbery."

"An *armed* robbery?"

"He robbed a bank with a sawed-off shotgun."

"Great," I said. "Very nice. So, if things get a little slow this afternoon, maybe we can knock off one of these chocolate shops or something."

"Ben, please, promise you'll behave."

"I promise. Where are we going to take him?"

"There's a fall fair just east of hear—an amusement park they've set up with rides and games."

"Will Bart enjoy that? How old is he?"

"He's fourteen, but he's hardly ever had these pleasures."

Bart was a surprisingly unimposing little guy with an army jacket that was at least two sizes too big and a crew cut that had grown a little too long, but was greased and carefully combed for the occasion. He kept his hands in his pockets when he was introduced to me. Then he climbed into the back of the Dioskouris' giant New Yorker and sat in the middle. He looked as though he was sitting on a living room couch.

At the amusement park, I stepped up to a sharpshooters' stand to win Diane a stuffed toy. All one had to do was to hit a moving target the approximate size of a pinhole while metal ducks, bears and crocodiles crossed rapidly in front of it. "Hold this," I said, handing Diane my candy apple. I took 105 shots for a mere $21.00 and handed Bart and Diane respectively a plastic whistle and a small rubber squirrel. Bart then stepped up, timidly handed his candy apple to Diane and fired two straight bull's-eyes.

"That's unbelievable!" said the proprietor.

"Isn't he astonishing?" I said. Diane glared at me.

"That's the most incredible thing I've ever seen," said the proprietor again. "I've been in this business twenty-five years and no one has hit that target twice in a row the way your brother there has."

"We're training him to guard the house," I said.

"That is truly amazing," said the proprietor.

"All right, just pay the kid his prizes already, will you?"

Bart picked the two ugliest stuffed animals he could find: a giant tiger and a pink snake with a red felt tongue. "The snake is for you," he said, handing it to me.

"Naturally," I said. "Thank you so much."

He then handed the tiger lying flat across his arms to Diane as if he were a knight presenting her with the corpse of a slain dragon. "Thank you," said Diane. "It's lovely."

The tiger, the snake and I stood at the foot of the Ferris wheel and watched Diane and Bart go round and round. Then we went to the roller coaster. Then the caterpillar. My furry companions and I learned some new vocabulary: "Spin," we said, and "slide." We waved at Diane and Bart as they came around corners and over slopes.

"Are you sure you don't want to try one of these?" asked Diane, as we lined up for *Tunnel of Ghosts and Vampires*.

"No, thanks," I said. "I have nightmares."

Tiggey, Snake and I became a little nervous when we realized that going into a dark tunnel with a young and slightly deranged rifleman would not rank high on a list of safe activities for Diane to do. We went around to the operator. "How long does this ride go on?" I asked.

"About five minutes," he said. He was helping people out of one of the cars.

"Do you have to take so long there?" I asked. He peered

over his shoulder at us. I had the feeling we didn't look very intimidating.

Then I heard Diane's voice in the tunnel: "Bart!" I dropped the stuffed toys. "Bart, please."

"Hurry this thing up!" I said to the guy. He didn't even turn around. "There's an emergency in there!" He pulled a lever and out came two cars, which he sent straight back into the entrance. Finally came Diane's car. Bart had his hands covering his face and Diane had a hand on his shoulder.

No one spoke until the ride back to the Centre. "Bart," Diane said, looking into her rear-view mirror at him, "you're going to find yourself a wonderful girl one of these days. I promise you will. Let's stay friends, please." He didn't answer. He was staring out the side window. "Wouldn't it be better if we were friends?"

A moment later, he said, "Okay." Diane reached around awkwardly and offered her hand. He took it; then he looked at me as I turned with Tig and Snake, and he smiled.

In a few short weeks, Diane and I went to the movies, to doughnut shops, to a party at the U of T, to the symphony, and most often to the university library, which stayed open later than anything else and was an acceptable place for Diane to be at one in the morning. The only drawback to meeting in the library was that her father always picked her up—forcing us to part company in the section of the stacks devoted to Old English.

But even this constraint soon vanished because John left for Greece, and the second car went to Diane. We grew inseparable. I wrote a song for her and played it on the piano one night in a sitting room at Hart House. Even though it was a silly song, she cried for an hour after. "How wonderful it must be," she said, as she had after the Dylan concert, "to be able to make music—to charge whatever feelings you have with sounds like a bird — and pretty sounds, not wails or grunts or cries, but melodious sounds whether the feeling is sad or happy." She ran her fingers through the hair at the back of my head as we sat together on the piano bench in the large empty room in which students, during the day, practiced on one of the three pianos, or sat on the leather couches to read.

"It's a tough profession, though," I said.

"Who cares?" said Diane. "You'll do something with your music and wherever you go to play you'll be making people happier—and *you* will always be happy; that's the important thing. I wish I had such an outlet."

"You could play music, too, if you wanted to learn."

"No, I did try to learn. I wanted very badly to play piano and, when I first began to take lessons, it was before my parents could afford a piano, so I practiced on a piece of cardboard with a keyboard printed on it. I heard how badly I played only once a week when I went to my piano teacher's house. When I finally got my piano, I tried and tried, but I never had it. It's not that I couldn't play. I did master the technique, but I just didn't have it—you know: the thing that enables you to tap into the rivers of your feeling and translate them into melodies."

"Well, I don't necessarily have it either. Maybe I've just studied music longer."

"No. *You* have it. It's not the studying that makes the difference. Some people never study anything and they have it. You can tell—in the way they hum or sing—in the way they beam with fulfillment. You can tell easily who has it, and *you* do. It makes no difference whether you're playing viola or piano or a comb. There's a special quality about the way you play—a kind of truth to your playing. I only wish I had a similar outlet," she said again, and sighed. "It's nice just to listen to you, though. Play me what you wrote one more time." I kissed her on the ear and played.

We came to know each other's class schedules by heart and we met twice and three times a day. She was asked to join a sorority and I fought with her because it cut into our time together. "How could you do this to me?"

"Do what? I thought you said it would be good for my confidence if I got involved in university life."

"So you joined a *sorority*?"

"Ben, they're all *girls* in the sorority. I don't see why you're so upset."

"That's below the belt, Diane."

"Well, I'm sorry, but we meet only once a week and my sisters and I plan very good activities."

"Oh, your *sisters*, now. Why don't you all open a convent with an orphanage out back!"

"You are mean—downright mean. I didn't know you had such a streak in you."

Diane and I did not speak for an entire day. But I broke down and waited for her outside of her last class. "Well, what do you want?" she said, crying immediately and rushing away.

"I'm sorry," I called after her.

"Those were cruel things you said—and unnecessary."

"I know. I'm sorry."

That Friday night I even went to a dance that her sorority had arranged. Diane, as part of her initiation duties, had to introduce the rock band. She rehearsed for hours. "I'd like you all to welcome the new rock sensation—*The Epiphany*!" she repeated a thousand times. "Do you think I should say 'the new rock *sensation*' or just 'new rock band?' "

"Say 'the tired young derivative band.' "

"Ben, please, I need your help."

"Okay. Just say 'new rock band,' then."

"Great, okay. Ladies and gentlemen, I'd like you all to welcome the new rock!"

"*—band.*"

"Oh, yes, 'band.' "

"Which one?" I said.

"Which one *what*?"

"Which *band*?"

"Oh—the Epiphany. I'd like you all to welcome the rock sensation Epiphany."

"Better; much better," I said.

"Ben, you don't have to patronize me. I know it's a dumb thing to do and I know I'm rotten doing it—"

"You're not; it's great, really. You've improved tremendously." What I liked best about the way she delivered the introduction was that the whole upper half of her frame bent forward, as if the imaginary microphone were ten feet away, but her hands remained pinned to her sides and her feet pinned to the floor. I stepped in front of her, inches away, and said, "Pretend I'm the microphone now."

"All right," she said with an earnest look, and just as she was about to hunch forward I kissed her. "Oh, Ben, you're no help at all. I'll never get this right."

"You'll be terrific. I think you missed your calling, really."

When her great moment came—The Epiphany waiting in the wings—she trembled up to the microphone, wearing the new burgundy silk scarf I had bought her for the occasion, raised her hands to her shoulders in that way she always did, and whispered the announcement so that it could be heard nowhere in the room—even if the microphone had been switched on. I died for her—would have given anything to steal her away from the hall.

When she joined me she said, "It was terrible, wasn't it?"

"No, you did a great job, really."

"Are you sure? Do you think anyone noticed I was nervous?"

"I'm positive not a single person noticed."

"Then it was okay?"

"Truly amazing."

The band's music was closer in impact to Diane's introduction than it was to an Epiphany. They played their giant electric guitars projecting from their groins without any real need of fingers. But during their slow numbers the quality of the music hardly mattered. Diane and I danced closely and I breathed her hyacinth fragrance for ten minutes at a time. My knees creaked to maintain the delicate sway of our hips, my arm trembling around her waist, my heart pounding against her warm plump breasts.

During the break, a couple of the band members mingled with the plebs. "Oh, look," Diane whispered. "Dan and Ted, the leads, are coming toward us." I was still dancing, my face buried at the juncture between Diane's neck and collarbone. "Ben, stop it. Look!" I slid off her and fell to my knees as she jerked herself away. "Hi," said Diane as *He* approached.

"Thanks for the fine introduction," He said. He had shades on, and He looked Diane over, inches from her face, and put his arm around her shoulder.

"Ben, I'd like you to meet Dan."

"Mr. Epiphany, a pleasure," I said shaking his hand vigorously. He still stared at Diane. "You'd be able to see her better," I said, "if you took your sunglasses off."

Dan looked at me, took his hand off Diane's shoulder and said, "Nice to meet you—both."

"Great, thanks," I said.

"Thanks, Dan," said Diane. "Great show."

As soon as he was out of earshot, Diane turned on me. "Why did you say that to him? Mr. *Epiphany*. He meant no harm. He was just being nice."

"*Very* nice. Beautiful, really." Diane left the hall in a hurry. She was halfway up Hoskin Avenue, the street that transected the campus, before I caught up to her. "How could you be so upset by this?" I said.

"You embarrassed me."

"The slime had his arm around you."

"He was just being friendly."

"Oh, yes, friendly. His next friendly question was going to be, 'Maybe you'd like to join the boys and me after the gig and partake in a little gang bang.' "

"That's disgusting," she said and huffed away.

I stopped. "He was an *OIL!*" I said.

Then she stopped and turned around. She was smiling. "You're jealous."

"Well, I'm glad we didn't have to turn down Philosopher's Walk for you to figure that out."

She ran to me and kissed me. We walked to her car and when I put my arm around her shoulder, she kissed my hand.

Ten times in as many days I had asked Diane back to my apartment and ten times she had said no. This time she agreed—but only for a cup of tea—and only if I could escort her in with her jacket wrapped around her head so that no one in the entire district could possibly recognize her. As I fumbled outside with my keys, one passerby paused to look at my bundled-up companion. "Under strict quarantine," I said. "Highly contagious—*leprosy*."

"Who was that downstairs?" asked Diane, before she'd sat down.

"Nobody. I don't know."

"You didn't recognize him? Did he recognize you?"

"Yes, it was my Uncle Milt—*of course* he didn't recognize me."

What about the restaurant? Was there anyone inside?"

"No, it was closed. The lights were off." So she sat. "Can I make you a grilled cheese sandwich?"

"No thanks. Just a cup of tea."

"Diane, why are you so nervous?"

"I'm not nervous exactly, Ben. It's just that I grew up in this place. Do you know that? This is the room I played in. That's where the TV was." She pointed to my stereo. "I sat at my father's feet and listened to him talk to my grandparents. It gives me a bit of the creeps. It was in this place I learned to tell right from wrong."

"Would you like to go somewhere else for a cup of tea?"

"No, I'll be all right in a few minutes. The tea will help." A streetcar screeched to a stop at the intersection and Diane leapt to her feet. I hugged her and then we kissed. Diane's lips were capable of igniting the entire laboratory of my body. "Please, Ben. It isn't right. Please."

We drank tea; I played my Tschaikovsky records; I even hummed the tune I had written for Diane; we kissed again and rolled onto the carpet where, over the next hour, we gave our Seempsone-Eatone garments the best test they could have had for durability. And then—my entire body pulsating, bleating like a lamb — I involved one of my hands.

"Please, Ben, don't."

Why are the hands the ambassadors of the sexual organs? I had rubbed my chest against her; ground my hips against hers; allowed my chin to graze upon the windward slopes. But why not my hands? "Diane, there are whole nations in which women go around with their entire breastal areas uncovered."

"Ben, we mustn't. *Please.*"

I walked her down into the cool autumn night around the corner to where she had parked the car out of sight, and we kissed again, but she left me. It was like hanging up the phone. Slamming the door. I watched her taillights fade up Parliament Street, watched them brighten as she stopped briefly, and then evaporate. What had I done? What had I not done?

I sat in my living room in the dark, except for the green light of my stereo. I played a Louis Armstrong record, but don't remember hearing much of it. Then I sat by my window. The streetcars were no longer running. I watched Mr. Seymour turn the corner and limp onto Queen Street and realized I didn't know where he lived—if anywhere. I wondered if I should call him up to spend the night at my place, but thought it better not to. One night when it was colder, maybe. I saw someone still working across the street in the pharmacy. It was Mr. Gray, the owner, taking inventory. He came out of his store to speak to Mr. Seymour when the latter paused at the window to wave, and I felt slightly relieved.

I turned in bed all night. I half-dreamed my Aunt Goldie came to visit.

Do you think it helped Mendelssohn that his family converted?

What does that have to do with anything, Aunt Goldie?

Do you think it helped Mahler that he converted? His descen-

183

dants still went to the camps. His music could not be played. Mendelssohn's music was not played.

That is true and it's terrible, but how does that relate to me? Music and Judaism. Do those things relate to you, smart guy?

Yes, vaguely. Generally.

What is VAGUE and GENERAL about it? They are the symbols of your birth and your calling—your talent. They ARE you.

But those labels diminish rather than enrich me. Labels diminish YOU, Aunt Goldie. You do yourself a disservice being nothing but Jewish, don't you see that?

DIMINISH. Is that what you learned in your Toronto University?

Oh no. You're not pulling that one on me, Aunt Goldie. You die when we don't go and you hold it against us when we do.

Diminish. Is that what the label does? I'll give you a better word—God knows I didn't learn it in any university. The word is dilute, Benny. DILUTE. That's what you do with Diane. That's what you do with a Greek Orthodox girl, Benny. You dilute your people. There's more Other than there is Jew, Benny boy, and enough diluting drowns, you know that?

Look at Mendelssohn and Mahler, Aunt Goldie. They converted completely—not half, but completely—and you're still calling them Jewish. They enriched the world with their work—the WORLD—not that that's what they wanted to do. Kissinger and Golda Meir didn't go around the world doing their thing so you could point at the TV every night and say, 'He's Jewish. She's Jewish.'

You hold your people in contempt, Ben, and that in itself wouldn't be so bad—your father does it, lots of Jews do it. What's bad is that you don't realize that your Jewish soul guides your work. Your own music—however good that may someday be—will have the Jewish soul singing behind it — the Jewish soul crying, Benny, remembering. And you can't have it both ways. You and that Diane, shlepping your half-Jewish children behind you and some day your quarter-Jewish grandchildren.

This is the New World, Aunt Goldie. Here we multiply traditions. We bring together the heritage of many great cultures to make the greatest culture. That's what our forefathers wanted when they came here. That's what YOU wanted.

Don't quote me the Declaration of Independence—I read it before you were born.

And don't you divide and segregate—divide and push. What does it get you? What has it gotten you? God of the Sea and Miss Nude World.

So that's what I get from my precious nephew after all these years. You can't have it both ways. You can't have your Jewish soul ENRICH the world—to use your word, smart guy—and dilute at the same time. What will your grandchildren use for a tradition, tell me.

And I see my Aunt Goldie's lights fade up Parliament Street. Why did Diane leave the way she did? Have I not won enough of her loyalty to deserve an explanation? Why does she serve those guests of her parents with such pleasure? She was loaned to her aunt in Greece—what kind of people are these? Why did she have to run off? Could she not be loaned to me? I care for her. I care too much for her.

But what kind of care is this? I've had nothing but problems since I've met this family. If John cracks up, who will deal with it? Diane will be too upset; her mother, desperate; her father, dead. But who am I kidding? It is *I*—not John—who will give Mr. Dioskouri his final blow. My fingers—not his—that pinch the valves of his heart. And she'll be there. Mrs. D. in black. Melancholy. A dark magnetic field with iron files of guilt scattered throughout our bodies. Diane's and mine. Me. Her child. Forever remembering. There, sitting, petting Lassie. Rememberr, rrememberr. Waiting for death. An invalid at forty-five. Her son mad. Her daughter diluted. She'll sit in the shadows of her palace. Eating. Eating quietly by herself. Turning into a heavenly body.

What beautiful chestnut eyes those half-children of ours would have!

I have fallen in love with Diane.

And it has begun to happen. As I lie in my bed, it has already begun to happen.

FIFTEEN

"Diane."

"Oh, Ben." She is crying.

"Diane, I'm calling because I love you." I hear a sob at the other end of the phone. "Did you hear me? I said I love you."

"I love you, too, Ben. I love you, too. Dear sweet Ben, the most terrible thing happened in the night."

"Are you all right? Did anything happen on the way home last night?"

"No. Nothing to me. It's my father, Ben." A wail rises out of her voice. "He had a heart attack. A very bad one."

"Oh, my God! Did he—? Is he—?"

"No, he didn't die. My sweet father. He can't die!" A sob.

"Where is he now, Diane?"

"He's in intensive care at North York General. We were there with him most of the night, my mother and I. That's when it happened—in the night. He got up to go to the bathroom. My mother thought nothing of it because he was saying he had indigestion all evening. And then from the bathroom there was a thud. We both heard it."

"Where's your mother now?"

"She's still at the hospital. I couldn't get her to leave, though we can't even go in to see him."

"Why didn't you call me? You could have called me."

"It was all so sudden and quick. I didn't know what to do. And why should we always involve you and upset you?"

"What do you mean always? When have you involved me before? I love you, Diane."

"Oh, Ben, I love you, too. I really do. I've never met anyone like you. I thought all boys were like John's friends."

"Diane, you have a rest now. I'll go to the hospital. Everything will be all right. You'll see."

"I can't rest now. Really I can't. I'll go back with you."

"Why don't I meet you there?"

We found Mrs. Dioskouri sitting outside intensive care, her feet crossed, her large elegant purse bulging in her lap, her dark eyes red at the corners, the great chiseled braids of her hair crumbling around her neck. The crucifix danced on her chest. "Ben, you hyev brreakfust?"

"Breakfast? Don't worry about me, please."

"You hyev to eat brreakfust you gonna get seeck you doan eat."

"How's Mr. Dioskouri? Have the doctors said anything?"

"I doan know. Doan say. My hyusbund verry goood man."

"I know. He's a great man." Diane sat beside her mother and put her arm around her. "Why don't you go home, Mrs. Dioskouri? You can come back a little later."

"Hyome. These my hyusbund."

So we sat there into the afternoon. A wise-looking doctor with gray sideburns, signing clipboards as he walked down the hall toward us, finally paused to give us news: Mr. Dioskouri would live—as long as he could live with certain restrictions.

The following day, Sunday, Mr. Dioskouri was taken out of intensive care and was to have two visitors at a time. It took the nurses coming by once every hour to keep the population in his room down to a dozen. I recognized many of them from the party: Mr. and Mrs. Christopoulos; Voula

Leftani with her olympic cleavage and her husband; Mr.
Gambros and his wife Kristina. Then the restaurant crowd.
They seemed to come in waves: Mr. Stanowicz with his
pale little wife; Magda, who cried uncontrollably; Mr.
Katz; even Moustaki, who brought expensive flowers and added
them to the garden sprouting everywhere—the window-
sills, the chairs, the two tables, the floor, anywhere there
was a flat surface except for the bed itself. Besides flowers,
people brought candies, books, liquor, one icon, and baskets and packages of cholesterol.

I came and went all day—mostly to make room for other
visitors—but Diane never left her father's side. Nor did her
mother, who saw to it that people had places to sit and
who distributed cakes and pita and chocolates, dipping
into the plates herself as they were returned to her. Fatigue
eventually led to boredom. Diane got into a quarrel with
her cousin Penny, who spoke wherever she went about the
oppression of women — and wherever she went, her
mother, Diane's Aunt Soula, tried to drag her away the
minute the subject arose.

"Look at all of you," said Penny, "with your crucifixes
and your worship of men."

"You leebarrashone o-woomun, Penny?" asked Mrs.
Dioskouri.

"What's wrong with it, *Thea*? Tell me."

"You may or may not have noticed," said Diane, "but
in our church, Mary is usually pictured as the central figure
holding a baby Jesus."

"Sure I've noticed, but read the Bible. Listen to what is
preached. Everything is male-centered. Even God is a
man."

"I don't believe God has a sex," said Diane.

"I believe God is a woman and let Her strike me dead
if I'm wrong!"

At this point, Mr. Dioskouri himself had to step in.
Sociable as he normally was, he looked pestered: he didn't
want visitors; he didn't want gifts or attention or concern
or gratitude that he was alive. He asked the doctor if he

could go home, and when his request was denied he asked if he could return to intensive care for the good of his health. Now the people who had gotten tired of the party in his room had begun to argue. He sat up noisily, groaningly, in the silence that had fallen after Penny's final declaration, looked around at all the visitors — Mrs. Leftani holding a box of chocolates and eating one after another — looked out the window at the cars going up and down Leslie Street, paused for a moment to listen to the P.A. calling a Dr. Brown to the maternity ward, and said, ''Penny, you rright. Now everrybody go hyome.''

That evening, Mrs. Dioskouri invited me back to her house for dinner. ''My hyouse empty, Ben. You come. You best boy.'' We were greeted by the beagle puppy that Mr. Dioskouri had received for his name day and that John had named Cerberus, ''except ours doesn't have three heads like the mythological one,'' said John. ''He has three asses.'' We came out of the doorway to find a small pile of droppings in the hall, another in the kitchen and a third in the living room. Mrs. Dioskouri cursed at ''*Kerberos*'' as she cleaned up, and then handed him a plate of leftover spareribs and poured milk into the porcelain bowl beside it.

Mrs. Dioskouri seemed distracted the whole time she cooked dinner. She put things in pots and turned on the stove, but spent more time walking from one room to another than she did in the kitchen. We ate sirloin steak that was, to put it figuratively, well done. Ancient lava would be a better description. Beside the steak on my plate was a clump of cauliflower that had been boiled for so long it no longer understood what it was supposed to be. It was just smell and texture mostly. Diane ate a couple of bites and said she wasn't hungry. She emptied her plate into Cerberus's and he scratched at the back door for several minutes so that he could be let out to bury his steak in the garden. That left Mrs. Dioskouri and me at the table sawing away until Diane said, ''You don't need to be polite, Ben. The meal is terrible.''

''No, it's fine,'' I said, and I went on eating, aiming to

finish half of what I'd been given. "How's John these days, by the way? Has he written or called?"

"Fine," said Mrs. Dioskouri and she let out a sigh that could have inflated a balloon. "My life brring verry bad luck, Ben."

"Oh, Ma!" said Diane. "You always say such stupid things."

"Ot kind stupeed? I hyev goood life, Thy-ane? My husband gonna die. My son, bum."

"And your daughter, Ma? Say it. What about your daughter?"

"My daughter verry nice. I say something, Ben?" I shrugged my shoulders.

"Your daughter," said Diane, "who's dating the nice Greek boy, right? Say it."

"I like Dzooeess pipple; you *know*, Thy-ane. I like Ben. I love Ben. Byooteefool boy."

"Oh, *please*, Ma."

"Ben, you tell me. You motherr hyeppy you see Grrik girrl? Ees gonna be morre hyeppy you see Dzooeess girrl. Not?" I nodded. "Any-oo-way. Gonna see. Not married now." Diane blushed and the two began to clear the table.

Mrs. Dioskouri washed the dishes while Diane and I sat in the den. "I'm sorry, Ben, but she's always depressed."

"Don't worry about it."

"If there isn't something to be miserable about, she'll invent something."

"It's okay. Forget it." I took her hand.

She let go and got up to pace. "I mean, there's real misery in the world: disease, poverty, hatred; and I have a mother who thinks she has it worse than anyone. It makes me so mad, I—"

"It's *okay*. *Forget* it now. I'm sorry I ever brought up the topic of John. I should have minded my own business."

"Well, he *is* your business. He's your friend. Why shouldn't you ask about him? — And that's the irony. John's in Greece partly to escape from her misery. He

190

couldn't stand to see it any more either — not that he's blameless—''

''Can we please drop it? I'm sorry I ever mentioned him.''

Mrs. Dioskouri brought us coffee and cake and, with a sigh, sat in the chair opposite me. Diane sat beside her. The tension of the last two days that was now visible on Diane's face seemed to blend into the subtle creases of her mother's face. What began next sounded like a confidential conversation, but Mrs. Dioskouri spoke in English. ''Neeck brring pepper to hosepeetull. Geeve me; you futhairr doan see.''

''What kind of paper, Ma?''

''Frrom lawyairr. Oo-want to buy rrestaurrant, I think so. Tole you futhairr beforre oo-one oo-wick.''

''That bastard!'' said Diane.

''Which bastard is that?'' I asked.

''My father's partner. My father took him in on credit —he had nothing—and for a couple of thousand dollars— which he could pay out of his first year's earnings, no papers signed—he got one-half ownership of the business. The only papers he insisted on signing were the ones that made him a full partner. Now Moustaki wants to buy my father off. He's been stealing left, right and center from the till; he's chased away some of my father's most loyal customers; he's insulted the staff; and a few weeks ago he emptied the cash drawer into his pockets instead of into the bank account. Let's face it: who else would have broken the glass *outward*? Why was *he* not outraged when he found out?''

''Well, isn't your father aware that Moustaki is pulling all these things on him?''

''Sure he's aware. He just doesn't want to deal with it. You don't know him. The restaurant's his kingdom. He goes there and feels successful. His people are there. His society. They love him and he loves them. They've all struggled in one way or another and they've all made it out now—even Mr. Seymour, in a way. The restaurant is

191

the place those people meet to remember the days before they were successful. My father doesn't *care* that Moustaki is stealing. What upsets him more is that Moustaki is breaking up the community. And my father is blowing up inside. He doesn't know what to do, and he hates talking about it with anyone. He took Moustaki in for a song because he thought he was giving someone a break. He's always done that, but it's never backfired before. And, worst of all, Moustaki has said terrible things about my father: he's said he was blind not to agree to open up a dance club; and a fool to let down-and-outs like Mr. Seymour into the place. And do you know who he tells these things to? His staff. He talks to Magda. Magda's been working at the Blue Sky for nearly ten years and she's always been happy. Now she's given notice she's leaving at the end of the month.''

"She *has*? Where is she going?''

"She'll find another place. She said Moustaki has made passes at her and threatened her. She can't stand it any more.''

"I'm surprised Magda hasn't belted him across the room. How does your father feel about being bought out?''

"Feel?'' said Mrs. Dioskouri. "Thut's oo-why een hosepeetull.''

"Oh, *Ma*,'' said Diane, rolling her eyes, ''*please*. You didn't want to buy the restaurant in the first place.'' And her mother rose to clear the coffee dishes away.

"Don't you think you're a little bit hard on her, Diane?'' I asked when her mother had left for the kitchen.

"Well, she *didn't* want the restaurant. She thought it would be too much of a risk. If decisions were left to her, none would ever get made. She couldn't decide to leave her village until my father dragged her away. She was unhappy. So he said they should leave Greece. She couldn't agree—or disagree. So he dragged her to Canada, then to the restaurant, then to the suburbs. And she's still unhappy. It drives you crazy. You get into a car with her because she wants to go to her friend Dimitra's place and, when you're half way there, she says she wants to go shopping. She can't decide where to go. Nor what clothes to put on in the morning. Nor what meal to cook. It's ridiculous."

"Isn't that all the more reason to make her happy — maybe give her more confidence?"

"We've *tried* to make her happy. If you bring home ten *A*'s and a *B* +, she'll want to know why you got the *B* +. That's what she's like."

"Then maybe what you should be doing," I began to say, but her mother returned to sit in her chair again.

"What should we be doing?" said Diane.

"But. . . ." I glanced at Mrs. Dioskouri.

"Don't worry about that. What should we do?"

"You should let her know you support her—and your father—in spite of the difficulties."

"Ma," Diane said, as she moved closer to her mother to kiss her, "do you love me?"

"You my tsild. Who I gonna love?" Diane hugged her mother, who like a squeeze-toy, let out another sigh. Minutes later, she nodded off in her chair. Not even Cerberus yelping at the back door could rouse her.

"Why don't you help her up to bed?" I said.

"Because she sleeps better here. If I turn on the TV now, she'll sleep for hours."

Diane offered to drive me home. A ride to the subway would have been generous enough, but she insisted. As we prepared to leave, not one but two cars pulled into the driveway one after the other. The first contained a young couple, the Pouloses, and their baby. They could not get into the hospital and wanted to know how Mr. Dioskouri was. The second car was a taxi, and all of us watched as Mr. Dioskouri himself disembarked. Diane was hysterical. Her mother came running. He'd had enough of the hospital and if they'd kept him there another day, he told us, he would surely have died. It was the first time I'd seen him without a tie.

We went inside again and sat in the living room. Diane and her mother were visibly delighted by Mr. Dioskouri's presence, but for an hour they pleaded with him to go back to the hospital. He finally agreed, but only if he could sleep at home that night. The Pouloses shared in both the delight and the persuasion. They drank tea and ate cake and were twice offered more tea and cake while their baby, "oo-William," went from knee to knee to couch to floor, where he was given a big marble egg to suck on. Mr. Dioskouri was particularly pleased to have the baby and he must have hinted about grandchildren because Diane blushed and took the baby over to hide behind it. I couldn't help but stare at the baby myself, partly because this baby had an unusually large head, and a thin down of blonde hair made it look even larger. I took William into my lap and pinched his giant cheeks. He gurgled and we smiled at each other.

After the Pouloses left, I volunteered to get home on my own in case Diane was needed to drive her father back to the hospital, but Mr. Dioskouri insisted that she drive me. "I gonna be okay. Thank you, Ben, you loook ufterr my fameely. I doan forgget. I gonna be okay. Go."

"Wasn't the Poulos baby cute?" asked Diane, as we pulled out of her driveway.

"Yes, very cute. It had a large head, but it was cute."

"All babies have large heads. It's because their heads don't grow as quickly as their bodies."

"Well, this one's body has a lot of catching up to do."

"You're so silly. You really are. William is going to be a very handsome boy; you'll see."

"Maybe, but right now he's got a giant head. Maybe it's the way they feed him—who knows?"

"What are you talking about?—the way they *feed* him."

"Maybe the food never gets beyond his head."

Half an hour later, Diane pulled over three blocks from my place. "We're not there yet," I said.

"I don't want to go closer. Someone might see us."

"Diane, both your parents know you drove me home! Pretty soon you'll be dropping me off at the end of your driveway."

"Don't you want to kiss me?"

"Of course I do."

"Well, I don't want to kiss in full view of everyone who knows us."

"There's no one there, Diane. It's midnight! It's Sunday! Everyone's gone home to bed!" And she stopped my mouth with a long, electrifying kiss. "Where did you learn to kiss that way?" I asked, my voice breaking from excitement.

"From you."

"I thought it was the Greeks who had a great oral tradition: Homer, Socrates—"

"The Jews have quite an oral tradition, too, don't they? I mean, the Bible is made up of stories—"

"No, ours is the nasal tradition," I said, and she laughed, her beautiful face releasing all the tension it had registered for two days.

We kissed and, over the next half hour, I learned again that the best contraception is to make love fully clothed.

"By the way," she said, as we pulled up in front of the restaurant, "I've been meaning to ask you: are you going with Carolyn to her boat?"

"To her boat?"

"Yes. She asked you at my father's party, didn't she?"

"Yes, she did."

"Well, are you going?"

"I told her I would."

"Oh."

"It really doesn't mean anything. I like her as a friend; that's all."

"Okay. Have a good time."

"It doesn't *mean* anything, Diane. We're just friends." She kissed me again, but not quite as warmly. "You're beautiful, Diane."

"You are, too, Ben." And she drove away, once again leaving me on the street to watch her car disappear.

SIXTEEN

Filet steaks sizzled on the barbecue as I lay back on the cool banks of the Trent River. Carolyn swam to shore again. "Are you sure you're not going to come in for a swim?" she said.

"Are you kidding?—the water's freezing!"

"Come on. Don't be a suck."

"You can get out now, too, young lady," said her father from the barbecue. "Lunch is almost ready."

Carolyn snuggled up beside me in a bath towel. "It's freezing," she said. "Feel my goose bumps."

I touched her arm, which bristled in the cool wind.

"And, darling, as soon as you're finished flirting with Ben," said Mrs. Drewry, "you can come help me set the picnic table. You can help, too, Ben." She winked at me.

"What are you having?" I asked Carolyn, as we got to our feet. "Dandelion salad and a glass of pollen?"

She elbowed me in the ribs. "No. Green salad. Is there something wrong with that?"

The rest of us ate the tenderest of steaks, the red juice flowing into our plates with every piece, and we ate slowly, noiselessly. Not a chomp could be heard. We drank red Burgundy wine out of clear plastic wine cups.

"So, Carolyn tells me you're studying music," said Professor Drewry. "Do you hope to be a composer or conductor?"

"I'd like to play and compose, I think."

"The Hendersons — they're my family," said Mrs. Drewry, "were great patrons of music. One of my ancestors was an accomplished conductor in London and I think that's where it all began."

"The Hendersons are related to Henry Purcell, aren't they, Mom?" asked Carolyn.

"Distantly, yes—so my father claimed. They were definitely related to James Timbrel. Have you heard of him?" I nodded, but only because my head was in the nodding mode—not because I'd heard of James Timbrel. "Oh, you *have*," said Mrs. Drewry. "You see, David, I told you he was well-known in his field. You collect stamps, do you, Ben?"

"Stamps?"

"James Timbrel was one of the most revered philatelists of his day, as you know."

"Yes, I have quite a collection of stamps."

Carolyn had stuck her thumbs through the short sleeves of her blouse and was provocatively snapping the straps of her bikini. "This bathing suit's had the biscuit."

"Yes, you've told me that twice now, dear," said her mother.

"I'm just reminding you I need a new one."

"Thank you."

"Does your family come from these parts, Ben?" asked Professor Drewry.

"No, they're in Montreal, but we originate from Eastern Europe mostly."

"We're part East-European, aren't we, Dad?"

"About one-sixteenth, I'd say. My family, Ben, came to Canada as United Empire Loyalists, and much of Mrs. Drewry's stayed in the States. That's part of the reason her brother is the Consul in New York."

"That's part of *your* reason," said Mrs. Drewry. "He's Consul in New York because he's a talented diplomat."

"Isn't your aunt an ambassador somewhere?" asked Carolyn.

"Really?" asked Mrs. Drewry.

"No, she almost became one. She—"

"I'm sure my brother knows her. What her name?"

"She has kind of a secret job, so—"

"Oh, hush-hush, is it?" she asked, laughing politely.

Carolyn and I helped clean up and then her parents sat in lounge chairs to read and take in the autumn sun, which was now directly overhead and warm. Carolyn asked me to take a walk with her along the riverbank, and Mrs. Drewry winked at us as we left. "Are you enjoying yourself with my family, Ben?" asked Carolyn.

"Sure. Why do you ask?"

"You seem so stiff and formal." And she took her blouse off and tied it around her waist. "Had you really heard of James Timbrel?"

"Who, the flagellist?"

"Philatelist. Oh, you cruel person," she said, laughing. "My mother's been trying to sell that guy for as long as I've known her and here she thought she'd finally found a customer. You mustn't tell her. My parents like you too much."

"They do?"

"Yes. They never forget a favor and my father liked the gutsy way you challenged his thesis about artistic responsibility. You were a hit."

I felt myself becoming tense and, when there was a sudden, sharp rustling in the bush beside us, I jumped. "Don't worry," said Carolyn. "It was probably just a chipmunk or something."

"Yeah, but don't they have these little beaks they use to take clumps out of your ankles?"

"Hardly," she said.

"Well, I'm sorry. I always changed the channel when Mr. Mutual of Omaha came on. Consequently, I know very little about wildlife, but I do have my own theory."

"And what might that be?"

"I group all plants and animals into three categories:

Humans, Food and Clothing. And it's a constant struggle to stay in the first category."

"You're cute. Do you know that?"

"You're cute, too." And, as she took my hand, I was willing to concede she was more than cute in her skimpy bikini—which did *not* need replacing. But I felt a strange lack of desire for Carolyn. It wasn't guilt, the way John had described it, nor at that moment even loyalty to Diane entirely; and I would have killed for this kind of attention from her the first time I met her. But her eyes—her *functional* eyes—had not warmed to me since that time on the train. What would eventually become of me? Would I be mounted on the wall like her giant wrist-watch clock? Would we sit and tell friends about James Timbrel and United Empire Loyalists and artistic responsibility? Would I be the bartender at *our* parties? Would she understand that, while her great-grandfather was collecting stamps, my great-grandmother was comparing gallstones in a *shtetl* somewhere?

That did not cover it, I knew. There was more to the Drewries than I had seen, and more, especially, to Carolyn. And there was a special appeal to living life—as I had gathered from my limited experience with the Drewries—in an uncomplicated way, and going off on your own to sort out your problems without forever having to complicate the lives of other people. I felt secure, too, in the knowledge that no moving bushes with Mr. and Mrs. Drewry behind them would be following Carolyn and me along the path through the forest. Yet, as we sat on the soft riverbank and she leaned in to me to kiss me, I was still thinking and not kissing properly. It was her father who had said that no one and no amount of guilt could make a person create what he needed to create.

That was not what I said to Carolyn, though. I said, "Carolyn, do you know I've been seeing Diane?"

"I had some idea. Does that make a big difference?"

"Doesn't it to you?"

"It does a bit, but Diane hasn't talked to me the way

she used to since that night you and her brother took us to a movie.''

"She hasn't?'' I had an uncontrollable desire to see Diane. "She hasn't mentioned that night to me either. Neither has John.''

"All I can say is, if Diane thinks I have to like her brother just for us to be friends, she can forget it.''

"I don't know if she thinks that.''

"And if I treated John half as badly as she does, people would think I was a fiend,'' she said snapping the straps of her bikini again.

We kissed again, and this time I reached beneath her bikini top to hold a breast in my hand. Then I withdrew my hand. "Let's not.''

She rose. "Come on. Let's go in for a swim.''

Carolyn swam down the river in the direction of the boat and never once looked back at me. I jumped in the freezing water and instantly shriveled to half my size. I had to struggle to keep up with her. She got out half way back and continued the rest of the way by foot, leaving me to retrieve her blouse and my shirt.

As we rode down the Trent in their boat, Carolyn seemed to have already forgotten what had nearly happened. "Someday, Ben, I'd like to sail around Cape Horn, like Magellan,'' she said.

Professor Drewry wore a skipper's hat and waved to someone on shore who wore the same hat and smoked a pipe. We all then waved again as our boat went by, with the exception of Mrs. Drewry who was reading *Anna Karenina* and could not be disturbed. I now felt strangely reassured by the company. Life could be worse than this. Maybe I should become a music professor and spend the academic year determining Rossini's influence on Mozart, and the summer sailing around Cape Horn. We waved once again to someone on shore and I stood this time as if part of the boat's company, and felt invisible.

SEVENTEEN

When the Drewries dropped me off on Monday afternoon, Mr. Dioskouri waved at me to come into the restaurant. He had two letters for me from John. They had been delivered to the restaurant. "Hyev a drreenk," he said.

"No, thanks, no."

"Send-oo-wich?"

"No, thanks."

Magda came out of the kitchen and, as the door flapped in and out, I noticed Moustaki. He had a young, pretty woman with him whom I had not seen before. "Is that a new waitress?" I asked Mr. Dioskouri.

"Yes, new. Marria. Chreestmus seasone — gonna be beesy. Nice garrl. Verry nice. You talk."

We heard a slightly muffled yelp from the kitchen. Maria came rushing out, her arms loaded with plates. As Mr. Dioskouri, Magda and I looked in her direction, we saw Moustaki's face at the small window of the kitchen door, but he vanished immediately. Mr. Dioskouri ran his palm over his mouth and chin. "Seet down, seet down oo-one meenoot," said Mr. Dioskouri, pointing to a table. "Magda, brreeng us coupla cognacs, please." Magda smiled at me and went to the bar. Mr. Dioskouri offered me a cigarette and, as we drank and smoked, it was impossible to tell from his expression that he even wanted to talk to me. He kept looking out the window at the traffic the way he usually did, his back straight, his look regal. "I gonna buy these rrestaurrant from these garrbeege," he finally said. "I doan carre coste me hyundrred thousand dollarrs I gonna buy *my* rrestaurrant."

"Is Magda going to stay with you?" I whispered.

"Gonna stay now. I talk to hyerr."

When I got up to leave, Mr. Dioskouri said, "Come back letterr. Come eat." And he left a generous tip on the table.

I ran upstairs to call Diane. There was a yelp from outside like the one I'd heard downstairs, and I went to my kitchen window, which overlooked the back alley, to watch Moustaki running his hand over Maria's bottom and trying to kiss her neck. She broke free and ran into the kitchen again.

I phoned Diane, but there was no answer, so I sat down with John's letters, as if they might give me a clue to her whereabouts. I opened the letter with the earlier postmark first.

September whatever, 1975.

Dear Ben,

So here I am. Weather is great. Wish you were here. My aunt is a pain.

xoxo
Johnny D.

October 2, 1975

Dear Nimrod,

I have to write more this time than last because my aunt said I wasted a piece of paper and a stamp. It's beautiful here. Everything's blue and white in Greece like the flag. My aunt's a crazy woman. She's just gone out to behead some bird for dinner. I can't believe my aunt and mother came from the same womb. *Thea* — that's *aunt* in Greek, in case you wanted to know — anyway, Thea's been trying to set me up with these fifteen-year-old girls. They marry kind of young in the village. (I met a thirty-one-year-old grandmother the other day.) Anway, she brought in one girl—very cute, but *fifteen*—and she put me into a room with her, locking the door from the *outside*, and she was yelling from the outside—no shame whatever—to get to know the girl because she has strong bones. Also, a gypsy came to the house. She wanted to trade something for my blue jeans—anything, jewelry. She had never met a Canadian before and she was rubbing her hands all over my body—my shoulders, my chest, my balls—wondering if we had all the same parts. I found her more attractive than that fifteen-year-old I was locked in with. I got a hard-on when she was exploring Canada, but my aunt threw her out. So I still haven't found myself a woman —it's the Palm sisters for me for at least another night.

Wait a sec. There's an old biddy coming in here looking for my aunt. I'm back. These people from Krokos— what would you call them, *Krokosians?*—are driving me crazy. They come in droves, kiss me, leave me cookies or something, ask the same questions — how's your mother, how's bla, bla, bla—and then they leave. The women all dress in black, too, if someone — *anyone* — dies. And they're all related to one another, so they're all in black—even Mary, my fifteen-year-old bride-to-be.

I've seen some of the countryside. There's a guy next door who drives Thea and me around in his BMW. He says one night we can go out in his car and pick up some women. I don't have much to talk about with this guy, but he's all I've got. He has a job in the marble works, but he makes extra money selling dope when he goes to the city. We'll be going down to Thessaloniki with him next weekend to visit *Theo*—that's my uncle. My aunt's practically in mourning because I haven't wanted to go down to see him. He's got some kind of heart condition and he's been recuperating in a clinic there. I'll write you from there if Thea gives me more paper. Be a good boy.

Yours Krokosiastically,
John.

I called Diane again and let the phone ring twenty times. Just as I forgot what I was doing and began thinking of the weekend and about Carolyn, a tiny voice said, "Hyellone?"

"Hi, Mrs. Dioskouri, is Diane there?"

"No. Out. You hyev nice oo-weekend?"

"Very nice, thank you. Do you know when Diane's going to be home?"

"Not too let. Ot Dzon say?"

"Pardon me?"

"Dzon. Ot say in letterr? Okay?"

"Oh, yes. He says he's having a wonderful time. He's met some nice girls and he's going to Thessaloniki to visit his uncle. He's having a good time." I listened for her neck to brush rhythmically against the receiver, but what I got instead was an earful of sigh. What reaction would I have gotten, I wondered, if I'd said John was syphilitic and living in the psychiatric ward of a hospital? "Would you mind having Diane call me?" I asked.

"Ots? . . . Thy-ane een rrestaurrant. Go see."

"I was in the restaurant. I didn't see her."

I went back to the restaurant to find that Mr. Dioskouri and the waitresses had left. Only Moustaki remained to serve the few customers. He came over to ask what I wanted and seemed to be brushing breadcrumbs off the tablecloth, though I couldn't see a single one. "I'll have an order of spareribs, please, and coffee after." He nodded and went into the kitchen. I was sitting with my back to the wall in the corner farthest from the door so that I could speak privately to Diane when she arrived. I turned to study the wall painting of a goatherd and his flock behind him. Across the room was the scene of his wife standing outside their house with her hands on her hips, waiting but evidently not unhappy. She was standing in a field of poppies. Everyone pictured on the wall seemed happy. John once told me that the goatherds and shepherds in the northern mountains were gone for months at a time with their flocks. "Don't they get lonely with no one to talk to?" I asked.

"Nope. They're content. If you ever see any of those

guys on the slopes, they're always beaming at you and waving. Mind you, some of them are a bit deranged.''

''In what way?''

''Well, as you say, it must get pretty lonely up there from time to time.''

''So?''

''So they pick out a shapely goat and—''

''They do *not*.''

''No, really. Take a close look at the flock, if you ever get a chance. You'll see a couple of centaurs hopping along with them.''

Mr. Stanowicz walked through the door just as my meal arrived. He headed over to the coffee pot. ''Hyey, hyey,'' said Moustaki. ''I'm gonna brreeng eet forr you.''

Mr. Stanowicz approached me and pointed with his thumb over his shoulder. ''Do you mind if I join you?'' he said.

''No, please,'' I said.

''What do you think of the new boss over there? Phew.'' I shrugged and took a bite out of a rib. I dropped it back into my plate and spit the piece into my napkin. ''What's the matter?'' asked Mr. Stanowicz.

''It's cold. It's got the horrible greasy taste ribs get when they're cold.''

''I wouldn't know,'' he said. But when Moustaki brought Mr. Stanowicz his coffee, the proprietor of Queen Rebuilt Auto Parts said, ''My friend here would like a fresh plate of ribs — except, this time, cook them properly.'' Moustaki took the plate as he muttered something about the cook having gone home with the flu. Without missing a beat, Mr. Stanowicz said to me, ''So tell me: how's school these days? Stavro tells me you're a straight-*A* student.''

''Not quite. I did have a *B*.''

''And the rest *A*'s?'' I nodded. ''That's a straight-*A* student where I come from. My son Hal's a pretty good student, too. Have you met him down at the university? He's a law student.''

"No, I don't get over to that part of the campus very often."

"Drop over there sometime. His name's Hal. You two should go out sometime. You'll like him; he's got a great sense of humor."

"I will, sure," I said. I felt a headache coming on and wondered if I had made a mistake going into the cold water. Not a minute had elapsed when Moustaki returned with the same plate as before. The half-eaten rib lay just where I'd dropped it. I bit into another cold rib and finished chewing so that Mr. Stanowicz wouldn't notice. "Is that better?" he said.

"Much, but I guess I've just lost my appetite."

"What's the matter? You coming down with something?"

"Maybe, yeah."

He paused to examine me. I averted his stare. "Girl problems?" he said.

"Sort of, yeah."

"You see: I got a sixth sense," he said, pointing to his temple with a fat index finger. "So what is it? You've been seeing a lot of Stavro's girl, haven't you?" I nodded. "She's a fine girl, a *very* fine human being—and pret-*ty* Phew!"

"She sure is."

"So what could be wrong? You young people get depressed over nothing these days. Tell me: where could you go wrong with Diane?—No, don't tell me. I got a sixth sense; I rebuild more than auto parts, believe me. Let me guess: your parents don't approve, right?"

"Well, I haven't really—"

"Dead on, right?" I nodded and kept on nodding through his next remark so as not to bruise his sixth sense. "She's not Jewish, is that it? Let me tell you: it doesn't make much of a difference. My eldest daughter married a supreme court justice—no less—and he gave her four beautiful children. And then what does he do? He runs off with some little tight-assed court reporter and leaves Essie with the four kids there. Oh, he pays her—very well, in fact; but what's a check compared to a father and husband? Mr. Supreme Justice: he was the right religion, but nothing else. You tell your parents *that*," he said. His eyes began to water. "Every time I see those kids, I . . ."

"It's OK, Mr. Stanowicz. Try not to think about it."

"You have that happen to you sometime, and *you* try not to think about it. It makes me very sad every once in awhile. He took a break and slurped loudly from his coffee. When he'd vacuumed up the whole cup, he said, "Diane isn't — J-you-know-what." His voice dropped when he heard Moustaki cleaning up behind us. "But believe me, it doesn't matter. You can't win 'em all, and she's one in a million. Believe me."

"Thanks for your advice," I said.

Moustaki handed us a check. Mine had ribs and coffee on it, and Mr. Stanowicz's had just coffee. "Two decades or more I've been coming here," said my companion, "and I have yet to pay for a cup of coffee. Do you think Steve would let me? Not in a million years. Never mind. I'll pay double. I'm not going to let him think things. Give me your check, too." He snatched it out of my hand. I tried to snatch it back. "Please," he said, "you'll make an old man happy."

Mr. Stanowicz didn't notice the coffee that I had not received included on my bill, and he paid far too much for the two of us. "Call my boy Hal sometime," he said, as he walked slowly away toward the door. He had his hands in his pant pockets.

"Thanks for everything," I said. He waved without turning around, and I went upstairs to wait the rest of the evening for Diane to call. But she didn't. I sat plucking my viola for hours. I opened my notebooks for a mid-term exam I had coming up in my Materials of Music II course. I read the heading I had written in my notes—underlined in red the way Mary Beth had always done—except, now that I was in university, underlined only once:

<u>Dominant Seventh and Derivatives</u>

How could music ever have come down to this? <u>Dominant Seventh and Derivatives</u>. Did Mozart think <u>Dominant Seventh and Derivatives</u> each morning before he sat at his piano to play? I'm sure Mary Beth House or whatever her name must be now—Mary Beth Mozart—believed he did. "Honey, I've packed you a nice tuna salad sandwich for the office today, but for heaven's sake don't forget your <u>Dominant Seventh and Derivatives</u> notes again because, as you know, your boss simply will not let you compose one single Divertimento more without them."

The next day, I rushed to Diane's class to find her, but found an empty room. The class must have been let out early. I didn't see her in the cafeteria where we usually ate together. I went to the library. I wandered around campus as if someone had dropped me off in a desert. I went home and spied through the corner of the restaurant window to see if she was there. "It's open, lad," said Mr. McConnell, who had come up behind me. I leapt back. "It's open."

"I was just trying to see if the window had been repaired properly," I said. "I thought I noticed a nick." Mr. McConnell bent down to look with me. "I guess not," I said and ran upstairs.

I sat in my apartment and smoked a pack of cigarettes while I waited for the phone to ring. When I finally reached her at home, she sounded as if I'd called her at her office somewhere. "Hello, Ben. Nice to hear from you again."

"What do you mean *nice to hear from me*! Didn't you get my message? I've looked everywhere for you."

"I've been in and out. Kept myself busy, I guess."

"What is this? Ontario Hydro? What do you mean, nice to hear from you—kept myself busy. This is Ben. I *missed* you. Where *were* you? You knew I was coming home yesterday afternoon."

"I didn't know I was accountable to you for all my activities. I was out with some friends."

"You're not accountable to me, but I wanted to see you. That's all. I couldn't find you after class. I looked everywhere."

"I had a sorority meeting this afternoon."

"On *Tuesday*, now?"

"I'm the new treasurer—or don't you listen to anything I tell you? We were planning our fiscal year."

"What do you mean your fiscal year, for Christ's sake! You've got twelve dollars in your budget."

"Thanks a million for calling, Ben."

"WHAT THE HELL DO YOU MEAN *THANKS A MILLION*! YOU'RE WELCOME SEVEN HUNDRED AND SIXTY-SIX THOUSAND!" But I said this last bit to a dial tone.

I did not get to speak to Diane for two weeks, but I followed her everywhere. I felt a longing for her that drained me of all energy. I saw her eating with friends; I saw her studying with a sorority sister in the library; and the only night I ate dinner at the Blue Sky was when I saw her car parked out front. But she brushed by me on her way out, saying only "Hello" with her Ontario Hydro voice. She looked pale and tired.

When I got upstairs, my phone was ringing. It was Sammy. "Guess what, Ben."

"What, Sammy?"

"I got my driver's license."

"You didn't."

"I did. And guess what else."

"Sammy, you're going to be a hazard to self, God and country."

"You haven't guessed what else yet."

"All right, let me guess: you've become Executive Vice President in charge of Human Resources at the Bank of Nova Scotia."

"No, but close."

"I give up. What?"

"We bought a brand new Oldsmobile and you get to have the Chevy—and I'm going to drive it down to Toronto for you."

"Sammy, have you discussed this with the Señor and Señora?"

"Si."

"I mean the 'driving down to Toronto' part."

"No."

"Well, maybe you should first."

"It's in the bag. Just leave it to me."

"This weekend may not be a great time, Sammy."

"Having problems with your girlfriend?" If anyone, *Sammy* had the sixth sense.

"How do you know?" I asked.

"If you had broken up with her by now, you'd say. 'No prob, come down.' If you were seeing her and not having troubles, you'd say, 'No prob, come on down. I'd like you to meet her.' But you must be having troubles, and you don't want me there because you want to lie around in your room and sulk and hope she drops in on you—"

"She's really great, Sammy."

"You're pretty hung up on this one. I'll be down this weekend to check her out. Just tell her you have to get together because your brother, a man of superior hand-someness and infinitely superior intelligence, wants to check her out."

"*Sammy.*"

"Good-bye. Just tell her—call her. Good-bye." And he hung up.

A couple of days later only minutes before Sammy happened to arrive, it was Diane who called me. I was stunned and delighted when I heard her voice. "I just wanted to see how you were keeping," she said.

"Where are you?"

"At the university—the library. I've got a big essay due on Monday and I haven't even started."

"Well, you've got all Sunday night. Can I meet you there?"

"I don't know, Ben. I've got to get going on this paper."

"So why are you calling, then?"

"Oh, stop. Because I can't keep my mind on it," she said, sniffling.

"I've got some work to do, too. How about if I meet you there and we'll work together?"

"Yes, okay." I could hardly hear her. "You never told me how your weekend was with Carolyn."

"I'll tell you when I get there—oh, I forgot; my brother's coming into town."

"Bring him. I'd love to meet him."

"Well, I'll wait for him but leave him here. I'd like to see you alone."

"No, bring him. I want to meet him."

"I want to tell you about Carolyn, though."

"And what you have to tell me is so private you can't tell me in front of your brother?"

"No, it's not private. I'll bring him."

But Sammy walked in the door with Crazy Sarah.

"Hello, Ben," she said and brushed by me to sit in the living room.

I pinned Sammy against the door and whispered, "Sammy, what the hell is this all about?"

"Ben, I couldn't help it. She heard I was coming and said she loved it in your apartment, so what could I do?"

"Does Aunt Hazel know she's here?"

"Of course. She *asked* me to bring her because she almost never gets out anywhere."

"So now she's gotten out to Toronto again."

"What could I do? It's just for a night."

"But I'm supposed to go meet Diane and she wants to meet you, too."

"We can go. Sarah will listen to the stereo or something."

"Ben, do you have an ashtray?" said Sarah over her shoulder.

I gave Sarah an ashtray, put on one of the Beethoven Romances and told her we were going out. "Go, go," she said. "Just tell the doorman not to let anyone in without the secret password."

Sammy and I found Diane sitting amidst a mountain of books, periodicals, scraps of paper and study cards. She pretended not to notice our approach, but she combed her hair with her fingers and pulled down her sweater. She then put one hand on her nose and, with the other, pointed to a spot in an open book. "Don't let us disturb you," I said.

"Oh, hello," said Diane, rising but still holding her nose. "You must be Sammy." She offered her other hand.

"Sammy, this is Diane."

"It must be a relief for you to meet a more distinguished member of the Beck family," said Sammy. Diane giggled nasally. "Is there something wrong with your nose?" he said.

"No, not really," she said.

"Then why are you holding it?" I asked.

"I have a big zit on it."

"Let me see," said Sammy. "I'm specializing in Zitology at McGill Med. May I?"

"No," she said.

"Okay, Sammy, I'll hold her and you remove her hand."

As I reached for her, she dropped her hand. "Oh, wow!" Sammy and I said in unison. "That calls for an immediate zitectomy," said Sammy.

"Don't," she said.

"Well, what did you expect?" I asked. "To hold your nose throughout the visit?"

"That is a major zit," said Sammy. "Thank you for cultivating it especially for my arrival."

Diane giggled. "Is it that terrible?" she whispered to me.

"Look at it shine," said Sammy. "Is it connected to a battery?"

"All right. Enough already about the zit." I said. "Can we go downstairs for some coffee?"

In the small library cafeteria equipped with a dozen vending machines, Sammy sat down while Diane and I went to get coffee. "Hi, Ben," she said, as I dropped in coins. "Why didn't you call me?"

"I *did* call you."

"Shh."

"Since then."

"I've been busy." I handed her a cup.

"So why have you been following me around if you've been busy?" I handed her a second cup and then stepped between the two coffees, held her head and kissed her passionately. Her lips were wonderful, but she was pulling back the whole time. "Not here," she said. "What if Sammy sees?"

Sammy was fidgeting with the salt and pepper shakers when we sat down. "You look very much like brothers. I never expected to see a blond, blue-eyed version of Ben."

"Our parents were merely experimenting with the brown-haired, brown-eyed variety before they perfected their technique," said Sammy.

"And the same silliness runs in the family, too," said Diane. Sammy fidgeted some more with the salt and pepper. Diane went on, "It really is nice to finally meet you."

"It's nice to meet you, too."

"What are you studying? Do you have any plans?"

"I'm still in high school, but I'd like to go on to study in the States. I'd like to become a pediatrician."

"You must like children very much," said Diane.

"I do."

"Sammy's being modest," I said. "He's planning to go to an Ivy League school and I'm sure he'll make it."

"I wouldn't be surprised," said Diane. "You must be very smart."

Sammy said, "If you'll excuse me, I think I'll just run upstairs to do some research for a paper I'm doing on the cardiovascular system of the gnat."

"I enjoyed meeting you," said Diane.

"Me too," said Sammy. "I'll see you at home, Ben."

"Don't be silly," said Diane. "I'll drive you."

"No, we have a car," I said. "Let's meet in the car."

"You don't have to leave, you know," said Diane.

"I do, really. It's a big paper."

When he left, Diane said, ''He's so cute. I can't believe what a cute brother you have.''

''Why not?'' I said.

''Oh, you know what I mean. Let's go upstairs before someone steals my stuff.''

Upstairs I kissed her again. She withdrew and sat before her books. ''Did you get what you wanted from Carolyn?''

''Yes I did.'' She went back to writing. ''Are you copying your whole essay?''

''It's a long quotation.''

''That's very clever. All you need to do is copy out all the books you need and then you don't have to carry them home with you.''

''Is that why you came here—to insult me?''

''You've insulted me.''

''I join a sorority and you become a raving lunatic, and you spend a weekend with a girl on her boat and I'm just supposed to forget it?''

''A girl *and her parents* on a boat.''

''Oh, I see: if her parents hadn't been along, you could have gotten a lot more accomplished.''

''I can see you've spent your break from me thinking this whole thing through very carefully.''

She began slapping books shut and putting her things away. ''So you feel you have nothing to explain to me,'' she said when we passed the check-out.

''I feel nothing for Carolyn. I don't know why I'm being expected to apologize.''

She walked — almost ran — toward her car and she wouldn't let me help her with her books—two of which she dropped and snapped off the sidewalk almost before they'd landed. ''You've got great reflexes,'' I said.

''You're disgusting.''

''Why am I disgusting? I didn't do anything wrong.''

''You went away for a weekend with a close friend of mine.'' We reached her car. ''And I don't understand why you did it.''

''And she's female.''

214

"*Yes*, she's female! Freud says there's no such thing as an innocent friendship between a male and female."

"Oh, I see. One lousy psychology course and you're analyzing my relationship with people."

Diane burned rubber as she streaked away.

When I got to the car, I found Sammy lying across the front seat and the radio blaring. "That was fast," he said, sitting up and turning off the radio. "You didn't work out your problem, did you?"

"Never mind, Sammy."

He left me alone for most of the drive home. Then he said, "Diane's really great, you know. I hope I find a girl like that some day."

"How can you tell?"

"She just is, and she's really beautiful, too, like you said. Zit or no zit." He paused before he said, "I don't know how you're going to break this to the family, but she really is terrific."

"Why do I have to break anything to the family?"

"You will have to, eventually."

"Not at this rate."

I parked the car right in front of Moustaki's and galumphed up the stairs with Sammy, who tried to pass me on the left and right until I grabbed him in a headlock.

Sarah was not in the living room. "Sarah!" I called out. "Oh, no, Sarah. . . ."

"Maybe she's in the bathroom," said Sammy.

She wasn't.

"She might have gone down to the restaurant," he said.

"But the restaurant's closed—oh no, Moustaki's car!"

We galloped down the stairs, but slowed at the bottom. I opened the door quietly. Sammy and I got down on our knees and spied at the corner of the window. "Oh, my God," I whispered. Sammy began to giggle and I covered his mouth. Moustaki was humping Sarah for all he was worth. They were both naked from the waist down and she sat straddling him in one of the restaurant's armchairs.

215

She bounced frantically, whinnying all the while, as Moustaki yelped and gasped.

"Holy mackerel," whispered Sammy.

"What are we going to do?" I said.

"You know, she hasn't got a bad body for her age," said Sammy.

"*Sammy*! What are we going to do?"

"Nothing. What are we supposed to do: barge in on them?" I sank to the sidewalk with my back against the wall. Sammy continued watching. "Come on, Sammy. Let's wait inside my door."

"You wait. I'll just make sure everything's okay in there."

A streetcar came and Sammy leapt after me. We waited with the door open an inch for at least a quarter of an hour. "What the hell's going on in there?" I said.

"Do you want me to check?" asked Sammy.

"No, stay here."

Then we heard the door and tore upstairs. We heard Sarah's footsteps and I looked out the window to see Moustaki running out to his car and pulling away in a hurry.

"Where have you *been*?" I asked Sarah, who was putting pins into the back of her hair.

"I used a man downstairs who was hung like a rhino. He was a foreign man. I liked him very much. Tell me, Ben, does he frequent the restaurant?"

"Yes he does, Sarah."

"Good. I'm exhausted now so I'll be going to bed."

"Good, Sarah. You do that."

EIGHTEEN

On Monday, Diane was waiting for *me* outside of my class. "I just wanted you to know I phoned Carolyn early this morning and told her I never wanted to see her again."

"That was a mistake, Diane. She did nothing wrong. *We* did nothing wrong. Did you at least ask her what went on between us before you broke it off?"

"I didn't see any need to." Diane's eyes were fiery.

"Of course not. Because then you'd find out the truth and we'd be on equal ground morally and you can't live with that. You always have to be offended — *martyred* in some way!"

She bashed me across the head with her briefcase and, for a split second I detected sympathy in the shooting stars of her eyes.

"Then why did you go? You *did* go, didn't you?"

"I went to be on a boat. We talked about stamp-collecting. *Nothing happened!*"

And she rushed away again, but this time I let her go. I stood in the middle of the Gothic hall of University College, viola case in hand, wondering what had hit me. I was dating Jesusa Christ. What had I done? I'd peeked at Carolyn's worn bikini. I'd checked to see what was inside. I'd *kissed* Carolyn. *Half*-kissed her. But I'd also kissed Mrs. Christopoulos and Mrs. Leftani. And *Mr.* Christopoulos. What would Freud have said about that! Dr. Freud, I'm wondering if you can help me: at a recent gathering I kissed seven hundred people of all age groups and sexes. And, oh, I mustn't forget: only last weekend I went out to a deli and ate a tongue sandwich. Is that considered the equivalent of French-kissing with a cow?

Why was Diane doing this to me? To *us*?

Part of my answer came the next time I saw her. She was having dinner with her parents at the restaurant. I walked in and both her parents stood to greet me and make room for me. Diane made the least fuss. She had circles under her eyes and looked paler than I'd ever seen her. But she looked lovely still—and familiar.

We spoke niceties. I spoke to her parents. She spoke to her parents—in Greek. And then came the question—like the question of a little girl recently adopted: "Daddy, do you love me?" He took her hand. She looked at her mother, and her mother took her other hand. I wondered at first if Diane's parents were consoling her and I tried to imagine how John would have reacted to this scene, when I remembered one time I'd heard him ask the question in only a slightly different way. And I realized how delicate was the filament of this girl's emotional life. I was moved beyond description. I felt again—as I had the night Diane introduced The Epiphany—the urge to steal her away to a safe place and protect her from facing the pain of her own responsibilities. But I knew I couldn't. I *shouldn't*. That if she were ever released to me directly—*officially*—she would never face up to her own doubts about Carolyn, about herself.

I asked her casually, as I finished swallowing a bite of my shish-kebab, if she would go out with me to a concert Saturday night. She looked at both her parents, who were busy eating, and said, "Sure I will. What time?"

"I don't know," I said.

"You don't know?"

"Well, I have to check if there *is* a concert."

The issue of Carolyn did not come up again that Saturday, but it still lurked behind some of Diane's remarks.

218

Everything was going well and we had once again become passionate when Diane said, "I'm still not ready for that, Ben," placing the emphasis on the *I*. I sat up, adjusted my sweater and lit a cigarette. We didn't talk for several minutes. "What are you thinking, Ben?"

"Nothing."

"You always do that," said Diane.

"You're beautiful; do you know that?" I said.

"No, I'm not."

"You *are*, though."

"Is that what you were thinking—how beautiful I am?"

"Maybe not, but I think you are. Do you believe me when I tell you that?"

"I don't know, Ben. You're a sweet person and I appreciate your trying to make me feel better."

"Why would I do that? Aren't you feeling well?"

"I am, but I tell you how I feel and I'm never sure *you* do."

"I think, you're *beautiful*! That's how I feel!"

"Don't yell. Okay, so you think I'm beautiful. That's not a feeling."

"Okay, I *love* you. Is that a feeling?"

"You really do?" she asked, rolling me onto my back.

"Yes, I really do." I ran my hands beneath her sweater to her breasts.

"Oh, Ben," she said and then she held her breath.

"Would you like a grilled cheese sandwich?" I asked. She laughed and, as the weeks passed, it became more and more difficult to part with Diane. Her parents were kind to me, but they were visibly apprehensive, wondering where all this would lead. One afternoon in December, when Diane and I were having a snowball fight on their front lawn, Mrs. Dioskouri came out a half-dozen times and said something in Greek to Diane.

"We'll be in when we're *in*!" said Diane, throwing a handful of snow up at her mother.

Diane was wearing a bright pink coat and, as she approached, I sensed the Fleurs de Temps perfume I had bought her. "What's the matter?" I asked, when her mother had left.

"She wants us inside. She probably doesn't want the neighbors to see us." And as if to defy her mother Diane flung snow in my face. I chased her to the flower bed where tulips had once sprouted from the snow and trapped her there, tackling her, kissing her frozen face, burning peepholes into the curtains of Oak Crescent.

Still, I worried, when we went inside, that we had upset Mrs. Dioskouri for the sake of it and that we would have to discuss it. But the subject never came up. She spoke about John, who was coming home in a few months, and about Christmas. "Ot gonna do these Chreestmuss, Ben? Gonna go hyome?"

"I usually do, yes."

"I like you come hyerre for Chreestmuss. You go oo-one oo-week oth you fumeely and coupla days—Chreestmuss Day—hyerre my hyome."

"Fine. That sounds fine. Thank you." Diane's look was unmistakably one of suspicion. Do they want to watch us? Do they want to ask pertinent questions? But I slipped into a trance. Christmas at the Dioskouris'. Christmas. The season that lasts a quarter of a year. A quarter of my life. Monkland Avenue High School. *High* School, not elementary. We sing, "Hark, the Herald Angels Sing" and "O Come, All Ye Faithful" and "Silent Night." I walk home and there are choruses everywhere. The snow is singing "Joy to the World." I rush inside and up to my room and fall to my knees—because Uncle Milt once said that *tushes* were Jewish, knees were Chrisitian—and I pray to Jesus. Not to God, but Jesus, asking him where I stand. I am in tenth grade and I look upon my knees with new interest— my Christian knees—and I am rewarded that Christmas by a visit to the Stockwells, the family of a client friend of my father's, a *diluted* family. She is Jewish. He is not. In deference to her there is a Chanukah bush in the living room and Chanukah presents beneath—wrapped ever so carefully in "Season's Greetings" paper only — one for

Sammy, one for me, and twelve each for the Stockwell children. My mother hands over — a look of veiled contempt on her face — a big poinsettia plant — the plant that was never to set foot in our house — the *Christian* plant. We listen to "A Child's Christmas in Wales" on Brian Stockwell's new record player and watch Scrooge on T.V. And back at Monkland, after the holidays, I can say what I got and make up the rest. A quarter of every year. January. Sometimes even February, when the Christmas skates and Christmas records and Christmas shoes become just skates and records and shoes — become absorbed finally into life. Yes, Virginia, there really is a Santa Claus *if* — if, of course. . . . And then there is only Boxing Day: the presents left behind. Give Virginia a cigar, anyway, and a moustache and she'll make jokes. She's really funny, really. "If God was a woman, what does that make Mary, tell me?" Ash-flick. Ash-flick. Yes, Ma, I am going to be eating grape leaves this Christmas — yes, no, *leaves* — stuffed with lamb. No, it's not an Italian dish. *Lamb.* I am going to be sitting among the Christian plants eating sacrificial lamb. Yes, Mrs. Dioskouri, there is your husband's heart and your son's mind and sex and drugs and rock 'n' roll, *but there really is a Santa Claus!*

"What are you thinking?" asks Diane, as I have my pant cuff shredded by Cerberus.

"Nothing."

"Are you offended by my mother's invitation?"

"No, of course not."

"Is that what you were thinking?"

"No."

"You won't have to go to church. That wouldn't be necessary. My mother was only thinking — since you've become so close — that you might like to spend part of the holiday with us."

"I know. It was very nice of her to invite me."

"Will it be hard to tell your family? Is that what you were thinking?"

"No, Diane. I want to tell them."

Luckily, Mr. Dioskouri arrived home and put an end to our conversation. Cerberus—with my sock in his mouth—ran to the door and tore at the bag Mr. Dioskouri had brought. The bag contained a one-pound hunk of roast beef for the dog, and in all the excitement of Diane's transferring the meat to a bowl Cerberus unloaded his previous meal on the kitchen floor.

My whole family came to pick me up in the new Oldsmobile because my mother didn't want me to drive "that old Chevy" all that way in the winter. They came on Saturday, planning to spend a night at a hotel in Toronto, but first my mother wanted to come upstairs to inspect my apartment. She examined the floors, which I had cleaned with a vacuum cleaner borrowed from the restaurant; the kitchen, which I had polished for the first time since it had been repaired after my grilled cheese fire; the bathroom, which Diane had helped me clean after I asked if I could borrow two pairs of rubber gloves (in case there was a microscopic hole in any of them); and the windows, which my mother ran her finger down. "They don't clean the windows on the outside for you?" was her first question.

"They do. Mr. Dioskouri has the guy who cleans the restaurant windows do mine sometimes," I said.

"Oh," she said, studying the dusty ghost of a previous snowfall on the edges of my front window.

"Did you work around the clock to get the place looking this way?" asked Sammy, hurling himself down on the couch.

"You've kept the place very nice," said my father. "What's your problem, Rita?"

"Nothing," she said, sitting in a chair she inspected first, the only person still in her coat.

"So, Benny boy, what have you got planned for the day?" asked my father.

"I thought we could see the CN Tower and maybe have lunch there, and then walk around downtown a bit."

"Oh, that sounds *truly* grand," said Sammy, rolling over on the couch.

"And this evening we're invited to have dinner with the Dioskouris downstairs. They wanted to thank us for looking after John."

"Tell them it was our pleasure," my mother said. "They don't need to repay us."

"Why not?" said my father. "I like the food in their restaurant. Call them and tell them we accept."

"Oh, and I took the liberty of inviting the Dioskouris' daughter, Diane, to join us today."

Sammy rolled over on the couch to face us again. My mother said, "The Dioskouris' *daughter*?" Sammy held up six fingers. "Why would you bother? Where's John?"

"John's in Greece and I asked Diane because—"

"Why is he in Greece?" my mother asked. "He's not going to school?"

"I think he's taking some courses there. I asked Diane because she's nice. She's very nice."

"Good, good," said my father. "But call her already because it's almost lunchtime and I'm starved."

You'd have thought we'd lined up at the CN Tower with Genghis Khan. My mother said nothing to Diane after "Hello," and a couple of times I thought Diane was going to leave us.

"Don't worry about her," Sammy said, falling back to join us. "She's weird about these things."

Diane tried to smile. "I know. It's all right."

When we stood in the line waiting to be seated, my mother was even worse. "What is this, Benny? The restaurant's moving."

"It's designed to allow you to see the panorama. It's a revolving restaurant."

"What do you mean *revolving*? It's not bad enough I have to eat my lunch ten miles in the sky—I have to spin around, too?"

"We're not spinning, Rita," said my father "Now, will you please relax?"

My mother asked the maître d' where the bathroom

was, and rejoined us just as we were being seated. "I feel much better now. I brought up my breakfast."

"Good," said my father, "so you have room for lunch."

That she was placed by the window so she could see the city my mother took as punishment. She ordered a mashed potato and a piece of dry toast and, when the waiter brought it, she pulled out the sprig of parsley and closely examined the striations on the potato. "Why do they bother with that?" she said. Then, before braving her potato, she looked out the window. "So tell me, Benny. Does the whole tower turn?"

"No, just the restaurant," said my father. "How could the whole tower turn?"

"Who knows?" said my mother. "It's no crazier than putting it here in the first place."

"Just the floor of the restaurant is turning," Sammy said. "Look, the window is stationary."

My mother put her hand on the pane and slowly it was pulled back. "How fascinating," she said. That matter settled, she picked up her fork, placed her napkin in her lap, pulled up her chair, the corner of which caught on the stationary windowsill, and was pulled backward away from the table into the person behind her. She stood up onto the windowsill and froze when she looked down. As our table passed her, we all stood to rescue her. Diane said, "Mrs. Beck, I'll be glad to let you have my chair."

"No, thank you, Donna. I'll wait for you all down in the car. Where's my purse?" The purse, which she had put on the windowsill, had now revolved a quarter of the way around the restaurant. Diane and I began to search for it.

When she left, only my father was able to finish his meal calmly. Diane excused herself and came back from the bathroom with red eyes.

"So," said Sammy, "when are you getting married?"

Diane ran to the bathroom again.

"What did you say that for?" I said.

"I was just trying to liven things up."

"Is she all right?" asked my father, tuning in for the first time.

"Yes, she's fine," I said.

"She's a nice girl," said my father. "I like her."

That night my mother refused to go to dinner at the Blue Sky. "Why not, Rita? You'll enjoy it," said my father.

"Maybe some other time," said my mother.

"But we already accepted an invitation," he said.

"Tell them I'm not feeling well," she said. "They'll understand."

Sammy rolled over on his bed in the hotel room. I sat looking out the window and said nothing. I could have said a great deal. I could have used the strategies I'd learned from my mother herself: that if she couldn't go to dinner I would rather not have dinner myself; nor see the people she had lined up for me in Montreal; nor go to Montreal at all for the holidays; nor return to Montreal *ever*. I could make myself sick. I could sit in the living room sighing until five in the morning. I could sit sighing without sleep for twenty years. I could become Neptune and call people F-en exploiters-this and F-en pigs-that. I could parade ghetto minorities of every description through the kitchen and into my bedroom night after night, week after week, until I produced a whole generation of grandchildren my mother could be proud of.

But I said nothing. So how did it come to pass that the stone woman was moved to sit across from the Dioskouris that evening at the Blue Sky? Sammy said, "If you think Ben and I are going to do things just because you get this way, you can forget it."

And so she came with us. And so she accepted a gift of table linen from Mrs. Dioskouri for looking after John. And so she listened as Mrs. Dioskouri solemnly told the story of John's demise, my mother twisting her face to understand. "And Thy-ane, too. *You* know," said Mrs. Dioskouri.

"Your daughter?" asked my mother.

"Yuh. Thy-ane. I tell ole life you gonna find nice Grrick

boy—goood boy. Ees doan hyev to be rreets. *You* know. You hyev sem prroblem.''

My mother reached across the table and took Mrs. Dioskouri's hands in hers. ''I know. I know.''

It was fortunate that the last memorable incident of the day happened after the Dioskouris had left for home and my family had left for the hotel to check out before returning to pick me up. The snow had begun to fall in great, light clumps when I heard Moustaki, who had been almost cordial throughout our dinner, shout in the street below. ''And neverr come back! *Neverr!''* I ran to my window to watch Mr. Seymour land with a thud on the sidewalk. By the time I got downstairs, the lights of the Blue Sky were out and Moustaki was locking the front door. He glanced at me over his shoulder before he rushed down the street to his car parked at a meter a half block away.

Mr. Seymour was lying on his back.

I crouched down beside him. ''Are you all right?''

''I think so. It's just my head.''

I propped up his head. ''There's no blood,'' I said. His eyelids fluttered as the snow fell on his face. ''Try to sit up,'' I said. ''I need to get you upstairs so I can call an ambulance.''

''No, I'll be all right. If my head's okay—that's what I hit—the rest of me will be fine, too.''

''Well, come upstairs anyway. You never know—''

''No. If you just walk me part of the way home, I'll make it.'' A woman who had been shopping put down her bags to help me get Mr. Seymour to his feet. She reminded me it was Saturday, though for some reason—probably because the street was so quiet—it felt like Sunday. ''Thank you so much,'' said Mr. Seymour to the woman. ''Bless you both.''

''Huchoo,'' I almost said.

As we headed down the street to the apartments a block away, I felt cold and realized only then that I was still in shirt-sleeves. Ironically, Mr. Seymour was walking more steadily than ever before. I also noticed he had on a new coat. "I'm sorry about what happened back there," I said to him, as we picked up our pace. I was trembling.

"Oh, it doesn't much matter," Mr. Seymour said. "I'll be moving right after Christmas."

"*Moving?*"

"Yes, I've found myself a lady friend."

"You're kid—I mean, you're—that's wonderful."

"And she has a nice little place in the east end—in Scarborough. And I've dried up now, Ben; it's been over a month."

"That's terrific, Mr. Seymour. We'll see you again though, won't we?"

"Oh, that boy back there doesn't scare me. Now, why don't you head back before you freeze to death? I'll be fine."

I skipped all the way home, incredulous, wondering the whole while if some hidden camera had not captured all this for a made-for-TV Christmas special.

NINETEEN

In Montreal, all my father wanted to talk about was the growing popularity of the *Parti Québécois* and what it would mean if Quebec became a country.

"How can they think it's better," he said, "just because one group is French-Canadian and the other is English-Canadian?"

"They feel threatened; they want to preserve their culture," I said.

"Threatened I can understand, but separation?"

"It doesn't sound like the right solution, does it?"

"I don't know, Ben. It's a crazy world."

All my mother wanted to talk about was the new house they had bought in TMR and how they were going to decorate it—small though it was. She didn't want anything big and wasteful. Except with Sammy, I could not even broach the subject of Diane without getting an icy glare. My father, who I had begun to think was part of the solution, became part of the problem.

"Look," he said, "you're seeing Diane; she's very nice; enjoy her company; get what you need out of it. But, if we're not talking about anything serious, why rock the boat?"

It was not until I went to Uncle Milt and Aunt Ida's jewelry and china shop on Sherbrooke Street to buy some Christmas gifts for the Dioskouris that anyone vaguely resembling my parents was willing to discuss Diane with me. The subject came up accidentally. I asked about their daughter, Linda, who had been looking for a job in psychology the last time I'd seen her a year before. "Oh, your mother hasn't told you?" asked Aunt Ida. "Linda's gone. What can I tell you? She met up with someone—a *goy*, needless to say—and they've returned to the land. He's some kind of wilderness nut."

"Where? What land?"

"I don't know, really and truly. Some place in B.C. The Rockies. You have to go by car, then by boat, then a dirt road. Who knows? It's in the wilderness. Why don't you sit down?" She pointed to the chair before the glass case containing engagement rings. There was a velvet cushion on top of the case. "Can I get you something from the back? A cup of coffee?"

"No, thank you."

"It's no trouble. Really and truly."

"No, really."

My father's sister then sat down across from me on the other side of the glass case and placed her delicate, white hands palms down on the velvet cushion. I could still clearly remember she was once a pretty woman with light blue eyes and brown hair. Even now she looked elegant in a gray dress and pearl necklace. The only real clues to her age, in fact, were the lines of her face and the fossilized ringlets of her hair. "Were they married before they left?" I asked.

"Secretly. She came home, told us and started packing. The following morning she was gone. We didn't know what hit us, really and truly. What could I do, except cry? One day we have an only daughter looking for a job and the next we have a correspondent from the wilderness."

Uncle Milt came in from the back just as she said this. "Oh, the Linda story again," he said. "So what do you think, Benjy? What do you think of your cousin, the cavewoman?"

"Please, Milt," said Aunt Ida.

229

"That's why she went to McGill," he said. "So she could find out why the elk are shy when it comes to grizzly bears."

"As long as she's healthy and happy," said Aunt Ida, "that's the most important thing. Anyway, Ben didn't come in to talk about Linda. He came for something else—a gift for someone, I bet."

"Don't tell me you're seeing someone it's so serious you came to a jewelry store?" asked Uncle Milt.

"Yes, I am."

"A *Christmas* gift?" he asked.

I hesitated, then nodded.

"So what do you want? You want an engagement ring? You want wedding bands? Here." He started pulling rings from beneath the glass and throwing them on the velvet cushion. "You can have them at cost. Take seventy-five percent off any price you see."

"No, I don't want a ring."

"Milt, leave the boy alone. They're kids. It's Canada. They meet other kinds of kids. What are we going to do? Really and truly?"

"So, what do you want from me? You want agreement? You got agreement," he said. "It's something my daughter never asked me for." Just as he choked up, Uncle Milt turned and went into the back again.

I picked out a Florentine candy dish for the Dioskouris' house and a gold necklace with a small heart pendant for Diane. "Is she nice?" asked my aunt as she wrapped the gifts.

"Yes, she's nice," I said, and I kissed her on the cheek.

"Are you moving to the woods?" she asked, as I opened the door.

"I don't think so, Aunt Ida."

That evening after dinner I tried to talk to my mother again. "You didn't tell me about Linda. I found out only today that she moved out west."

"How did you find that out?"

"I was in to see Uncle Milt and Aunt Ida."

"At their store?"

"I wanted to go there to get some gifts."

"What kind of gifts?"

"For the Dioskouris."

"For *Diane*," she said, and she left me in the kitchen to go into the living room.

I followed her. "Why can't we have a normal conversation?" I asked her.

"Because there's nothing to talk about."

"So the only criterion is that somebody be Jewish?"

"Is that all your father and I have?" she asked. "Is that all your grandparents had?"

"You know, I found out that Linda—"

"Linda is somebody else's child. You're mine."

"I want you to know that I'm going back to Toronto early this Christmas."

"Go! Do what you want." And she went into her bedroom and slammed the door.

TWENTY

Mr. Dioskouri sat in the den, in a shirt, tie and his new silk robe, his arms spread across the back of the couch. Diane knelt beside the tree and handed her mother the gift I had brought. "Wrapping service?" she asked.

"No, I did that one myself. The gift," I said to Mrs. Dioskouri as she slowly unwrapped it, careful not to tear the paper, "is from my parents."

"Oh, . . . verry nice, verry kind," she said, hardly looking at the dish, and she pushed forward a couple of times until she was able to rise from beside her husband to give me a kiss. From Mr. Dioskouri I received a gold lighter and a bottle of brandy; from Mrs. Dioskouri, a monogrammed wallet; and from Diane, a big picture biography of Beethoven. When Diane opened her gift from me, the entire room blushed. I rose to kiss Diane and she gave me her cheek as she went on blushing.

The day was spent with people coming and going a dozen at a time. They came with sweets and gifts and kisses. They ate; they drank; they played *Tavli*; and then they went on to someone else's house. The phone rang every quarter of an hour and, when it was John and his aunt, everyone got on the extension.

So memorable was the spirit of the day at the Dioskouris' house that its warmth continued to preside over all my times with Diane until we could smell the very first blooms of spring. She wore the heart necklace everywhere —wore it even on the night we lay together on my couch for long hours, and she announced suddenly that she had seen Carolyn.

"Did she call you?" I asked.

"No, I ran into her at school."

"Did you at least say hello to her?"

"Oh, I did more than that. We had a long talk."

"She asked you to talk to her again?"

"No, I asked her."

"And what did you find out?" I asked, kissing her chin. She turned her back to me. "I found out you didn't tell me the whole truth."

"What kind of crap is that!" I said, sitting up.

"If it weren't the truth, why would you get so angry right away?" she asked.

"What did Carolyn say?" I leapt to my feet.

"She said you had a very nice time together, that her parents liked you very much, and that it's too bad things didn't work out between you."

"And why didn't they work out? Did she tell you that?"

"Stop yelling. You always start yelling," she said, about to cry. "No, she didn't. She said you kissed—and it wasn't the first time—and she said . . . you touched her. She was kind of surprised anyway that the two of you didn't hit it off because you were *kindred spirits*—those were the words she used."

"And you believe that I was her *kindred spirit* and that I got involved in a romance with her that got so hot it burned itself out? Is that what you believe?"

"It doesn't matter."

"Obviously it does matter, or you wouldn't have asked Carolyn for a nice talk." Tears were now flowing down Diane's face. "Is it not possible," I said, "that the burning romance I had with Carolyn was a figment of her imagination—that Miss Magellan was having a little adventure with me, like sailing merrily around Cape Horn?"

"So none of it is true."

233

"Well, who do you believe?"

"I don't know, Ben. Please don't yell any more."

"How can you not know? What has all this between you and me meant to you? Has it amounted to nothing?"

"So you didn't touch Carolyn? She lied?"

I hesitated a moment and, in that moment, the world crumbled. "Yes, we kissed," I said quietly, "but it was Carolyn who kissed me."

"Ben, it's not what you did with Carolyn that upsets me."

"What is it, then?"

"Why don't you take a little time to work it out," she said.

Those two kisses cost me three months each of celibacy. If I had dated Carolyn any longer, I could have joined the priesthood. For a period, I purposely avoided Diane: rushing upstairs when I saw her car parked on Queen Street, dodging the halls I knew she took classes in, eating off campus, and studying at home. Later, when my feelings of longing and loneliness weighed heavier than my need for mutual forgiveness, I began returning to our old haunts hoping, at least, to catch a glimpse of her. It was then that I discovered *she* no longer studied in the same spot in the library, nor ate in the same cafeteria, nor even at the Blue Sky. I began to get worried. I was tempted to speak to Mr. Dioskouri, who still waved at me whenever he saw me, just to find out if she was all right; but I put off even that. Then, one day, on St. George Street near the campus, I thought I saw from a distance a yellow Dodge just like Diane's pulled over to the side. I stepped up my pace to see if it was her car. I decided I would talk to her, that we could reason things out, that we were meant for each other. I would ask her how she was—not pushing, not pleading—just how she was. How was her brother? Was he back from Greece? Her father? Her mother? As I approached, I noticed there was someone in a white jacket leaning in the window. And it was definitely Diane's car. I slowed my pace. It was not a white jacket, but an intern's shirt. Was there something wrong? Her father? I waited behind a car on the other side of the street. There was nothing wrong. Just a chat. With a bearded intern, who laughed and kept raising one eyebrow—a trick that comes more easily to a doctor, I'm sure. What an oil he was! What a slime! He combed his beard with his fingers and laughed again. Then more finger-combing. Laughing. Eyebrow-lifting. How long could this go on? When they parted, I would check the other side of the street to see if I could find an oil slick trickling into the sewer. They waved at each other finally and she drove off.

I did not sleep well that night. At first, I resolved to talk to her the next day. By morning, though, I wanted only to know if she was still wearing her heart necklace. I would go by her class toward the end of her lecture—rush by just to steal a look at her neck.

But, when I got there early, who should be waiting outside the door ahead of me? Dr. Mazola himself. What did he want? If she was discouraging his advances, why did he persist? And, if she was really only a victim of this guy, but he sprouted up everywhere anyway, why was she less guilty than I was? Now it was Diane who had to call me.

But she didn't. At worst, she didn't want to call and I would be relegated to memory alongside the football player who cut off the circulation in her hands. At best, I'd confirmed her worst doubts about herself. But, if I had, who was this *guy*? On several occasions, I drove all the way up to Willowdale and roared around the circle of her street to see if I could catch her — catch them — at an awkward moment. Did she not miss me? Had she gotten over me? Where was John? Why hadn't he called? What was wrong with everyone!

On the day of my last exam before the summer break, my car wouldn't start. I rushed to catch a streetcar and realized, just as I got on, that I'd forgotten my viola. I ran back to my apartment, hopped another streetcar and arrived a quarter of an hour late for my exam. It was clear from the start I hadn't practiced enough. My professor, an aging man who'd been concert master of the Toronto Symphony, stopped me halfway through. "You do not have the proper feeling for this instrument," he said. "Your high keys are too strident and your low ones too melancholy. You are not subtle is what I'm trying to say."

"May I start again? I'm sure—"

"No. I'm not going to fail you this time because I know you're a good student. I've watched you through the year and I've discovered that your greatest virtue as a musician is your versatility. You have a feel for quite a variety of musical forms. Perhaps you should try a different instrument. If that makes you happy, continue in the fall. If not, well . . ."

As I boarded the Queen streetcar home, I was depressed beyond description. I took a seat in the back, holding my viola case close to my side, and I remembered the thousand occasions my mother had sat with me, encouraging me to play—filling me with a sense of confidence that saw me through the days I could neither hit a baseball, nor pass a math test, nor find the courage to ask a girl to dance. I remembered Sammy lying on his back on my bed conducting as I rehearsed for my first school concert. And Sarah. What would I tell Sarah? And *Diane*.

Just as the streetcar passed the Blue Sky, I saw the yellow Dodge in front. I rushed to the door and, when the streetcar stopped, leapt off into the path of a screeching car that struck me—struck my viola case at my side—and sent me flying. I felt as if I was in another TV movie. My leg was sore and I was still holding the handle of my case; I got to my feet to see if the leg was broken, but it wasn't. The driver of the car rushed over and took hold of one of my arms. Mr. Katz left his store to take my other elbow. People stared from the streetcar windows.

"I'm all right," I said. "I live just over there. I'll be all right."

The streetcar driver gave me a slip of paper with his name and number on it. "If you need a witness, just call."

"I'll be fine, thanks," I said.

And then I saw my viola smashed on the road, like some strange punctuation to the morning's events. Mr. Dioskouri's arm was around my shoulder. "Come insigh, Ben. You okay?"

I nodded. Where was Diane?

The driver of the car pulled out a wad of bills from his pocket. "Look, buy yourself a new violin." He was pressing bills into my hand and shirt pocket.

"It was a viola."

"Then, buy a viola and have a night on the town after, okay? No hard feelings?"

"No, okay, thanks." As he drove away, I asked myself, how many people would thank the person who'd just run them down? What a *shmegeggy* I was turning into!

I went inside with Mr. Dioskouri, hoping at last to see Diane. Instead, there was John.

"Was that *you* out there? Jesus!" he said. "Why don't you watch where the hell you're walking!"

I sat down and John told me all about Greece, and I told him all about my morning. He seemed much more cheerful than he'd been a year before. "When did you get back?" I asked. My knees were trembling from the shock of the accident.

"Just last Sunday. Do you have to go to the bathroom, or something?"

"John, how's Diane these days?"

"Oh, she just left for Greece last night. You really broke her up. I've never seen her so wrecked in my life."

"Why did she go?" I asked. I was fighting back tears.

"She needed some rest and some sun, I guess. And she needed to straighten out her mind. There's been a guy who keeps proposing marriage to her and I don't think she's ready for that. Who knows?"

I tried to contain myself, but this last bit of news crushed me. "I'll see you, John. I'll call you," I said and ran out of the restaurant and upstairs to my apartment. When John came up minutes later and let himself in, I was lying on my bed smoking. He was carrying a bottle of wine.

"I can't believe she did this to me," I said.

"That's what Diane said."

"How could she just go off to Greece without calling me?"

"Is it true about Carolyn, you prick?"

"Nothing happened between Carolyn and me. *Nothing.*"

"Do you have a corkscrew?"

John and I sat in the living room, drinking wine and listening to Mahler records. "Maybe it's better this way," John said. "Maybe you need some time away from each other to think things through."

"John, I've never felt this way about anyone before. I can't even describe what it's like. I'm constantly thinking about her."

"If you two get back together, you're going to have to make some pretty serious decisions. Are you ready to do that?" I didn't answer. "Have you decided what you want to do with yourself, with your life?"

"Look who's talking."

"Hey, listen, I don't have to worry yet. I don't have girls falling all over me the way you do. Who'd have thought when we went out on a double date that you'd end up with both girls."

"I did *not* end up with both girls. You don't understand: I *love* your sister."

The word seemed to startle John, as if he hadn't believed, until I'd said it, that I'd even taken an interest in Diane. "I'm glad. I really am," he said quietly, and he took a throaty swig of wine.

"The only two things I care for are Diane and my music. In fact, the two are connected: being with Diane and playing music are like expressing my feelings in two different languages."

"What will you do with your music?"

"Maybe I'll open a club somewhere and—"

"*Buy* into the Blue Sky. Buy over that dick's share."

"Who knows?" I said.

"And what about Diane?"

"I'll just have to wait for her to come back, that's all."

The following day, my classmate Martin Stitzky and I auditioned for a blues band that had advertised in the university paper, the *Varsity*. The father of one of the band members owned a club downtown and he'd offered to give the band its first job.

They accepted me on the basis of my piano playing, but one of the guys, a clarinet player who recognized me from school, offered to lend me a fiddle I could also practice on. Martin was hired to play the double bass.

I called home that night to tell my parents I was staying in Toronto for the summer. It was my mother I spoke to. "But I made up your room in the new house. What do you mean you're not coming?"

"I've lined up a job in a band here and we're already booked in a club. And, Ma," I said anticipating her next comment, "I can't face another summer with Benny Altar. It's my career I'm talking about—*real music*. I'll come home once in awhile, I promise."

She hesitated a few seconds. "You're staying to be with Diane, aren't you?"

It was a comment I should have expected but hadn't because of the circumstances. "Think what you want," I said. "I'm staying in Toronto this summer."

The band had played in the Puerto Azul Club on Gerrard Street for two weeks when the night manager told us we hadn't chased away any customers, so he was extending our contract for another two weeks. The other guys were experienced jazz musicians and they were patient with me as I braved the great tunes of Louis Armstrong, Fats Waller, Bessie Smith and Oscar Peterson. We played "Honeysuckle Rose," and "The Laughin' Cryin' Blues" and "Rockin' Chair" and "Mood Indigo." And, when we were on, my whole being was in the music, my fingers becoming the back alleys of my soul and nerves, sending the thieves and the lovers and the rubbies out through the keys into the resonating strings of the instrument.

At first, it hardly mattered to me what effect our music was having on the audience, many of whom came to drink first and listen second, but the glass I'd inadvertently left on the piano after a break one night had a few bills stuffed into it. After that, I always left a glass. One lady, who wore a feather hat, requested "Blueberry Hill" and gave us ten dollars each because we made her cry. John came to see us play and said he'd come back. Sammy brought a friend from Montreal and they came both nights they were in Toronto, Sammy requesting "Those Were the Days" at all the breaks and offering me a nickel.

When John came to hear us again, it was at the Blue Sky, which Mr. Dioskouri had fashioned into a club for us by shining dim, colored lights onto the Mediterranean village painted on the walls, and which he kept open for longer hours during our two-week stint. This time John brought Ron or Don and Nancy Nash and Carolyn Drewry.

"How long has it been since we last saw you, Ben?" asked Nancy, during one of our breaks. "Has it been two years?"

"Almost," I said.

"Guess what," said Nancy. "I'm pregnant."

For Nancy and Ron or Don, the band played "The Anniversary Song" and a jazzed-up version of "Twinkle, Twinkle, Little Star." I could hear Nancy cackling through both after I announced the dedication, and she told me later that we should be recording we were so wonderful.

At the next break, Nancy patted her abdomen and said she thought it was time to go. "Do you have to go, too?" John asked Carolyn.

"No, I'd like to stay," she said.

"Okay, I'll drive the Nashes to the subway," said John, "and you entertain Carolyn, but no groping — all right, Nimrod?" Nancy cackled and saved us from having to respond.

I felt uncomfortable being left with Carolyn. I had worried from the moment she walked in that at some point during the evening she would raise the subject of Diane and the last conversation they'd had. Here was her opportunity. As I watched her run her hands down the sides of her glass to clean off the mist, I realized I had lost all desire for her. Yet I felt a faint sense of jealousy mixed with guilt, recognizing that I had erased whatever potential we might have had as a couple. "How have you been keeping?" I said.

"Fine, fine."

"Your parents?"

"Oh, the same—you know." She took a sip of her drink and crunched on an ice cube.

"I've been meaning to tell you—"

"It's okay, Ben. We don't need to go into it. It was nice while it lasted, but it's over. *C'est la vie.*"

"Yeah, but there was hardly anything to *last*. I mean—"

"So you had Diane step in for you—and in the process put an end to the friendship she and I had, too."

"I did not have Diane *step in* anywhere. She steps with her own feet, and I did not appreciate some of the things you told her."

"I told her the truth."

"And you allowed her imagination to fill in the rest. What kind of friend were you, anyway?"

"I'm leaving," she said.

"Carolyn, stay. This is stupid. We can all be friends again. Let's forget what happened. Diane was more my type, that's all." Was this really me talking? Telling one beautiful girl she could stop chasing after me because I had become devoted to another beautiful girl? Where was Sammy now? Where was *Hollywood*?

During the band's last job, which I was now calling a "gig" to match the pathetic little goatee I had grown, Debbie Poltzer came to see us. We were playing on the Danforth at the Agora Restaurant and Tavern, owned by a friend of Mr. Dioskouri's. I saw Debbie at one of the tables but couldn't place her until she opened her mouth.

241

"I heard you were playing in this band," she said when I came over to her table, "and I figured (a) you needed a break from studying foot medicine; or (b) you needed a break from your regular friends; or (c) you have a really bizarre hobby; or (d) you needed a break from—"

"Conversation," I said.

"That's really rude," said Debbie.

"I know. I'm very sorry," I said. "I've been having a bad night."

"On the contrary. I think you're really good up there, and you're cute with your new beard and your eyes closed when you play."

I went to the bathroom and looked at myself in the mirror with one eye closed, then the other, then both nearly closed.

It is a testament to my state of mind that summer that this was the girl I went out with twice. She was a kind enough girl who offered to type all my medical papers and wore too much makeup. But was she in a hurry! The first night she kissed me after a heavy application of lipstick and left a waxy residue all over my mouth and ears. The second night she had me eating with her family and discussing the intricacies of the foot for hours. Afterward, in her room downstairs, which her parents "never enter after nine p.m.—never so much as knock on the door even," Debbie Poltzer was ready to bear my child. For hours she tried, the poor girl. For hours we rolled together and rubbed and kissed each other until I lost the sensation in most of my body. But the Beck seed held fast—determined not to blend with the Poltzers'. And Debbie and I parted on good terms. She looked pretty, suddenly, but sad. "At least promise me," she said at the door, "that you won't mind a call in the middle of the night if ever I have medical problems."

"With your feet?"

"Whatever." She kissed me again and, if I hadn't kept my eyes open, I would not have known when it ended. Then I waved and staggered out into the night.

TWENTY-ONE

I shaved my goatee, which didn't look good when my eyes were open, and I went to Montreal for a week before school was to begin. When I returned, I found Magda sitting on the steps outside my door. "How long have you been sitting there?"

"Just a few minutes. Vhere have you been? I vas looking for you for days. Please, I have to talk vit you."

"Sure, come in."

When I sat down, Magda began to pace back and forth in front of me and to bring her hands together at her chin, as if she were praying. "A few days ago," she began, "Mr. Dioskouri had a terrible heart attack."

"Oh, my God," I said, jumping to my feet. "Not again."

"He's still alive, but it's very serious. If he gets better, dey do not know how vell he vill be—you know." I nodded. I wanted to rush to the phone. "But someting terrible happened—da vorst ting I ever saw in my life—and only I saw, nobody else."

"Worse than the heart attack?"

"Vorse." Her voice sped up. "Nobody knows. Only you vill, but I do not know vhat to do and you must tell me."

"What happened?"

"Dere vas a plumbing problem in da restaurant, vater

everyvhere and da plumbers came, but dere vas still a big mess. Mr. Dioskouri asked me to come in please and help clean up early before da restaurant vas opening. I came and, vhen I valked by da front vindow, I saw dat Moustaki vas vacuuming da floor. Fine. But den I saw somebody lying on da floor. I couldn't see who it vas. I stopped just for a few seconds. Moustaki still vacuumed. I run inside. It vas Mr. Dioskouri. Moustaki yelled, 'Oh, no look!' And he run to the phone to call da hospital. How long vas he lying dere before I came? Five minutes? Ten minutes? A half hour? Moustaki saw and he vacuumed, you know. Oh, God, my God," said Magda, and with a great sob she dropped into a chair.

"What can we do? Have you thought of calling the police?"

"Vhat could I tell dem? Dat he gave him a heart attack? I don't know how long he vas dere?"

"Is there a possibility he didn't notice Mr. Dioskouri until you came?"

"No chance. He vas vacuuming *around* him."

"Look, Magda, I have to go to the hospital. Tell me where Mr. Dioskouri is, and come back later. We'll talk some more about this. I will take care of Moustaki, I promise."

"How can you take care? Nobody can take care of dat man?"

"Leave it to me. I promise."

Once I got to the Toronto General Hospital, it took me a half hour of walking through a giant old seedy wing and a brand new white wing to find Mr. Dioskouri's room. Outside were John, Diane, their mother and, lo and behold, Moustaki. Sitting almost exactly as she had at the other hospital, Mrs. Dioskouri hardly noticed me as I rushed by her to hug Diane. We held each other for a long minute. Diane seemed but a remnant of her former self.

"If your father okay?" I whispered.

"No, he hardly even wakes up. He's still in intensive

care," she said. "And look at my mother. She's spent most of the week on that bench there."

I approached Mrs. Dioskouri and crouched down beside her. "Hyellone, Ben," she said, without looking at me.

I shook John's hand and glared at Moustaki's back. He was leaning against the doorpost of the room. I had to fight the urge to pound him into the intensive care room with Mr. Dioskouri, but he looked pathetic himself.

"The guy's amazing," whispered John, as I continued to stare at his back. "He's been here more than I have this week. He opens the restaurant, gets it rolling and comes straight here every day. You'd think they'd been the best of friends. Why does he feel he needs to put in so many appearances, I wonder."

"That's a good question," I said.

John, Diane and I went down to the cafeteria to have coffee. I learned that Mr. Dioskouri had only a fifty-fifty chance of recovery. "Can you imagine my family without my father?" asked John. "There would be bedlam. We'd kill each other off in no time."

"Oh, be quiet, John. Stop talking that way all the time," said Diane.

I thought for a minute, but didn't know what else to say about Mr. Dioskouri's health. "So how was Greece?" I asked Diane.

"Oh, it was okay, *you* know," said Diane.

"Look," said John. "Why don't you two just get married and cut the Romeo and Juliet routine, do me a favor." Diane was ripping off tiny bits of her styrofoam cup and dropping them back into the cup. I watched the meticulous process as if it were some kind of experiment. "All I'm saying," said John, "is I've never in my life seen two people fart around so much."

"Will you be quiet already!" said Diane.

"You should see the gift Diane bought you."

"Shut up!" said Diane.

"It's unbelievable."

"I said *shut up*!"

245

"Will you drive Diane and my mother home, Ben? I've got to get out of this place."

"No. Why should Ben have to do that?" said Diane.

"I don't mind," I said. "I'd be glad to."

"Great," said John and he left us there. Diane continued ripping bits of the cup. It now looked as if it had almost completely digested itself. "So how's your doctor friend?" I asked.

"Oh, he's not. He's just a pain. How did you know about him?"

"Oh, I have my sources."

"Yeah, I know about your sources."

"I've been seeing someone else, too," I said. Diane didn't look up. "She's Jewish, too. Very gorgeous."

"Good," she said.

"Maybe you know her. Her name is Debbie Alphaghetti."

"Debbie *Alphaghetti*?"

"An Italian Jew—you know: prominent Roman family; sold a controlling interest to Chef Boy-ar-dee."

"No." She rose to leave. "Ben, you don't have to bother driving us home. It's such a long way."

"I insist."

"No. We can take a cab." She headed for the door.

"Diane, you're the most wonderful girl I've ever met. How could you leave me the way you did?" I took her in my arms.

"I'm not, and I didn't leave you, Ben. I waited so long for you to call."

I backed her into the coffee machine and kissed her passionately. "Diane, I'd like to marry you."

We stopped moving. I tried to separate from Diane so I could see her expression, but she held onto my neck tightly, her head on my shoulder. "Will you marry me?" I asked again.

Still no answer and no movement. "What about Debbie?" said a little voice.

"Don't be ridiculous," I said. "*Will you marry me!*" I pulled free.

She was crying. "Don't yell, please. How can we, Ben, with my father the way he is?"

"I don't mean tonight. We'll wait until he's better. *Okay?*"

"What about your parents?"

"Yes, I have parents."

"They hate me."

"They'll love you. Let me take care of them. *Okay?*"

"Okay."

"Does that mean *yes?*"

"Yes."

That night, Diane presented me with a perfectly wrapped gift in the shape of a violin case. "What is this?" I said, ripping the paper off like a maniac. "A submachine gun?"

"Don't be silly," she said.

I unlatched the case. I was speechless. I caressed the instrument.

"This is a Roth violin," I said.

"Yes, I know," said Diane.

"Look at the label: it's patterned after an Amati."

"I know," said Diane.

"It's beautiful, Diane."

"John told me the story of your final exam and your accident, and I couldn't afford a piano, so. . . ."

"Well, this must have cost you nearly as much," I said, gently holding the violin under one arm and putting the other around Diane.

Magda did not come back to speak to me. She didn't come to work for a week, from what I heard, or even call to say she wasn't coming. When I finally ran into her, I was on my way into the hospital and she was running past me the other way, with a handkerchief up to her nose. I said hello, but she only waved and continued on. My first thought was that something had happened to Mr. Dioskouri. I rushed inside and ran down the corridor toward the elevator. Upstairs, a small crowd had gathered around someone who had apparently fallen. It was Moustaki. A nurse was tending to him. "What happened?"

"Who are you?" asked the nurse. "Do you know this man?"

"Yes, I do."

"There was someone here a few minutes ago," said a woman standing beside me. "She was a fairly large woman. I saw it all from down the hall there. She came up to this man, called his name and then smashed him over the head with her huge handbag."

"Do you know who the woman might have been?" asked the nurse.

"No idea," I said.

Mrs. Dioskouri arrived with several Seempsone-Eatone bags. "Ot hyappun? Ot hyappun hyerre?"

"It'll be okay," I said to her. "I'll explain in a minute." I helped two orderlies load Moustaki onto a stretcher, and they wheeled him away.

"Ot hyappun, Ben? You tell me."

"I guess he got too excited and passed out."

Diane soon came and everyone quickly forgot about Moustaki when we were told that Mr. Dioskouri would be coming out of intensive care. The gates once again opened and the party arrived. They came with the flowers, the candy, the liquor, the cakes, the fruits, the discussion, the kisses, and this time Mr. Dioskouri was not as impatient. As I watched the color slowly return to his face, I began to wonder what I was going to say to him about Diane and me.

But first I had to speak to my parents. My father was scheduled to come to town to meet with a customer at the beginning of October and I insisted that he come stay at my place. Initially, my mother was going to join him, but he talked her out of it, saying that he and I would both be busy and what would she do all day.

Diane and I spent the evening before my father's arrival

sprucing up the apartment. "Will you talk to him with me?" I asked.

"No, Ben. It would be better if you explained it to him alone. I don't want him worrying about my feelings. Trust me—it's better if you tell him alone."

"But then I have to tell your parents, too."

"That's different, though. They know you and like you so much already."

"What should I tell my father about the Jewish thing?" My mind was racing. "It's going to come up, I'm positive."

"Well, I told you already. I'm willing to consider converting but not just for the sake of saying Ben Beck married a Jewish girl. I want to look into it. I want to do it properly if I'm going to do it."

"I don't know how well that's going to go over, Diane. You know, my parents—"

"There are *four* parents involved here. One thing at a time, please, Ben. My parents are not going to have a Greek Orthodox wedding either."

"Okay, I'll do my best."

By the time my father got to my place, I had prepared a speech on the future of the world. "So, you're playing violin now," he said, picking the instrument off the chair I had been practicing in. "That's quite an instrument," he said. "It was nice of the school to lend it to you after the accident."

"Yeah," I said, laughing uncontrollably.

"I just hope you're not throwing away your future. You know, music is a tough—"

"I know, Dad."

"Well, just don't—"

"I won't."

"Hey, listen, Benny, we don't have to talk at all. I'll just make like I'm going to say something—I'll grunt, maybe—and you make like you understand right away without telling me; then I'll pretend I'm making another comment, and so on."

"Dad, please, I have something important to tell you."

"What is it—school? Something wrong—"

"No, not school. I—"

"You're not feeling well?"

"No, I'm fine. I—"

"The car's okay?"

"Yes! What I want to tell you is that the school didn't lend me the violin. Diane bought it for me."

"As a gift?"

"Yes, as a gift."

"That's a very generous gift."

"Dad, we're very serious about each other."

"She's a nice girl," said my father. "I don't blame you, really, but—"

"But what? If she's a nice girl, why do there have to be any *buts* about it."

"Okay, so what are you telling me? Give it to me straight, Benny. Tell me what hard truths you've learned so far."

"Have I ever been dishonest with you before, Dad?"

"Telling the truth depends on ability, not honesty. Now, look me straight in the face." I looked at his nose. "Tell me, what are you going to do with this Diane—with your life?"

"The truth, Dad, is that I love Diane and I'm going to marry her. I'm going to continue my career in music, and I'll start by becoming a junior partner of Mr. Dioskouri's and playing jazz downstairs. The Blue Sky could become a jazz club. We filled the place in the summer when we played and—"

"Now, back up, back up, please. Let's not talk about the jazz club for the moment—though, God knows, worse fates could befall you as a musician. But let's back up here a moment." My father walked to the window and rubbed his face with the palms of his hands. "Ben," he said, "Diane's not Jewish."

"And I'm not Greek Orthodox."

"That's what I'm saying."

"No, you're not. You're saying *she's not Jewish*. That's all you see."

"Benny, it's *different*. You grew up Jewish; I grew up Jewish. How many times in your twenty years did you wish you were something else? What will your children say? They'll have a choice. They'll ask themselves: do I want this? Do I *need* this? What the hell for? How many children in Europe would have said it thirty-five years ago, Benny? Look at your Aunt Goldie. The very fact that she was born what she was turned her into a maniac. You can forswear many things, but you cannot forswear your blood."

"Diane is very sympathetic to all that. She—"

"Sympathy is not blood. The Jews have suffered for centuries just for being what they were. Generation after generation, Benny."

"If all those generations in heaven have been suffering because of people like Diane and me, then they've been suffering unnecessarily. They could have put their time to better use making clouds or mixing with the Phoenicians."

"Well, I must say you have a point there. You're not the same guy who left Montreal a couple of years ago— that's for sure." He paused here a moment and, in that moment, I felt the weight of the Earth roll off my shoulders. "And what does her father say?"

"Her father?" I said. "I haven't spoken to anyone else yet."

"I appreciate that, Benny. Well, they're decent people. I don't deny that. God knows, I've known a few of ours who—*you* know. . . . Let me sleep on it, all right?"

He did more than sleep on it. When I saw him the following evening, he said, "I took the liberty of speaking to Mr. Dioskouri."

"*What! Where?*"

"Don't yell, Ben. In the restaurant. Isn't that where he works? I just wanted to hear what he would say—that's all."

"How could you do that to me!"

"What? I'm not allowed to find out how someone else feels?"

"No!"

"He was pleased."

"What?"

"Amazingly enough, he was pleased. He said it would be hard to find a Greek boy like you. You've made quite an impression on these people."

"And then what happened?"

"We drank some brandy together and he said he was going to help you. You won't believe it: *he* was the one who suggested the jazz club."

I put on my shoes and rushed to the door. "Ben I have to leave tonight. I probably won't see you."

I stepped into the room again. "Dad, you don't know what this visit has meant to me."

"I'm sure," he said. And then, as awkward as it felt for both of us, he hugged me for the first time since I was a child. "So what's the next step? You seem to be calling the shots now. What about your mother? Is Diane willing to convert?"

"She said she'd give it serious consideration. I'll talk to Ma and explain."

"Never mind," he said. "*I'll* speak to your mother. You'll start all over with your Phoenician story."

I hugged my father again and then ran down to the restaurant. I found only Moustaki. "Where's Mr. Dioskouri?" I asked him.

"Go hyome. Thrree hourrs ago."

"Will you be here tomorrow?" I asked.

"Surre. Oo-wherre gonna be. Stavro hyes to tek eet easy now. I gonna be hyerre." His eyes and lips narrowed. "Oo-why?" he asked.

"I just want to know—I thought we could have a little chat tomorrow."

"Oo-why not now?"

"No, tomorrow. I'll see you."

On my way out, Mr. McConnell stopped me. "At your wedding, lad," he said, "I'll address a haggis."

"Great," I said. "Thank you." And I rushed to the car. Mrs. Dioskouri met me at the door. She kissed my cheek, said, "I verry hyeppy" without a smile and then went into the living room to sit in the dark.

Diane ran down the stairs to meet me. "Oh, Ben."

"*What happened now!* They *know* now, don't they?"

"It's not that."

"You were crying again! They're upset about us."

"My father came home and he was so happy."

"Sit down over here and tell me." I led her into the kitchen.

"Your father spoke to him and he came home to tell my mother. He brought a bottle of champagne with him and he and John toasted our health. Then my father went up to the bedroom and, when he came back, his face was white as a sheet. He was holding a leather glove they've had for decades. There were some gold coins inside—it's just a dumb custom. You give coins to newlyweds for good luck."

"And?" I asked.

"And they were gone. Someone had taken them."

"Where are they now? Your father and John?"

"That's what I'm trying to tell you. My father was hysterical. My mother said we could get other coins—it was no big deal. But he wouldn't hear of it. Those were the coins they'd brought from Greece, and *those* were the coins he wanted to give us. So he was yelling for about a half hour, and we all thought he was going to drop dead."

"And?" I did not want to hear the conclusion.

"And finally John said he knew where the coins were. He told us he'd sold them a long time ago—to a teacher."

"Where are they now?"

"They looked up the teacher's number in the phone book and my father made John call and then he left."

"Who?"

"My *father.*"

"Where's John?"

"He went out somewhere. He was upset too."

I drove to the address Diane and I had found written on a scrap of paper. Mr. Dioskouri's car was in the driveway. A small, severe-looking woman, who smelled of celery and wore an apron, asked me to sit down in the living room. That's where I found Mr. Dioskouri, sitting alone beside the fireplace.

"Hyello, Ben," he said, as if I'd just walked into the restaurant. He squeezed my hand in both of his. "I'm verry hyeppy," he said. "Verry hyeppy." Then he looked straight ahead again, anything but happy, his posture stiff and upright. He had not taken off his hat.

A balding man who wore spectacles and a vest and looked as if he'd just stepped off a canvas by Grant Wood came into the living room. *Prowled* better describes the way he tiptoed and hunched forward. He held a small jewelry box in his hands. "Oh," he said, noticing me for the first time as he turned and sat. "You brought someone with you."

"These my son," said Mr. Dioskouri.

"Oh, you're John's brother," he said. "I'm Mr. Milbury." I did my best to smile. "Did you not go to Hedgemont School?" he asked.

"No."

"Oh," he said, waiting for more. "Well, Mr. Dioskouri." He opened the little box, pulled out a bundle of tissue fastened with elastics and delicately uncovered five gold coins. "Here are the sovereigns," he said.

"Hyow muts?" asked Mr. Dioskouri, standing up and pulling a wad of bills from his pocket.

"Now, just a minute. I didn't even say I wanted to sell them. I bought these coins when gold was thirty-five dollars an ounce, and it's worth three times as much today. And, don't forget, there's over an ounce here, not to mention the historical value of the coins."

Mr. Dioskouri pulled three fifty-dollar bills from his wad and threw them in Mr. Milbury's lap. "These more than ounce. Geeve me coins."

254

Mr. Milbury rolled his eyes and handed over the coins.

That same evening, I looked up Mr. Stanowicz's phone number and called to ask about his son. "Oh, Hal's doing just great. He's getting ready to write his bar exams so, in no time, we're going to have a new lawyer in the family. Believe me, we're all excited. Have you had a chance to get together with Hal yet?"

"No. That's why I'm calling. I thought we could get together."

"Oh, he'd love to. He's a nice boy, like you. Let me give you his number—*call* him, by all means."

I called Hal and told him the long story of Mr. Dioskouri and Moustaki, including the tragic tale Magda had recently told me. "That's terrible," he said. "That Mr. Dioskouri is one of a kind. My father always talks about him, and of course I've known him since I was a child, though I haven't had a chance to drop in to the Blue Sky these past few years—"

"Hal, I have a tremendous favor to ask of you. It would help Mr. Dioskouri."

"I'd love to help, but if there were no witnesses to that heart attack incident—other than Magda, after the fact—there's practically nothing we can do."

"No, it's easier than that case. I can expain the details to you. Would you be willing to help?"

"Sure, anything."

"It has to be right away, though—tomorrow."

"Well, tomorrow I've got—"

"It will take only an hour, I promise. Please meet me tomorrow for an hour."

"Where?"

"In my apartment above the Blue Sky."

"Okay, I'll be there at eight-thirty."

"You don't know how much I appreciate this."

"Don't mention it."

"Thanks, Hal—oh, and one more thing: do you have a three-piece suit you might be able to wear? I know I'm asking a bit much, but—"

"I'll wear the suit. See you at eight-thirty."

At 9:15 the following morning, I walked into the Blue Sky with Hal. He was tall, slightly older than I was, wore a gray suit and carried my briefcase filled with music sheets. We walked by the counter behind which Moustaki stood; he didn't acknowledge me. His thin-lipped look was severe that morning, and I almost lost my resolve.

Maria brought us coffee, and Moustaki took so long to come over to our table I was afraid I was going to have to go get him. Gradually, though, brushing crumbs off one table, then another, he wended his way toward us.

"Sit down, sit down," I said. He had not yet smiled. "I'd like you to meet my friend and lawyer, Hal—ah—Mahovlich. I like to call him The Big M."

"Glad to meet you," said Hal, not missing a beat. He was better at this than I was. "And you're—?"

"Moustaki."

"Oh, that's a nice name."

We all sat. "Let me come straight to the point," I said. "I'd like you to sell your partnership of the restaurant."

"Why, you got a buyerr?" he asked, turning up his face.

"Yes. My client here," said The Big M.

"So, the leetle shysterr oo-wants to move in, eh?" said The Little M. "Eet's going to cost you plenty—*eef* I decide to sell."

"I'm willing to pay you what you paid for the partnership, plus interest and any increase in the cost of living." Moustaki laughed and began to rise from his chair. "What if I were willing to tell your wife you've been leaping on the waitresses around here?" He laughed even more loudly and stood straight up. "What if I told you I have evidence that will send you to jail for two to five years? What kind of restauranteur would you be then?"

He blanched and sat down again. "Oo-what do you mean?"

"You know where I live, don't you, Mr. Moustaki?"

"Upstairrs."

"Do you know what I heard in the small hours of the morning on September 14th of last year?"

"Oo-what?"

"I heard the sound of a window being smashed." A rivulet of perspiration made its way down Moustaki's temple. Hal sat with his hands folded in his lap. "Then I looked out my window, and do you know who I saw with a little bundle under his arm running down the street to where he always parks that familiar lime-green Javelin? I saw *you*, Mr. Moustaki. You. Plain as day."

"Oo-what arre you going to do?"

"I'm going to call the police."

"You hyave nothing you can—"

"He has," said Hal, "and he can and *we* will. Two years minimum. Five years max."

"I'm going to think about eet," said Moustaki. He turned to leave.

"Mr. Moustaki," I called after him. He turned. "You have until my wedding day to make up your mind."

TWENTY-TWO

Diane and I were to meet her parents at 4:30 p.m. at Plato's Symposium to check out the banquet facilities. She was to meet me at my car on campus no later than 4:00. She arrived at 4:35. "Okay, let's go," she said, as she jumped in.

I tore down College Street. "Do you know where it is at least?" I asked.

"I told you I did. Just relax."

A half hour later we pulled over on the Danforth to ask a woman if she knew. The woman was dressed in black. Diane asked her first in English, then in Greek. The woman pointed down the road, turned her hand northward and said, "Rra-rre Avenue."

"What the hell is Rra-rre Avenue?" I asked, as we pulled away.

"Pape," said Diane. "It's just up ahead."

Only Mr. Dioskouri was there when we arrived. He was having a cup of coffee and a smoke with Plato. As they talked, I surveyed the vast hall. There were mirrors on all the walls and they had some kind of marble complexion, meant to look, I suppose, like marble mirrors. At one end of the hall overlooking a dance floor, there was a giant painting of the Parthenon and, at the other, mounted on a plaster column, a bust of Plato. He presided over forty or fifty tables with white tablecloths and centerpieces with polyester floral arrangements. Diane joined me. "We're going to go in a minute. The place is too small."

"Too *small*!"

"Sshh. Yes."

"How many people are there going to be at this wedding?"

"I'm not sure."

"Give me a ball-park figure."

"I don't know. A few hundred, I guess."

"A few hundred! Do I know anyone who's coming?"

"If your parents invite any guests, you will."

"That's below the belt, Diane." My mother now knew of our plans, but she and I had not exchanged a dozen words on the subject. "My parents will invite guests, don't worry."

Mr. Dioskouri was now ready to leave. As he opened the door, Mrs. Dioskouri walked in with Seempsone-Eatone bulging at her sides. She yelled at Diane because she had worn jeans to visit one of her father's friends.

It was late January before we found a suitable hall — suitable, at least, for our parents. My father had finally persuaded my mother to come to Toronto to make arrangements, but she did not contribute a word to the conversation at the Blue Sky and pretended not even to listen. Mr. Dioskouri said we would all fit in his car and, as we were leaving the restaurant, Mr. McConnell tugged at my arm. Diane stopped with me. "I'm glad for the two of you," he said. "You make a handsome couple. At your wedding I'll address a haggis."

"Thank you very much, Mr. McConnell," said Diane.

"What the hell is a haggis?" I asked at the door.

"It doesn't matter. He's so nice."

When we arrived at Paradise Gardens, the four parents were visibly impressed, even my mother, who uncrossed her arms. To get to the front door, we had to pass over a moat by way of a drawbridge. We were greeted by a man who said, "Hello, I am Oliver Boyer," and then shook his own hands. "How are we all today?"

"A bit better, thanks," said my mother, as we stepped in.

Mr. Boyer was the uncontested winner of the Oil of the Year Award. When he walked, his shoes barely touched the floor. When he spoke, every word was wrapped in silk. When he sat, he seemed hardly to need a chair. We walked through a hall with an excess of fairy-tale curtains, to a glass-enclosed courtyard with a kidney-shaped turquoise pool. "Look Diane," I said, "that's where Adam and Eve did most of their swimming." We saw Valhalla Hall, where Mrs. Dioskouri kept pointing to the crystal chandeliers, and Eden Room, where Botticelli's "The Birth of Venus" was guarded on one side by Venus de Milo herself, and on the other—because, having no arms, Venus de Milo was at a distinct disadvantage—by a suit of armour. At the back of the Eden Room was the Harmonium Suite. "Here," said Mr. Boyer, "the happy newlyweds can have a quiet moment, and there are facilities, as you can see, for them to change into their going-away outfits." There was an immense, round, white, fur bed, a marble bathroom complete with bathtub, a vanity room, and a closet. I sat on the bed to check its spring. "The bed, of course, is not to be slept in," said Mr. Boyer, "but merely to create the proper mood."

We arrived, finally, at a room called Office. My father asked, "Is this where the happy newlyweds study?" Mr. Boyer smiled for an appropriate length of time and then put back his here-we-are look.

He escorted us into a room with a desk and eight or nine thrones all around it. We each pulled up a throne, except my mother. "Paradise Gardens, of course," said Mr. Boyer, "has its own hostess who will make your guests feel at home and who will discreetly see to it that tiny catastrophes do not occur. She carries aspirin, a needle and thread and many other little remedies," he said, winking at Diane and me. "We also have our own minister, who is ordained and can perform a non-denominational service on the premises, if that is what you wish." I cringed and avoided looking around. "Now, how many people are we expecting at this festive occasion?"

"A half dozen or so," said my mother.

"Oh," said Mr. Boyer, scratching his upholstered head with a gold pen.

"Meesees Beck, we gonna pay," said Mrs. Dioskouri. "You doan oo-woarry. A-oourr parry."

"I wouldn't hear of it," said my mother, and she put her hand on Mrs. Dioskouri's shoulder

On my wedding day, June 21st, 1977, I could not find my family anywhere. They were to arrive at their hotel the night before and to call me to confirm the time they were to pick me up. When I didn't hear from them, I called the hotel several times and then Montreal several more times. The following morning I left a half dozen messages but still no word. Finally, at noon, two hours before the wedding, the phone rang. "Sammy, where the hell have you guys been? I'm frantic here."

"Ben, Mom is not coming to your wedding."

"What?" I sank into a chair. "Where are you now? Put her on the line."

"We're here at the hotel, but she's gone out somewhere. Dad went looking for her."

"What happened, Sammy?"

"We got an anonymous call from a Greek man yesterday—that Moustaki guy, I'm assuming. We already had the car packed—everything."

"Tell me exactly what he said."

"I don't know exactly, but he said a number of terrible things about Diane."

"Like what?" I was seething.

"He said Diane had become pregnant by another man and that she had an abortion last month."

"And Ma believed him?"

"She didn't know what to think. She hardly knows Diane. I told her it was a malicious lie. Dad told her, too. But Mom couldn't figure out what this guy's motivation could have been. I told her he was just an evil guy, but that wasn't enough for her. She still had a small bit of doubt. I told her he'd humped Sarah, and she went wild, cursing you and me for our irresponsibility. We did finally calm her down, though. And she came along with us last night. Then, half way to Toronto, she asked Dad to drop her off. She said all those terrible things might not be true, but she was in no mood to find out at her son's wedding. So we drove back to Montreal. By morning, Dad had talked her into coming again. But she took off when we got here, Ben, and I don't think she'll come back in time.''

''Then you and Dad have to come without her, and you have to leave in an hour.''

''I know, Ben. I'll see you.''

When we got to the hall—my father, Sammy and I—I took Sammy aside and told him I needed to speak to him and John. But first I had to find Mr. Dioskouri. He kissed me on both cheeks and said I looked handsome. ''Mr. Dioskouri, I have to know if Moustaki is going to be here today.''

''Overr therre,'' he said, pointing with his thumb over his shoulder at Moustaki, his wife and two children. The *audacity*! He was here to gloat: to assert that no one was going to intimidate him. I went into a huddle with John and Sammy. Then I straightened up and cleared my mind. This, after all, was the day I was to be married.

And married I was. When I first beheld Diane—a sylph from Homer draped in white — and then lifted her veil finally to kiss her, I could feel only the sweet sting of love and victory. I squeezed her too hard against me, and she beamed and called me her ''husband.''

At no extra charge, Benny Altar and his boys came in from Montreal to play mood music. That there was no seating plan Diane and I regarded as our small wall against a hurricane of wedding arrangements. That there was a reception line for me was the ultimate blow. Down the Valley of the Shadow they came — kissing, squeezing, pressing money at us, smiling, chuckling, guffawing. My cheek muscles had never known such exercise. 'You arre

Ben's broatherr?'' they asked Sammy, the master of ceremonies.

''Yes, his younger brother.''

''Hyow muts youngerr?''

''Three months.''

''Nice. Verry nice.''

Next to Sammy stood Carolyn, the maid of honor, and then John, the best man.

''Your mother really isn't coming, is she?'' said Diane during a lull in the line-up of guests.

''I *told* you: she took seriously ill. She had to be hospitalized.''

''And I didn't believe you then either.''

''Do you think your parents did?''

''My father did, maybe.''

We were interrupted by more guests and still more until the line began to taper off. I could not have planned it better if I had tried: the very last family, led by his wife and children, was Moustaki's. The children ran ahead toward the tables and Mrs. Moustaki had to chase after them. When he got to me, I shook Moustaki's hand and said, ''Come.'' John and Sammy joined us.

''Where are you going?'' asked Diane.

''We have a little private matter to discuss,'' I said. ''We'll be right back.''

The three of us led Moustaki into the Harmonium Suite and surrounded him. ''Oo-what do you oo-want, boys?'' he said, pulling up his pants too high and crossing his arms.

John pulled an envelope from the inside pocket of his jacket. ''I have in this envelope,'' he said, holding it up to his ear, ''two signed and notarized statements to the police: one, signed by Ben here,says that he saw you break the window of the restaurant and make away with a money bag; the second one is signed by Magda . . .'' Moustaki's eyes widened. ''It says she witnessed you stand by while my father—'' John's voice broke—''lay dying on the floor of the restaurant. I should rip your face—''

"*Stop*, John," I said. Moustaki pulled back.

"*I* have here an envelope," said Sammy, drawing it from his pocket, "addressed to the *Toronto Star*. A friend of the family works in the editorial department there. In this envelope is a description of the night, a year and a half ago, when you raped my father's mentally disturbed cousin—"

"Oo-wait a meenute," said Moustaki, trying unsuccessfully to grab the envelope.

" 'Nine months almost to the day after that incident,' the story reads, 'Sarah gave birth to a boy who looks very much like his daddy. Now nine months old, the boy — unkempt and underfed — goes in the arms of his disturbed mother from establishment to establishment as she looks for employment — all the while his fat cat father nightly drops bags of loot on his kitchen table in suburban Toronto.' "

"Oo-what do you want, boys? Tell me oo-what you oo-want."

I pulled an envelope from my pocket. "I want you to sign this contract selling your partnership of the restaurant to me. I have a deposit attached." I took out a pen.

Moustaki opened the envelope and went over to the fur bed to sit down. "Oo-well," he said, scanning its pages.

"Sign or die!" said John. Moustaki snatched the pen and signed, pulling the check off almost in the same motion.

Just as we closed the door behind us, I heard a familiar voice: "*There* he is!" And we turned just in time to see my mother, ablaze in sequins, swing her familiar matching purse covered in nickel coins all the way around until it clanged against the side of Moustaki's head. He fell to his knees. "That's what you get from me, you lying whoreson," she said and then turned to kiss me. "Congratulations, son. Your bride is beautiful."

I stood open-mouthed.

My mother patted my cheek. "Close your mouth,

Benny. Mrs. Dioskouri told me everything. She called at the hotel to see how I was.''

Then, as if she had done nothing more than straighten my tie, she strode across the hushed room and seated herself at the parents' table. Benny Altar struck up the band in a rapid version of Mendelssohn's ''Wedding March'' from *A Midsummer Night's Dream*. Moustaki staggered toward his table with the help of his wife and plopped himself in a chair. A buzz of conversation could be heard all around the room, just beneath the volume of the music, as people watched and waited for Moustaki to leave. But he sat. Defiant and stone-faced, he crossed his arms and sat.

I took my place beside Diane, who stared at me for a moment as I sipped some water, and together we surveyed the room: the two hundred and thirty Greeks on the left, the seventy-two Jews on the right, and the fifty-six Other scattered throughout. It's true not every one was there.

My Uncle Milt said he couldn't leave the jewelry store and sent Aunt Ida alone. Magda hadn't come because she was sure Moustaki would. Aunt Goldie and Uncle Mort had brought only Heshele. Mr. and Mrs. Ioannou, lifelong friends of the Dioskouris, had not even returned the invitation. Nor had Cousin Harry, who, my father said, did not want to set an example for his children. But he sent along a check with my parents.

Diane and I smiled at one another until we heard the single clattering of a spoon against a wine cup. It was coming from Mrs. Dioskouri. Then more clattering, and more, until the sound filled the room like a gust of wind through a giant chandelier. Diane and I kissed.

It was not until we were partway through dessert and all of us finally calm that the very last guest arrived. A minute before, I'd heard what I thought was the distant blast of a bagpipe, but the sound was lost in more clinking of wine glasses with spoons. After Diane and I kissed, the siren-sound quickened. Suddenly, through the doors came the hostess carrying a large silver tray with a bundle covered by a cloth. Behind her marched Mr. McConnell, wearing a tartan kilt, a ceremonial sword, and playing "Scotland, the Brave." The hostess put down the tray beside the wedding cake. The music tapered off with a drone. There was once again not a sound in the room. Mr. McConnell unsheathed his sword and a hundred people leapt to their feet. The hostess lifted her hand and pulled the cloth from the tray. Before us lay a dark, grotesque, beastly affair wrapped in some kind of membrane. It looked as one would expect the kidney of a mastodon to look. Mr. McConnell proceeded to pass the sword over it and pronounce upon it in Gaelic. He then turned toward the guests. "This," he said, "is a haggis, a traditional Scottish food made of the organs of a sheep and wrapped in its stomach. I offer it today to the new couple that they have a long and healthy life together."

The crowd applauded and Mr. McConnell turned to his right. He played "The Flowers of the Forest" and marched out the door again.

When he was gone, Sammy slowly approached the microphone. He stopped there a moment and the room fell silent yet again. "When we put on a wedding," he said, "we like to give people their money's worth. But let me ask you—" he spoke through the laughter—"let me ask you: at what other time in history, and in what other place, except in this best of all possible worlds, could a guest who was attending the wedding of a Jewish man to a Greek woman address a haggis?"

The crowd roared again.

And shock upon shock, Diane, who had been silent much of the afternoon, who could barely be heard when the minister asked us for our vows, who had forgotten to let go of her father's arm through the service as he had forgotten to let go of hers, now walked over to the microphone beside Sammy and said in a clear confident voice, "Thank you all for making this occasion possible, and . . ." She stopped and looked toward me, brilliant in her white gown, the dark eyes peering from beneath the upturned veil. "And I am so very happy."

As if on cue, Benny Altar preempted the rest of the speeches by striking up the band and calling out, "Let's dance, everybody!" No one moved. He was halfway through "Those Were the Days" when Sarah strode across the floor, a cigarette stuck to her lipstick, waited for the song to finish and whispered something to Benny Altar. The band played "The Lion Sleeps Tonight." Sarah walked directly to the Greek side of the room, plucked Moustaki from his seat and pulled him to the dance floor. She flung her arms around his neck and swept him in great circles around the room. I took Diane to dance. Then Aunt Goldie and Uncle Mort joined us. Then Mr. and Mrs. Dioskouri. Then my parents. Soon the floor was filled with dancers. The band played "Hava Nagila," then "Zorba," then "Samiotisa," Benny Altar announcing one as a hora, another as a horo. Circle formed within circle of dancers holding hands, pulling outward and pushing inward, the lead dancer, Mr. Christopoulos, connected to the line by a handkerchief. He spun himself into a frenzy, slapping the floor, springing toward the chandelier, unraveling the line and weaving it through the tables, adding one person after another to the far end of the line.

Diane and I ducked into the Harmonium Suite. I leaned her against the back of the door and kissed her, the veil brushing against my forehead, until our breathing slowed beneath the throb of the music beating against the wall. "Diane, do you think we can do it here?"

"No," came a voice from within the room. It was Sarah. She was lying on her back on the fur bed, the small black feather of her hat curling toward her forehead. "Ben, do you have a cigarette?"

"Sarah, what are you doing in here?" I asked.

"I'm having a rest," she said.

"Leave her," said Diane. "She isn't doing any harm."

"Ben, call me a taxi," said Sarah. "I think I'll go back to my hotel room."

"Sarah—"

"It's okay," said Diane. "I'll go have the hostess call you one."

"Diane," I said. I was about to stop her because Sarah was liable to get into a cab and give the driver her Montreal address, or ask him to take her to *Buffalo* or who knows where. "Nothing," I said. "See if you can find the hostess."

TWENTY-THREE

I wanted to spend the second twenty-four hours of my married life naked with Diane. And her aunt agreed with me. She locked the bedroom door from the outside and came by every so often to rap at the door and shout, ''Bebby! Meck bebby!''

She had met us at the airport in Thessaloniki, carrying a great bouquet of lilacs, which she'd brought all the way from her garden in Krokos and which she ground into our faces, rather than handing them to us, as if she were anointing us. Bits of lilac rolled down our necks and the front of our clothes. She then felt my shoulders and my arms, squeezing here and there, before she kissed me. Thea, as I was told to call her from the start, was shorter and rounder than her sister. She had dark shrewd eyes, wore layers of black clothing and walked like a sergeant major. Unlike Mrs. Dioskouri, who spoke like the smallest girl at a school of etiquette, Thea squawked like a crow as she hoisted our suitcases jammed with a hundred pounds of gifts, and squawked again outside the terminal at a taxi driver who was reading a newspaper.

In the ride to the bus station, Diane must have asked if we were going to see her uncle in the clinic because Thea turned from the front and said, ''Theo move—Athena— doketorr—Athena.'' I presumed this meant we would be taking a trip south eventually. Thea suddenly let out a wail like someone just wounded, but the wail trailed off into anger. "Stup-ed Theo!" She looked directly at me. "Motherr-low die five yearr beforre. Fatherr-low die seex monss beforre. I loook everrything. Stup-ed Theo, seeck, seeck."

I nodded sympathetically. "She means her in-laws both died," said Diane, " and left her to look after everything because my uncle's been so sick."

"I know," I said. "She wasn't speaking Greek." Diane laughed just as the pilot of the cab turned the corner on two wheels.

On the bus ride through the mythic mountains of northern Greece, I was struck by the azure color of the sky—a quality of blue I had never before seen. "That's why she didn't come to the wedding, you know," said Diane.

"Who? Why?"

"My *aunt*. Because of her in-laws and her husband's condition. That's why she did the wail for you."

"Oh . . . The countryside's beautiful, Diane."

"Tell me what you think after you've seen Krokos."

The bus creaked higher into the mountains. A turquoise Mary, a string of worry beads and a silver crucifix clattered against the driver's mirror. A warm breeze from my window pulled at my eyelids and filled the back of the bus with the scent of the drying lilacs in Diane's arms.

"There are still Jews here, you know," said Diane.

"*Jews*?" I asked.

"Yes. Are you surprised?"

"No. I wasn't sure I heard you, that's all."

"There were quite a few in Greece—more than seventy-five thousand—and most of them lived in the north. There aren't many left, though."

"The war?"

Diane nodded. "They lived well with the Greeks."

"I'm sure they did," I said.

Krokos was a dusty village not far from the dusty town of Kozani. "Welcome to the Laredo of Greece," said Diane, as children swarmed all around us and followed us down a lane lush with flowers toward Thea's house. There was hardly a straight line to be seen anywhere, as if the houses had been built without the use even of a ruler. White paint was applied holus-bolus over most of the walls, and the edges, the window frames and the doors were an uneven blue, as if an artist had wheeled through town with a giant can of paint. Mules wheezed, roosters crowed and the odd car honked at chickens bawk-bawking in the lane. Thea's house seemed to have been built one room at a time, because every room but the bathroom was a kitchen with beds in it. And every bed was piled high with linen, wool blankets and an eiderdown. I was enchanted by the place.

One artifact in particular welcomed me with a power I cannot account for. Smiling down at us from above the sink in the kitchen designated as Thea's bedroom—the master kitchen—was the exact same green Buddha clock as the one in my parents' kitchen. "Look!" I said to Diane the moment we walked in.

"Otch?" said Thea.

"I can't believe it!"

"You like?" asked Thea. "I geeve you. Buy in Torroano. Krresge. Loang time beforre."

And how quickly I was spoiled! When I said I was tired, Thea forced me down on a bed and with the strength of a sumo wrestler cracked the bones in my back. When I approached the sink with a plate, she hooted at me and snatched it away. Visitors came one after the other, but only Diane was made to sit with them. I sat in the garden reading, and plates of luscious melon or bowls of almonds freshly picked from Thea's field a mile away appeared magically beside me. She was a terrible cook. She made up a batch of her secret recipe of Chicken Rigor Mortis but, when we left ours on our plates, Thea hustled us off to a *cafenion*, where we feasted on fresh trout and *Demestica* wine. And best of all she allowed Diane and me to have time alone together. When we weren't interested, she *insisted*.

The first night in Krokos we were locked in our kitchen and, exhausted through we were, made wild, passionate love, the pent-up liquids of three years of incomplete nights and frustrated fantasies emptying into the layers of bed-clothes. At dawn, just before I drifted into a canyon of sleep, I remember wondering how it could have been that people were ever herded out of such places, and how, if history ever tipped that way again, Diane would be dragged down one of these lanes with me. I turned toward her and felt her warm breath flow down over my face as I fell asleep.

A couple of days before we were to leave Krokos for the south I woke to find a gnarled hand resting on my cheek. It took me a few seconds to process the information, but I bolted upright to find a tiny old woman dressed in black sitting in bed with me. I shrieked and shot out of bed, forgetting I was naked. I pulled a pillow up to cover myself and the woman started cackling.

Diane came running into the room. "What's the matter!"

"This woman was sitting in bed with me, under the covers!" She was still laughing. "Who the hell is she?"

"Oh, don't worry about her," said Diane. "That's just Kostina."

"What do you mean, it's *Kostina*?"

"Oh, it's the feminine form of Kosta."

"But what was she doing in our bed?"

"She didn't mean any harm, Benny. She's a bit senile, that's all, and I guess she likes you."

That afternoon Kostina walked with us to the grave-yard. Diane and I fell back. "You're not going to like this," said Diane.

"No, I don't mind," I said.

"We're not exactly going to Mount Pleasant Cemetary, you know."

"I know."

"No, you don't. This is a small village and they don't have all kinds of land to spare here, so each family gets a single plot."

"What do you mean?" I asked.

"I mean, you get to lie in your grave for five years and then you get dug up."

"Then what?"

"Then your bones are put in a box and the box is placed in an ossuary, which is a small building made for that purpose."

As we approached the graveyard, I could see a half dozen women all in black tending to their families' graves. From a distance they looked like large crows. Kostina began to wail. Out of this little woman came an operatic myriologue full of pain and sorrow, but she shed no tears. When she finished, she rose from her knees and said something in Greek directly to me.

"She says she's sorry she isn't singing properly," said Diane. "She has a sore throat today."

"Fine," I shouted at her. "You did a great job." And she smiled at me, a senile little smile.

Thea called us over to the grave of her in-laws. "Both hyerre," she said.

"Did she say they were both here?" I asked.

Diane asked her aunt and, as she got her answer in Greek, she translated for me. "She says her mother-in-law was supposed to be dug up when her father-in-law died six months ago. But she didn't let the men who usually do the digging . . . do it this time . . . Instead, she came at night, dug up her mother-in-law . . . because she'd forgotten to pull out her gold teeth anyway . . . and the next day, before they lowered her father-in-law into the grave, she put the bones of her mother-in-law . . . in a shopping bag and slipped the bag into the coffin . . . so she could have an extra five years in the grave. Wasn't that smart, she's asking."

"Very," I said, nodding vigorously at Thea.

We strolled toward the ossuary. The building was no more than a large shed. Diane stayed outside. The door creaked open and Thea pointed to the corner. "Thy-ane grrendfatherr, grrendmotherr." She dashed across and stuffed a bone back in the box and pulled a few dried flowers from around it. Their skulls peered out of the partially closed lid, and on the front of the box were two pictures. In the one of Diane's grandfather, the smile looked exactly like that of the skull. I recognized the irregularities of the teeth. The pattern was the same throughout the room: photos, flowers, the odd crucifix and boxes of bones.

I heard Diane shuffling through the grass outside. "Your ancestors have good strong bones, Diane," I called to her.

"Oh, stop," she said, as I emerged. "Are you finished?"

"Diane, do you realize I could never die here—I mean, in Krokos?"

"Of course you're not going to die here." She laughed at first but stopped.

"I mean, I *couldn't*. What would they do with *my* bones in a little ossuary like that?"

Diane took my hand and squeezed it. "Why do you always have to think of such things?"

"I'm sorry."

That night Thea pulled a bundled-up handkerchief from behind a loose brick. "Forr you—you oo-wedding," she said.

I offered it to Diane, who shook her head. "You open it," she said.

Inside the bundle there were a half dozen gold teeth and a British sovereign. I hugged Thea and kissed her. She was crying. "Meck bebby," she said, and left the room.

The following afternoon just before we were to head south, Thea said we should both call home. We sat in the kitchen—the one *used* as a kitchen—and Diane called first. I studied a photo above the sink of the Dioskouris—except it was not a single photo, but four that someone had blended together for Thea into a collage. The collage was absurd, though, because the individual pictures were taken years apart, so that Diane was a young girl of three or four;

John, a twenty-year-old; Mr. Dioskouri, fifty; and Mrs. Dioskouri, a teenager.

"How is everyone?" I asked, as I dialed Montreal.

"They're great," said Diane. "My father's better, John's working in the restaurant and my mother actually sounded cheerful. I miss them."

I heard the phone connect. "Hello?" said my father.

"Hi, Dad. It's Ben, calling from Greece."

"It's six-thirty in the morning!" he said.

"I'm sorry. I just wanted to see how everyone was."

"Fine, fine, " he said. "We've been thinking a lot about you and your new bride—just wondering how you were getting along in Greece there?—Oh, I must tell you what happened. I won't keep you. Your Great-Aunt Hazel and Sarah were standing at a bus stop the other day and some crazy kid was practicing his marksmanship out an apartment window. He was shooting a pellet rifle or something and, of all the people in Montreal, who should he shoot right in the temple?"

"Oh, no."

"Sarah, that crazy, unfortunate woman."

"And?"

"And, who knows? She's in the hospital. It didn't kill her, but it must have come close."

"And?"

"And they had to operate. She's conscious now. But you know the funniest thing of all?"

"What?"

"She won't say a word to anyone. Not one single word."